GATEWAY
TO
HELL

WWII COLLECTION

Books by James Rouch

The Zone Series
#1: Hard Target
#2: Blind Fire
#3: Hunter Killer
#4: Sky Strike
#5: Overkill
#6: Plague Bomb
#7: Killing Ground
#8: Civilian Slaughter
#9: Body Count
#10: Death March

World War II Collection
      Gateway To Hell
      Tiger
      The War Machines

GATEWAY
TO
HELL

WWII COLLECTION

James Rouch

SPEAKING VOLUMES, LLC

NAPLES, FLORIDA

2012

GATEWAY TO HELL

Copyright © 1979 by James Rouch

ISBN 978-1-61232-925-3

For Sylvia

25 October 1943

From the Office of the Reichsfuehrer (Special Directive 43/777)

To Generalmajor Weichs, Officer Commanding Engineers, 10th Army, Italy. (Copy to Herr Doctor Gersdorf, Director, Todt Labour Organisation, Central and Southern Italy)

The Fuehrer has personally inspected the plans for the fortification of the Gustav Line. The Fuehrer recognises the vital importance of Monte Cassino, overlooking and controlling as it does Highway 6 and the entrance to the Liri Valley; the so-called 'Gateway to Rome'. The Fuehrer is determined that any attempt by the Allies to cross the Rapido River to gain access to the valley should be smashed in its opening stages and to that end orders that the following work be carried out immediately:

1. The building of an emplacement on the south slope of Monte Cassino to accommodate two Pak 43 88mm anti-tank guns.

2. The emplacement to be so sited that the guns can bring direct fire to bear on any attempt to bridge the Rapido between the railway line west of Cassino town and the village of Sant'Angelo.

3. The structure to be sited taking every advantage of natural protection for the guns and magazines (i.e. caves or overhangs).

4. The structure to be of composite steel/concrete construction and proof against aerial bombs (to 1,000kg) and artillery fire (to 150mm).

5. The emplacement to have a screen of mutually supporting close defence positions to enable it to resist infantry assault and remain in action even if it should be isolated from the other defences for a period.

This work is to be carried out under an order of the highest authority and to be given the first priority in men and materials. The task is to be executed under the continuous supervision of an officer of proven ability. The Fuehrer requires that this work be completed by 15 January 1944,

Heil Hitler

*   *   *   *   *   *

The Bedford's three-ton load of ammunition had not all detonated at once. For an hour after the 152mm howitzer shell had crashed into the road beside it the truck and its cargo had burned steadily, occasionally blazing up in a fountain of white and brown flame as the contents of another box ignited. At last, though, at two in the morning, the fire had reached fifteen cases of 3in mortar bombs.

As the vehicle disintegrated jagged lengths of chassis member lanced into the ground, and the compacted stone surface of the narrow road was torn open and scattered by the massive blast.

'We'll give it another minute.' Two hundred yards away, from a spot that had been safely beyond the wide circle of illumination the blazing truck had shed, Sergeant Lucas watched the last guttering flames playing among the mangled debris.

Nearby stood a huge D8 caterpillar tractor, its drab green paint rendering it almost invisible in the darkness, save for the bright leading edge of its wide bulldozer blade. The machine's powerful engine was ticking over with a slow *chug-chugging* noise. A loose bracket securing its high-set vertical exhaust rattled in time to its beat. About it stood the small group of Royal Engineers who had been waiting for the opportunity to move forward and clear the road.

One by one the last few small fires went out, and the distant site was merged once more with the darkness.

'OK. Let's go. Mount up, Russell, and keep the noise down with that thing. It's not a bloody race.'

The young sapper's grin flashed perfect teeth at the sergeant, and he vaulted into the driving seat.

Flanked by the other men of the section the tractor moved forward along the road. The big diesel rarely rose above a muted rumble that failed to drown out the continuous thunder of the British and German artillery and mortars engaged on their night's work of bombardment and counter-bombardment.

Two miles away a star shell burst into dazzling light at six thousand feet and began its slow gyrating descent, leaving a faintly visible white spiral tail behind it as it fell. The harsh glare of the burning magnesium lit the ruins of the monastery directly below it and threw into sharp relief the boulder-strewn slopes, criss-crossed with ravines, of Monte Cassino. Grey-white billows of smoke sprouted on the hill, throwing deep shadows that reached down to the cluster of shattered walls, that had been the town of Cassino, at its foot. A moment later, just before the sinking flare dipped from sight behind the ruins crowning the hill, the reports of the shells' impacts came to the cautiously advancing men.

'I bet that lot has given a few Jerries a headache.' Sapper Harris hefted his pick and shovel from one shoulder to the other.

'Don't be daft, Slacker. We've been slinging stuff at that slag heap since January. It must have soaked up half a ton of bombs and a couple of dozen shells for every sodding yard, and still every time we have a go at taking it we get a bloody nose.' There was resignation in Alf Porter's voice.

'Shut up gabbing, you lot,' Sergeant Lucas called out of the dark behind them. 'Reilly, go on ahead and guide Russell over this bridge. I don't want him ditching this wagon and leaving it out here until broad daylight for the Jerry gunners to use for target practice.'

The broken section of road lay a few yards the other side of a narrow stone bridge over a small culvert. Its span was not more than eight feet and the masonry thick. It held under the tractor's weight, but the edges of the bulldozer blade took chunks out of the parapet as the big machine crawled over.

Pieces of the Bedford littered the road. A scorched and battered cab rested upside down in an overgrown crater nearby, the heated metalwork being slowly cooled by the stagnant water.

'It's not too bad, Sarge. Shouldn't take long.' Corporal Clark kicked aside a chunk of oil-coated engine casing as he surveyed the damage.

'Sure, and we'll have it done in no time. No time at all.'

'Shut up, Reilly.'

'Whatever you say, Sergeant.'

Lucas opened his mouth to repeat the instruction, but cancelled the idea before forming the words. He'd never yet won a satisfactory victory over the Irishman's mouth, and had given up trying. But the overweight oaf giggling somewhere on the other side of the D8 was another matter.

'Tatman, you shut up as well.'

The giggling stopped and was immediately followed by a sustained attack of violent hiccoughs that had an artificial timbre.

'Get them to work, Corporal.' Lucas knew that he could safely leave the running of the job in Clark's hands. His junior NCO was a bit of a fusspot, but he was thorough and always got a job done. It wouldn't be long before he got his third stripe and a transfer, and then he'd be lumbered with a fresh-faced lance-jack, still wet behind the ears and needing breaking in.

The sergeant smiled approvingly as he heard Clark rousting Porter from some nook he had found to rest in, unobserved and, he hoped, unmissed. Porter was an 'old soldier', the father figure of the section, and reckoned in his seniority that he had already done his bit. Perhaps it was because they were alike in several ways that Lucas frequently overlooked the older man's skiving.

Clark was in his early twenties, shared no affinity with the more mature members of the squad and consequently had no compunction about extracting the last ounce of effort from every man. He'd make a good sergeant and would in all probability go on from there if he decided to stay in. Lucas had no such ambition. As long as things ran smoothly he was quite content to stay where he was.

Mike Russell was leaning back in the tractor seat, waiting for the next call for his charge's services; the rest shovelled loose material towards its dipped blade.

It was a little while before Lucas realized he had been screwing up his eyes, trying to pierce the darkness to make out Monastery Hill. It was something he'd been doing increasingly often of late. That great forbidding dome of land, painted an almost uniform pale grey by the masses of dust and powdered stone produced and thrown up by the round-the-clock shelling, had come to dominate every aspect of his life.

During the day the German artillery observers, perched among the shattered fabric of the ancient building at its top, dictated where he could go and where he couldn't, how he travelled and even at what speed – if he was in a vehicle. To break the unwritten rules those invisible eyes imposed was to invite a storm of devastatingly accurate artillery or mortar fire.

At night if the moon was up it exercised the same malevolent influence upon everyone who lived within its field of vision. Even now, when darkness cloaked the low lying land about it, it would jump disconcertingly into vision again, without notice, under the glare of short-lived artificial suns.

'Here, Tatty. Have you got wind? Something don't half pong round here.'

Harris didn't get an answer. At least, not the one he'd expected. Corporal Clark interjected,

'Get on with your work, Harris. No wonder they call you Slacker. And if there is anything that pongs round here it's not Tatman, it's that ruddy muck you bought from that Wop ponce.'

'That's good stuff, is that. All the birds like it.' Harris leapt to the defence of his choice of cologne.

'And the only women you go with don't give a damn what you smell like. It's your money they love.' Reilly threw in his inevitable contribution.

'And the usual thing *you* love is the sound of your voice.'

With Harris getting that small measure of revenge on Reilly, Lucas stepped in to restore order, half a second before Clark started to do the same.

The work progressed swiftly. With the last of the spoil pushed back into the hole the D8 waddled back and forth across it, feathering its blade as it went until the original contour of the slightly cambered surface was restored.

A shout and a wave to Russell signalled the sergeant's satisfaction with the finished product.

'Turn this mechanical marvel round and we'll get out of here before the sun comes up and catches us with our smoke-screens down.'

Applying a lock to the left track, Russell eased the right lever forward and the tractor began a smooth pivoting turn. The clanking, squealing and grating of the steel links on the road filled the air with ugly discord that smothered the sharp crack of the shell that burst high overhead. But an instant later the men on the road knew what had happened, as suddenly they found themselves in shadowless light that took the night and replaced it with bleaching brightness.

'Under the bridge! Under the bridge!'

Mike Russell was already leaping from his seat and the others throwing down their tools as Lucas bellowed. Before two of the star shells' twenty-five seconds of life had elapsed, the men were tumbling and jumping down the steep sides of the culvert, into the several inches of water running along

10

its bottom and under the protecting stonework of the little bridge.

They crouched there, each to himself counting off the time of the parachute-suspended flares' fall.

'Holy Mary, Mother of . . .' If Reilly finished the prayer nobody heard him.

In swift succession five colossal concussions assaulted the men's ears, and jarred their feet as the shock travelled to them through the ground. A pause, a moment only, but one to be savoured, then started a ferocious deluge of high explosive that saturated the surrounding area in overlapping blast waves that pummelled at the sheltering sappers. The air grew thick with dust and they tied cloths over their mouths so that they could go on breathing. The ground heaved, and they knelt down on the sharp gravel of the stream bed in the cold water, so as not to be knocked off their feet. And they put their hands tight over their ears as they huddled against the damp walls to preserve their hearing, and to find some imagined safety amid the storm of high explosive that burst about them.

The room smelt musty. Blending with the odours of stale tobacco was the hint of age and recent neglect exuding from the tassel-trimmed heavy drapes and the faded brocade of the chair backs and seat covers. Large gold swirls of design that snaked across the once royal blue carpet were now mostly hidden by masses of dusty footprints and drifts of carelessly crumpled paper.

Lieutenant Roy Saville stood before one of the dozen plain desks scattered about the big room. He and the staff officer sprawled behind it were the only ones there.

Two minutes, the major had said. Well, he'd taken ten and still he'd got nowhere.

The major had only half listened. To him, Saville was just another of an endless stream of similar supplicants who had battened on to him in the last few days. Some were chasing medals, some promotion, many like this lieutenant felt that they were being under-used, that they were wasted where they were. Each in turn had begged, or argued or done both in a vain attempt to be re-assigned. He realized the flow had ceased, and made an effort to hoist himself into a proper seated position, from which with more conviction he might deliver the short thirty-second speech that by practice he had

11

honed to the bare essentials and reduced to a machine-gun-like gabble.

Adopting the more businesslike pose was as close as he came to launching into his 'sorry wish I could help' dismissal.

'Damn it, Major. My men are Assault Engineers, not damned road menders. There must be something more important for them to do.' Saville had uttered the words with more force than he'd intended, but at least he had at last said what he really felt. To the major it must have sounded loutish and arrogant, probably come as a bit of a surprise after the reasoned, even flowery way he had submitted his case earlier. But now he had no regrets, he'd said what he'd really wanted to say.

Initially the staff-officer's face registered no reaction. He rocked his chair back onto two legs and for a moment appeared lost in intense contemplation of the patterns of light made by the dust-covered chandelier on the yellowed plaster scrolls studding the ceiling. When he spoke at last it was without inflexion in his voice, a neutral tone that gave nothing away.

'What job is your platoon allotted in Diadem?'

The lieutenant was quick to answer. 'We're to maintain and keep open the immediate approaches to one of the bridges over the Rapido, as soon as it's built.'

'Which one?'

There was a perceptible hesitation this time before the response.

'Amazon.'

The chair thumped back onto all fours. 'Good God, man, isn't that enough for you? On that job you'll be within spitting distance of Monastery Hill. You'll be a sitting target. Jerry will be throwing everything he's got in your direction.'

'Major, it's a job that pioneers could do, or a general construction platoon, humping logs and steel mesh around. My men have had enough of being a target. Jerry artillery and Nebelwerfers have been using them as a punch bag every night for the last three weeks. Give us a chance to hit back.'

'In –' the major consulted his watch, 'in twenty-one hours a hundred thousand men, Americans, British, Indian, Polish and every other nationality you can think of are going to get up and start walking towards the Gustav Line. This attack has been planned down to the last soldier, the last bullet. Even if I wanted to I couldn't start shuffling men about just because you think you should be doing something rather more glamorous than you've been given.'

'It's not that, Major.' Saville took a step nearer the desk and leant over it. 'My men are the best in the Eighth Army. There isn't a pill-box or blockhouse we can't crack wide open. All I'm asking is that we're used for the sort of job we've been trained for. Give us a real job.'

In a far corner of the room stood a large easel. Its utilitarian lines, like those of the desks, were in stark contrast to the dated elegance of the other furnishings. Thumbtacked to it was a large scale map of the Cassino sector.

The major found his eyes straying to it. Abruptly he pushed his chair back, rose, and strode over to it. He knew Saville would be watching him. For a minute he just stood there, deep in thought, then he returned to his desk and reached for the telephone.

'Wait outside, will you.'

Behind him as he closed the door the lieutenant heard the staff-officer asking the operator for Divisional Headquarters.

As he stood in the corridor, awaiting the outcome of the major's call, Saville was surprised at how quiet the old hotel was. From a room further down the passageway came the hesitant clatter of inexpert typing. The ancient lift creaked and clanked its way past his floor to stop at the one above. He heard the ornate wrought-iron gate rattle open and, faintly, the noises of conversation. Apart from those signs of habitation the place might have been deserted. Hardly the hive of activity he'd been expecting.

Even though it was a little after two in the morning, he'd expected the usual bustle and seeming confusion of a Brigade Headquarters on the eve of a big push. The absence of either was strange, but an indicator of how well the preparatory work had been done. This late in the day, with only hours to go before the offensive began, for most of the Staff it was now a time of waiting for the first results to come in.

Four miles away the guns could be heard pounding at each other, and at their respective targets on and about Monte Cassino.

'Right, come with me.' The major burst from the room and at a brisk walk led the way to the service stairs, and up to the top of the building.

A military police sergeant checked their papers scrupulously before taking a key from his belt and unlocking a felt-covered door.

What must once have been the largest room of the best

13

suite in the establishment had been stripped of most of its furniture and filled with serried ranks of assorted chairs. They all faced a huge map that completely covered one wall.

At the same fast pace as before, the major led Saville to a paper-strewn table immediately in front of it. Without any preamble he stabbed a nail against a location on the map: a point where the close-spaced contour lines denoting the steep south face of Monte Cassino merged almost to run as one. The neat crescent underlined a short, curved symbol that resembled a miniature gap-toothed comb.

Saville examined the anonymous ridge thus indicated, and waited for the major to speak.

'A couple of days ago, a pair of Yank medium bombers had a go at knocking out a Jerry mortar battery situated in what is left of one of the monastery's courtyards. As is usual with the very appropriately titled US Airforce, they missed. But just for once the bombs weren't entirely wasted. They overshot and clouted this ridge. In doing so they blew away the camouflage of a Jerry position we hadn't even suspected existed until then. It showed up on some routine aerial reconnaissance photographs taken before they'd had a chance to do another vanishing trick on it.'

This was just the background information, Saville realised, the preliminaries before the main announcement. He felt a quickening of his pulse rate and there was a feeling of tightness in his chest. A bead of moisture was forming over his top lip. Well, he'd asked, and now he was getting. Precisely what, he'd know within the minute.

From the table the major took a plain brown envelope, and from it a clutch of photographs. He sifted through them, selected one and handed it over. 'This is quite a clear shot. As you can see, they've tucked it in beneath an overhang.'

The large gloss print showed an expanse of rock-strewn hillside. It was a scene of utter desolation, broken only by an occasional patch of gorse or outcrop of weather-worn boulders. The picture was sharp and clear, taken in good early-morning light, to judge by the shadows. A blur of hazy white that cut across a corner of the print betrayed the path of a tracer-shell aimed at the aircraft.

Tilting the print to orientate the view, the lieutenant made out what appeared to be a blank slab of concrete set against the face of a small cliff, near its top. A second, closer scrutiny and he saw two step-sided rectangular openings in the otherwise unbroken façade it presented.

14

'Do we have any idea what they've got in there?'

A slow shake of the head was the major's first answer. 'A pair of eighty-eights is the most likely guess.'

The information prompted a long low whistle from the lieutenant as he realised the implications of what he was being told. He looked back to the map and in his mind fixed the emplacement's position upon it.

With a loud smack the major slapped his hand against the map, the heel of his palm on the south slope of Monte Cassino, the fingers spread out to cover the mouth of the Liri valley, covering the Rapido River and its approaches as far south as the Sant'Angelo.

'You get the picture, I see. That's about the ground they'll cover. From there they can bring down direct fire on any attempt we make to erect bridges. Without bridges we can't get tanks and guns across to support the first waves of infantry. If we're unable to reinforce the bridgehead with armour and anti-tank guns quickly, we could suffer losses that would make the massacre of the American 36th Division back in January look like a picnic.'

'And you want my men in the front rank, so that those guns can be taken care of as early as possible?' Saville tried to anticipate what was coming.

Again there was the slow shake of the head from the major. 'I didn't wake a brace of colonels and a major-general and his aide just to arrange something as simple as that. When the position was first discovered, the planning staff were thrown into a minor panic. They worked through a whole alphabet of lunatic ideas as to how we could neutralise those guns as quickly as possible. Eventually they just had to settle for an intensification of the smoke programme, to blind the Germans and mask the bridges.'

The major paused, trying to read in the lieutenant's face his reaction to what he'd been told so far, but he learnt nothing from the calm brown eyes and unmoving expression. Whatever turmoil there might be inside him, it didn't show on the outside. He wondered if the officer of engineers was one of those rare cold fish who went through life without the burden of emotion, or passion, or fear. But there was something there, concentration. It was as though he were devouring the maps and photographs through his eyes, and soaking up the words.

'I know that the General had a pet scheme, though he didn't push it, of slipping a small group through the Jerry

15

lines in the confusion of the opening moves and tackling the place by direct assault. Well, I phoned him just now, and told him we had a volunteer. That's you.'

Saville used a small cough behind his hand as a cover for wiping the perspiration from his face. The photograph felt tacky in his hands and he looked down, thinking the print must still be wet, then he realised it was his hands sweating. His back was prickling and he had to make a conscious effort to catch and understand the major's next words.

'Well, you said you wanted something important. I'm not expecting a torrent of thanks, but if you've got any immediate questions I'd appreciate it if we got through them fairly briskly. I want to get my head down for a couple of hours. It may be my last chance for a while.'

'It's going to be a bit sticky trying to sneak a platoon of men through the Jerry lines, confusion or no.'

'Not your whole platoon, just one section. You'll have a small infantry escort and, within reason, anything that you might need for the job. You've no reservations, I hope. I believe you did a job a bit like this on Monte Camino.'

'That was rather different, Major. Two attacks had already gone in before we had a go at that strongpoint. We knew the ground, knew what stores to take. Is this all the information we have?' He tapped the print he held and indicated the envelope.

'I've got this for you as well.' The major partially withdrew a slim sheaf of papers from the envelope. 'The very best photographic interpreters Intelligence has in the whole of the Med worked on this. From it you should be able to formulate some sort of plan. I should imagine, though, that improvisation will be the order of the day. I'll arrange things with your CO and arrange for you and your men to attend a briefing with one of the assault battalions some time later today. The rest will be up to you. Think you can handle it?'

'Yes, sir. We'll crack the place in half.'

'I'll settle for just having the guns spiked. I know that concrete busting is your speciality, but don't forget you've to get there first. Apart from anything else you'll be running the gauntlet of our own artillery fire, at least until you get across Route 6, then it should be mainly smoke. Nasty stuff, but better than HE. It should give you some cover, if you're able to move during daylight, which I rather doubt.'

'What do we do after the job is done?'

'That's up to you. Again, you'll have to play it by ear.

You can either sit tight and wait for us, but that might take a week or more, or you can try and make your way back and establish contact with our leading elements. There are risks either way.' The major injected a note of flippancy into the conversation. 'Might be an idea if you take a coin with you.' He pushed the prints back into the envelope and handed it over as he made a move to the door.

'There is just one last thing, Major. Have we already tried to bust that emplacement?'

There was a long pause before the reply. 'It's in the report. Eh, but I might as well tell you. First thing we did was to ask the RAF if they could flatten it for us. They gave us a very quick "no". Too small a target; and as they went to some lengths to point out, that overhang is fifteen to twenty feet thick. Even a direct hit with a thousand-pounder, if they were able to score one, would barely scratch it. So we gave it to the gunners. When they finished enthusing over the genius of the German engineer who sited the thing, they condescended to give it the undivided attention of a couple of their super-heavies for an hour or so. Eight-inch jobs I think.'

'And?' Saville sensed that he knew the answer before he asked.

'The spotters on Monte Trocchio reported six direct hits, five near misses on the front of the emplacement, and seven hits on the face of the overhang. When the smoke cleared they couldn't see a scratch on it.'

The MP held the door open for them as they left, and locked it after them.

They paused at the lift gate. The major offered his hand. Saville surreptitiously wiped his before taking it.

'It's all a bit of a rush job, but I'm sure you'll manage it. Well, good luck.' He declined the lieutenant's offer to let him into the lift first. 'No thanks. I'll take the stairs. I don't like these things, don't trust them.'

As the major's belt, then knees, then highly polished shoes disappeared from his sight and were replaced by the black wall of the lift shaft, it occurred to Saville to reflect how different was the world of a staff-officer. He didn't dwell on the thought. There were other, more immediate things to think about.

Each massive concussion as a shell exploded was preceded by a short-lived flash of vivid light. They came so close after

17

one another that, to the men cowering in the damp unsure security of the tunnel beneath the road, those of them that dared risk opening their eyes to the flickering white hell, it was as though they were watching a lunatic film show. The limited view that they had of the ground beyond their shelter blinked in and out of vision as each detonating round for an instant illuminated it from a different angle. Wild shadows grew and melted, formed and vanished, in rapid succession.

The air filled fast with dust and grit, flying mud and stone. Broken brick fell on and about the men as shells pummelled the mercifully thick bridge and road-bed above them.

The shell fire slackened and petered out. Still the doubled figures held their cramped positions. A minute passed, two, then three, and still they made no move to stretch aching limbs, unlock the hands they clamped to the sides of their heads.

In a steep walled gully behind Monte Cassino a German gun-layer, anticipating by a split second his battery commander's order to fire, sent from his elderly captured Russian howitzer a single round that preceded by a fraction of time those of the other spoke-wheeled pieces.

A rising noise like an express train heralded its approach and announced that of the others. The barrage was much shorter this time, only two rounds from each gun, but the last two struck a different note on landing, adding to the roaring boom of their instantaneously consumed explosive content the ugly sounds of rending metal as they struck something more resistant than the road or surrounding fields.

With the passing of the deluge the throat-rasping smoke began to thin, and as the first man took his palms from his ears he heard a new noise.

The stream had fallen to a meagre trickle that meandered aimlessly from one shallow dip in the gravel to the next. A little distance up-stream from the bridge the water could be heard splashing into the depths of a crater it would have to fill before seeking its original path.

'Jesus bloody Christ. They gave us a right bloody pasting that time, and no mistake.' Reilly was the first to stand, wiping the slime of the walls from his sleeves and the impressed small stones of the stream bed from his knees.

'Right, on your feet. Let's see what the damage is.'

Mike Russell was already out of the tunnel and scrambling up the steel-gouged side of the culvert as Lucas spoke. 'I'll go over and skin the bastards if they've knackered my 'dozer.'

'What's up, Mike? Afraid you might have to start learning how to use a shovel again if they have?'

It was evident both to Russell and Harris, before they ever reached the level of the road, that the D8 had been hit. As they hauled themselves up they saw red tongues of flame close to the holed engine-casing, and brighter flames laced with yellow, that spun in a pillar to the height of the exhaust from the punctured and ignited fuel tank.

'She's finished.' There was relish in Harris's voice as he walked to the front of the tractor and ran his hand along the top of the blade, having to reach up to do it. The great concave wall of metal had been raised at one side by an explosion-warped hydraulic ram. 'That's the end of our night's work.'

'Don't get your hopes up, Slacker. Here comes the old woman.'

'Harris, round up any tools you can find in one piece.' Corporal Clark turned to Porter. 'And you can help him.' Having satisfied himself that the section's least keen workers had a specific task that would keep them busy and swearing for a few minutes, Clark turned to help Sergeant Lucas, who was attempting to organise an impromptu fire brigade to tackle the burning machine.

The small fire near the engine had succumbed to the first well-directed helmetful of water that had been thrown at it. But that was only after Tatman had been dissuaded from further attempts to extinguish it with handfuls of dirt and dust. Lucas had forcefully brought to his notice the fact that the vehicle's chances of salvage were already remote enough, without his compounding the damage by adding abrasives to the machine's guts.

The flames fed by the gallons of fuel in the large tank were not quenched so easily. The metal about the entry point of the red-hot fragment that had started the fire was twisted into fantastic shapes which prevented it from being reached and smothered.

'It's no good, Sarge. We'll have to let it burn itself out. How about pushing off until it does? I feel bloody conspicuous next to this bonfire.' Russell wiped his face on his sleeve, streaking himself with bars of soot.

'Keep trying. The lieutenant will be back soon, and I don't want him to find this mess and us gone. Now have another go at putting it out.'

'Jeep coming, Sarge.' Harris felt it necessary to put down

the two shovels he was holding in order to make the announcement.

Parking the jeep some distance the other side of the bridge, Lieutenant Saville made his way to where Lucas was directing operations.

With a critical air and growing impatience the sergeant was watching Tatman's pathetic attempts to smother the fire with an armful of wet grass. He snorted his contempt and turned from the scene to salute his officer as Tatman disappeared from vision, instantly wreathed in volumes of dense white smoke.

'Is he fighting or stoking that fire, Sergeant Lucas?'

'Corporal Clark!' There was an edge to the sergeant's voice. 'Get that oaf down and move back until the air clears, then see if you can pull some of that metal aside to reach it better.' He saw Tatman jump off the D8, so full of smoke that it continued to exude from his clothing even after he was clear of the pall. 'They should have it out in just a minute, sir.'

Saville looked back across the bridge towards his jeep, at all the craters he had skirted, and then forward to the road beyond the bulldozer, now heavily pock-marked by more of the same. 'Bit of a mess, Sergeant, but as of right now it's someone else's. Tell the men to . . .'

Beneath the flames a hydraulic fluid reservoir, its contents heated to boiling point, suddenly ruptured under pressures it had never been designed to resist. There was a loud explosion and a large puff of grey fumes as the evaporated contents were freed of their constraints, and the flames died.

At the report every man had ducked and shielded his face, or sought cover. From the direction which one unidentified pair of heels had taken came a frightened wailing that grew louder and more hysterical as everyone raced to the spot.

'I'm hit! I'm hit, oh, oh, I'm hit!'

Clark was the first to reach Tatman. 'Where? Where is it?'

The big man lay face down in the foul-smelling mud at the bottom of an overgrown crater. Beside him lay the bloated carcass of a long dead goat. Tatman didn't notice either of those unpleasant factors. Arching to get his face out of the glutinous mixture so that he could at least breathe, he tried ineffectually with his short pudgy arms to reach a spreading stain in the middle of his back.

Many hands reached down, and it took all of them to haul

him out. Throughout the process he continued to give vent to cries of fear and pain.

'I can't bloody see it.' With difficulty, having constantly to avoid the flailing arms, Sergeant Lucas pulled the wounded man's clothes up his back to bunch them about his shoulders.

'I'm hit. I know I'm hit. I felt it burn.'

'Maybe it's a flake of metal. They're like razors, go in without hardly leaving a mark.' Clark had pulled off Tatman's jacket.

'That's right, kill you quickly as anything they will. Slice up your insides like you was the Sunday roast.'

At those comforting words from Reilly, Tatman, who under Lucas's urging had managed to attain a degree of self-control, started howling in earnest.

The lieutenant took the jacket from Clark, and something about the feel of it made him unbunch it and look at the stain they'd automatically assumed to be blood. He rubbed his fingers over the darkened area, then sniffed it. 'It's oil, Sergeant. This stain, it's oil.'

'Shut up.' With less gentleness and concern than he'd displayed so far, Lucas cuffed Tatman across the back of the head. He peered closer at the expanse of pale flesh, and just above an area corrugated by several rolls of fat, he stabbed his finger down hard.

There was no doubting the genuine nature of the scream the action elicited as a freshly formed blister was burst.

'On your feet, you malingering coward. That wasn't metal that hit you, it was hot oil. Bloody hell, you stink.' In company with all of the others Lucas backed away.

'It's that bloody goat. Some of the muck must have got on him. Phew!' Porter pinched his nose between thumb and forefinger and waved Tatman away as he shamefacedly tried to edge back into the group.

While Lucas and Saville went ahead in the jeep, Corporal Clark led the rest of the section back to their company headquarters. Not through any lack of energy on his part, but because the stench of his battledress had grown to be overpowering, Tatman trailed a long way to the rear of the file.

They left behind them a lot of urgent work that another section would have to tackle in daylight, with only such smokescreens as could be laid for cover. But that was no concern of the sappers who followed the route the jeep had taken. They had done their stint, and now they were quite happy to let others take the risks for a while. Although they didn't yet know the reason why they'd been taken off the road job, the change held out at least the hope that they might be getting a softer number.

As they reached a stretch of road artfully concealed from the observers on Monte Cassino by huge screens of camouflage net, their pace became brisker. Despite the work and dangers of the night their step became jaunty as they moved further from that hated hill. Harris even tried a snatch of unrecognisable tune. Things were looking brighter.

Sergeant Lucas looked up from his study of the photographs as the lieutenant climbed into the passenger seat of the Morris 15cwt truck.

'Well, what do you think, Sergeant?'

'It's a bit of a tall order, sir. There are a lot of risks to be taken and a tough job to do at the end of them, if we make it. Do we know who we'll be getting as an escort?'

'Not a clue. This is very much a last-minute affair. I'm hoping it'll be an outfit with a bit of experience. I'll admit it's difficult to imagine any CO will be happy to give up some of his best men just when they're needed most, but I'm certain Division will come up with something.'

'We'll have to get inside the place to be sure of doing a thorough job on those guns, otherwise the minute we clear off the Jerry gunners might pop up again and do a few quick repairs.'

'Yes, I'd come to the same conclusion.' Saville took one of the photographs and examined it. 'I should imagine our only hope is to find the back door, the one the gun crews use.'

'If you look here, sir —' The sergeant's finger traced along a faint line that snaked up the hillside and turned in to vanish from sight behind the ridge that held the emplacement. 'That might be the path they use for re-supply.'

'Hmm, there certainly don't appear to be any other tracks that pass even remotely near to it. If the only entrance to the place is in the back of the ridge, then that must mean they've driven a tunnel right through it to the gun position in the front. That's a hell of a piece of engineering.'

'Yes, sir, and there are these as well.' Lucas indicated two small white arrows painted onto the print. Without them the small features they highlighted would have completely escaped notice.

'Machine-gun posts, either end of the ridge. Yes, they do add a complication.' Saville tapped his teeth with the edge of the print as he gave them thought. 'There's a chance of course, that one or both of them might be knocked out by the barrage. I believe the artillery boys are going to put on quite a show.'

'And if they don't, sir?'

'Then our escort will have to winkle one of them out for us. With the field of fire they've got there's no way we can detour round them, and the only other alternative is to scale the front of the ridge itself. I doubt if we could make that thirty-foot climb even if we were fresh, and not loaded down with a mass of stores.'

The more Saville became embroiled in the planning for the operation, the greater became his awareness of precisely how difficult was the task that faced them. It called for the skills of a commando in getting through the German wire, mines and fixed defences of the valley floor, and the ability of a mountain goat to scale Monte Cassino itself. And only then would their talents as assault engineers be called for.

'How do you think the men will receive the news?' The answer he got would give him an insight into his sergeant's mind as well as serving the purpose of giving him an idea as to how best to present it to the section. It was a minor irritation he found in Lucas that the NCO rarely volunteered information, nearly always waiting to be asked. It was as though he lacked the ability to anticipate, though he displayed that facility in every other aspect of their work.

Lucas pretended intense preoccupation with the suddenly difficult job of putting the photographs back into the now dogeared envelope. He knew what the reactions would be from each of his men.

Clark would make no comment, just listen intently. Reilly would whisper a snatch of prayer, swear under his breath and then grin at the prospect of another fight. Harris and Porter would groan a protest, as was their inevitable custom, and then accept the situation. Russell wasn't quite as predictable. He'd only been in action with them once, though he'd done all right. Doubtless after joining in the ritualistic groan that always greeted a new assignment he'd go along with the others, coming out with his usual stream of not always relevant questions. That left . . .

'Tatman, sir. The others will be OK, but I don't think Tatman is right for this sort of job. He's all right if it's a straightforward head-on job, but he's not the quietest man in the company and he'll make a terrible racket if he's hit. And if we're near a Jerry post at the time . . .'

'I'm inclined to agree with you, but he has one outstanding virtue we can make use of: do you know anyone else in the whole of the company who could carry an eighty-pound beehive charge all that way? We've got to have one, and I can't spare two men for it. There's a lot of other stuff to take as well.'

Lucas said nothing. The lieutenant was quite right. Tatman was as strong as an ox, with incredible stamina. If he hadn't been such a bloody great baby about being hurt he'd have had a walkover in the Eighth Army heavyweight boxing tournament. Certainly no one else sprang to mind who was even remotely capable of lugging the dome-shaped demolition device up Monte Cassino.

'Well, let's get started. The first thing is to spell it out to the men, then we'll work out what stores we need and figure out how much of it we can actually carry.'

Dawn was just breaking as Lucas engaged first gear and eased the Morris onto the rough track that led to the field kitchens. Their tiny self-contained encampment was just one of hundreds that jostled for room in the narrow strip of safe ground behind the two-mile-long, twelve-hundred-foot-high spine of Monte Trocchio, running parallel to the Rapido and the Gustav Line. Here, in one of the few places for miles about that was screened from the all-seeing eyes of the German observers in the monastery, were packed more than two whole divisions with all their complement of transport and armour. In addition there were huge dumps of supplies of every description.

The few tracks were busy with scuttling jeeps and despatch riders, noisy with the rumble of the last of the long lines of trucks that had brought still more materials of war during the hours of darkness. Every inch of ground flanking the routes was lined with serried ranks of bren carriers, Sherman tanks and M10 tank destroyers, close-spaced parks of armoured cars and occasionally, standing out monstrously huge and dwarfing even the massive Churchill tanks, the lattice-steel crescents of Valentine bridge-layers.

Gangs of pioneers and men from the labour battalions stood stripped to the waist at the roadside. As pot-holes appeared in the surface they would dart forward and hurl shovelsful of shale into the damaged section, and dodge back before the

24

next vehicle passed. A chorus of shouted obscenity followed any driver, regardless of rank, who put his wheels too near the edge and caused it to crumble.

Having taken fifteen minutes to traverse a hundred yards, Lucas pulled the Morris off the road and parked it between two radio vans.

Lieutenant Saville waited a moment before getting out. There was a fluttery feeling in his gut and by sitting still and concentrating he hoped to put off for a while yet a visit to the latrine. If he could put it off long enough he'd only have to go the once. If he went now there would have to be a second visit.

It was the first time he'd ever had a reaction like this to the realisation that he was shortly going into action. He'd stuck his neck out before, and got away with it. But this time it seemed his neck was out further and the axe was nearer and keener.

A puckered circular scar in his left arm and a dull piece of metal on a strip of garish ribbon were all that he had to show for the other times. Why the bloody hell did he do it? Because he thought he was the only one who could do these jobs? Balls. If he didn't do them someone else would, maybe not so well or as fast, but they'd do them. But maybe that was what it did boil down to. He was a bugger-sight better at breaking concrete than anyone else, he'd proved it. And now he had the toughest one of them all. God only knew how thick was the construction of the emplacement they were attacking; possibly yards, to judge from its invulnerability to conventional long-range attack.

And now in words that didn't say as much he'd have to explain to Corporal Clark and the others where they were going, and why; only the *why* he would explain as 'because we've been ordered to', instead of a more truthful 'because I wanted to'. Did he want to? The hell with it. He was going to, that was all there was to it.

He'd feel better when the guns started up. Then the need to concentrate on the job in hand would swamp all else, force his mind onto a single track from which it would not have the time to deviate.

A last twinge in his bowels was brought under control. 'Right, Sergeant. Let's go and give them the good news.'

*　　*　　*　　*　　*　　*

Hauptmann Franz Wolff was already at his desk as the first shades of dawn came in through the ground-floor window of the town hall. He took his gold-rimmed glasses from their neat black case and proceeded to clean the round lenses with economical motions of the small square of chamois his wife had so thoughtfully sent him in the parcel before last. At the thought it provoked he looked at the ornately framed photograph on the corner of his desk. It was a very good likeness; she really did look very lovely in that print dress he'd bought in Rome for her. It was time he sent her another gift, but that would have to wait until he could get to the city again. Here in Piedmonte was nothing save growing dereliction. Piece by piece the Allied bombers and artillery were dismantling the old walled town.

In front of Wolff was a cleared space on his desk top. He looked at his watch: he had another five minutes before the first reports came in and laid a foundation for a stack that would grow and grow no matter how fast he worked through it, until at about ten o'clock the last would arrive and he could begin to take stock.

Each day it seemed the pile grew taller as the lists of damage to fixed defences within his sector became longer and longer. The Allied artillery and airforce bombardment was making more work than his men could cope with, coming as it did on top of the already lagging list of new works to be completed. Everything was being rushed, nothing being done properly, certainly not the way he'd done things back in Munich. There he had established an envied reputation for meticulous planning. When a structure he had designed was erected he could go and look at it with a feeling of pride.

Not now though, not here. Here it was rush and patch and improvise. He was glad his recent promotion had brought with it a change of duty. It was marginally less distasteful for him to inspect the shoddy work of others than to have to do such things himself. In his nine months in Italy he could count on the fingers of one hand the number of emplacements and strongpoints he had designed which when completed he could view with any degree of satisfaction.

Gefreiter Henschel was suddenly in front of the desk, his ugly face leering down at Wolff over the top of a half-metre stack of reports.

"Looks like the Britishers have been beating the shit out of your pill-boxes again, eh Hauptmann?' White-blotched pink gums were exposed as Henschel widened the leer. The single tooth that was left to him after his many brawls displayed its tobacco stains as it stood sole guardian of the cavern beyond.

Wolff winced, and patted the pile straight after the NCO dropped it carelessly. He knew why he had been given this coarse oaf; it was because he alone of the Engineers Headquarters Staff was prepared to tolerate him. The Hauptmann would not have readily admitted to anyone that his seeming tolerance had more to do with his being ill at ease with the processes of military discipline and his reluctance to invoke them, rather than any virtue of forgiveness for Henschel's crass stupidity and loutishness.

In his business practice Wolff had maintained standards by a quiet firmness, tempered with fairness and humanity. He had found the army more inclined to use shouting and brutality.

Henschel, not waiting to be dismissed, stuck his hands in his pockets, belched loudly and sauntered out of the room.

The telephone shrilled. Wolff cleared his throat with a small cough shielded behind his hand, and picked it up.

'Good morning. This is Hauptmann Wolff, Inspector of Fortifications, Cassino sector.'

'Wolff, this is the bloody army, not the business quarter of Munich or wherever it is you come from. I waste an hour a week waiting for you to finish that announcement. Get down here, now!'

Gently Wolff replaced the receiver. Although his caller had not given his name he knew full well who it was. Oberstleutnant Steiger had a style all of his own.

The walk down to the basement was a draughty one. When the fighter-bombers had struck the column of supply trucks weaving its way through the town two bombs had landed beside the building, collapsing part of the outside wall. Through the hole Wolff could see the crater and a dead dog that someone had thrown into it.

'Come in. Sit down. Drink? Oh I forgot, you don't, do you? Well I do. These days it takes the place of sleep.'

And of washing, Wolff thought to himself as he took in his senior officer's ill-kempt appearance.

'Got any reports in yet?' Steiger poured himself a tumbler full of Martell brandy and lounged back in an expensive-looking winged leather armchair.

'They arrived as you called, Oberstleutnant.'

'Lot of them are there, for this time of day?'

27

'There would seem to be more than there were yesterday at this time, yes . . .'

'And yesterday there were more than the day before that, and so on and so on.' Steiger waved his glass about as he spoke, slopping more stains onto his unbuttoned jacket. 'Every day there are bloody more than the day before.'

Wolff was rapidly gaining the impression that the drink in Steiger's hand was not the first of the day. More likely it was the last of the night.

'Word has come down from the gods at Army HQ that we are to expect large-scale Allied attacks some time on or after,' he paused and consulted a scrap of paper on his desk, 'some time on or after the twenty-fourth of this month. Now I don't know how they know that. Maybe they've invested in a crystal ball, or maybe they read it in the guts of a ritually slaughtered chicken, I don't care. All I care about is that we have our house in order by then. I have no intention of losing my balls, crystal or otherwise, in a clear-out and general hatchet job just because of some slack-arse working under me.'

The Hauptman reddened. 'Is the Oberstleutnant referring to me?'

Steiger was taken aback for a moment, then burst into a loud guffaw of laughter. 'Wolff, you really are a prize. I got you down here because you're the only one who does work. Ten like you and I could have built the Great Wall of China by the twenty-fourth. Tell me, frankly, can we be on top of our work load by then?'

'We can try, Oberstleutnant, but in all honesty, with the volume of work . . .'

Steiger interrupted him. 'We can't, can we? There's not a Jew's chance in Berlin of having everything built or repaired by then, and we both know it. Look at this.'

He stood up and walked to a large model of central Italy that dominated the middle of the room. 'Look at it. There's the Gustav Line, the Caesar Line, the Hitler Line,' he looked up and grinned at Wolff, 'and I'll lay money on that one suddenly changing its name if it looks like the Allies are going to get through it; there's the Senger extension, the Dora extension,' he threw his hands in the air. 'The list is endless. There is simply a limit to what we and the Todt Organisation can do in the time with the resources we've got.'

'What is the Oberstleutnant suggesting.' Wolff had more than a suspicion of what was coming. Steiger was like an old fox, sly and cunning, with a potential escape route from any situation that might arise.

How the man had hung on for so long was incredible, his vices being so gross, so many, and so well known. It made one suspect that the widely whispered rumours about a certain gift to Reichsmarschall Goering at the time a lorry load of paintings vanished from a palace being used as an Engineers' HQ might just have some substance. Certainly the man's guardian angel appeared to have impressive powers.

'Very direct, Wolff. I like that. Let me put it in a nutshell. I want you to mark a proportion of the damage reports as satisfactorily repaired. You can't get round to them all, for all you know they could have been.' Steiger turned on a conspiratorial smile that was more a smirk.

'What proportion of the records would you like me to falsify?'

The Oberstleutnant didn't notice that the usually very correct Wolff had addressed him without the usual courtesies. 'Adjust, Wolff, adjust.' He gently corrected his subordinate. 'I think, oh let me see, shall we say eighty per cent?' Again the smirk was in play. 'A little more impressive than our current average of thirty-one, don't you think?'

'Why not make it ninety, or ninety-nine?'

'Now let's not get carried away. I think eighty will be sufficient.' A note of concern had crept into Steiger's voice, he adopted a tone of conciliation. 'We must be realistic . . .'

It was Wolff's turn to butt in. 'Precisely, Oberstleutnant, and that is what my reports will continue to be. I must reject your suggestion.' With that he left the room.

When he got back to his office he found it necessary to sit down and wipe his glasses for a full three minutes before he could regain some measure of his usual state of composure. He couldn't recall having been so upset since 1937, when a city councillor had approached him with the suggestion of an arrangement they might come to over the voting at a forthcoming planning committee meeting to discuss the allocation of city contracts, for which Wolff's firm had tendered.

He could only hope that he had not made trouble for himself. But he knew he had done the right thing. Decencies were difficult enough to preserve in wartime, certainly his integrity was not going to be one of the casualties. Having achieved a state of mind in which he felt he could work, he took the top report from the stack and started to read.

It was about an emplacement he knew well, having personally supervised its construction. It was the last job he had completed before his promotion, and one of the few he felt a pride in. The engineering problems had been considerable, not least that of tunnelling through a particularly unstable ridge. He read quickly, eager to see how it was standing up to the non-stop bombardments pounding Monte Cassino.

*　　*　　*　　*　　*　　*

'Well, there it is. Has anyone got any questions, or suggestions?' Lieutenant Saville was sitting on the tailboard of a Guy platoon truck, and the men were on the ground around him. He took a long time over fishing out cigarettes and matches from various pockets, to give them time to think.

'You said we were crossing the river after the first wave, sir.' It was Porter who broke the silence, at least the silence of the group; the guns and traffic were making enough noise to warrant his raising the volume of his usual gruff tones. 'How soon is "after"?'

'At this stage I don't know. We should find out at the briefing. We won't be right on their heels, if that's what you're thinking. We'd just get in everybody's way. The boats and rafts will be ferrying assault infantry for at least the first couple of hours, we could go any time after that. Depends on how many boats are knocked out, how stiff the opposition is, and so on.' He glanced over the other men. 'Anyone else have something they want to raise at this stage? There'll be another chance later, but by then not so much time to do anything about it if it's a real problem.'

'What about weapons, sir?' The questioner was Russell.

Saville glanced at Lucas before answering. The sergeant avoided his eye. 'None, apart from the items we are taking that'll be used to crack the emplacement. I've worked out what we're going to need in the way of stores. To be sure of doing the job we'll all be taking maximum loads, that includes me and the sergeant as well. I think every man will have quite enough without adding personal arms. For protection we'll rely on our escort.'

'I don't fancy that, sir. I don't fancy that at all.' Reilly's voice was audible from among the general hubbub that the unexpected announcement created. 'What if this escort of ours gets bumped off, or buggers off? What then? We'd be

30

left right in the shit and no mistake. We don't know these fellas at all. For all we know they might piss themselves at the first bang and run like scalded cats.'

'Watch your language, Reilly.'

'It's all right, Sergeant Lucas. I can appreciate their concern, and I'm having second thoughts myself, but we're still left with the problem of weight. When we're getting near the top of the hill every ounce will make a difference. What do you suggest?'

Lucas was rather pleased at his advice being sought in front of the men. He regarded Saville as a good officer, never expecting anyone to do something he wouldn't, always leading from the front. But he'd never been able to strike up the same sort of relationship with him that other sergeants managed to with their platoon or company commanders. They had remained strictly sergeant and officer; they worked together but it wasn't really a partnership. He didn't feel that the cause was snobbery, or lack of trust on the lieutenant's part. It was just that there was some indefinable barrier there and sometimes he sensed the men realised it as well, and so he was glad of this opportunity to display cooperation in front of them.

'Well, sir, the Lee-Enfield .303 and Thompson sub-machine gun are both over nine pounds, so they're out. The sten is lighter, but it can be an awkward shape to handle when you're carrying a full-weight pack as well. That just leaves pistols, the .38 Webley or Enfield. Better than nothing, but not a lot to choose between them, just a case of which we can get a hold of.'

While Lucas had been listing the alternatives there had been whispering among the men. It was Harris who was prompted into being a reluctant spokesman.

'Eh, Lieutenant, we'd be a lot happier about this whole show if we could have something that would really stop any Jerry who got in our way.'

'What had you in mind?'

It took a poke in the back from Russell to get Harris to say, and then he took so long over an apologetic preamble that Reilly lost patience and took over. He was blunt about it.

'What we want is those big .45 automatics the Yanks have, sir.'

Lucas snorted with derision. 'What use is a ruddy great hand cannon like that. The chances any of you would get even your first shot into the target are remote, and with the kick they've got the second shot, if you ever got one off, could go anywhere.'

Reilly was not to be put off. 'But if we do hit the target we know it'll go down and stay down.'

The growing heat of the exchange was clear to the lieutenant. He sought a way to quench it. 'I think they might be a good idea, but there's no way we can get hold of them. They're not standard issue and I doubt we could prise any away from the Yanks, even if there was time.'

Corporal Clark had hesitated a long time before speaking. What he had to offer might bring him praise for initiative or just a lot of trouble. He decided to chance it.

'There is one way we might get hold of a few Colts, Lieutenant. I've heard that some Yanks have set up a sort of black market in a village about eight miles from here. If we pooled our money, and got going now, we could be back in time for the briefing.'

Lucas kept his expression straight, waiting to take his cue from his officer. It was a long time in coming.

Saville was aware of the conflict that must have gone on in Clark's mind before he came out with that snippet of information, but that was secondary. What he said now would probably be a major factor in forming the men's attitude to the job that lay ahead of them.

His alternatives were to pour cold water on the whole idea of weapons, or talk the men into accepting standard issue revolvers; or he could go the whole hog and try to get the Colts. Chances were that the black market was just a myth, a rumour. But if he tried at least the men would have seen that, and would then readily accept Webleys as the best available.

The whole mission was loaded with risk, the comforting presence of pistols with such awesome and deserved reputations as man-stoppers might just tip the balance from pessimism to confidence.

He unbuttoned a pocket and pulled out all the money he had on him. 'Does anyone know the going rate for a .45?'

There was an instant change in the men's expressions. Tatman in particular modified his from morose discontent to beaming expectation. That was not necessarily a good sign in his case, but it was most definitely an improvement.

'I hope we've brought enough.' Russell tried lifting his backside from the hard bench to avoid the effects of the bumps the Morris was continually finding. Unfortunately the irregularities in the road came at irregular intervals and he wasn't able to synchronise his movements with those of the bench.

'Seeing as it's every bloody lira we have it'll have to be, won't it?' Harris was not happy. 'I was saving mine for my next leave. I've got a couple of birds in Naples all lined up.'

'I suppose you have to pay them plenty, Slacker, so they'll put up with that ugly mug of yours.'

Harris came back at Mike Russell very fast. 'Well at least the birds I go with are real women who want a bloke with a bit of experience, not a skinny kid who doesn't know what it's for yet.'

'You're both mad. Women are nothing but a pain in the arse.' Having delivered that weighty piece of philosophy, Alf Porter went back to sucking on his empty pipe.

'Your trouble, Alf, is that you've been a ruddy bachelor for too long. What you want to do is to find some healthy old girl, a widow with a bit of property . . .'

'So what makes you think I couldn't get a young one if I cared to?'

Harris backed off. 'All right, all right, don't get touchy, I was only saying . . .'

Saville could hear snatches of the exchange going on in the back of the truck. The men were keyed up, ready to jump down each other's throats. It was a sign of the inevitable build up of tension that would continue to grow until the guns started in fourteen hours' time.

Fourteen hours. There was a lot still to do, and if it was humanly possible they had to find the time to get their heads down for a while. There weren't enough hours in the day.

'I think this is it.' Corporal Clark was riding in the cab between Saville and Lucas. He'd offered to drive, but the sergeant, who so confidently handled any type of explosive device, was nervous of being driven by other people.

The Morris stopped on a dusty unpaved road that served as the main and only street of the small village. Gawky off-white houses topped by tiles of contrasting blue and red and umber loomed two and three storeys high over them. War had spared this hamlet, passed it by completely. Apart from a burned-out German armoured car, an obvious victim of a strafe attack, half a mile outside of it, there was no evidence anywhere of the vicious battles and rearguard actions that had littered the hills and valleys all around with a heavy sprinkling

33

of white wooden crosses.

'Perhaps if you and Sergeant Lucas stayed in the truck, sir. Otherwise it might put them off.'

'Good idea, Corporal. We don't want to ruin everything after coming all this way. We have to keep an eye on the truck, anyway. I don't fancy walking back just because an Italian brat has swiped a couple of wheels.'

The street was almost empty. There was none of the mass of urchins and young pimps who littered the streets and squares of Naples. Nor any of the attractive dark-eyed girls who touted for the various cafés and bars. For a hundred yards in either direction there was not a living soul in sight, save for an old woman who sat in a rickety cane-back chair outside one particularly seedy and dilapidated property. Unmoving, dressed all in black, she was as much a part of the furniture of the street as the gutter down its middle and the washing lines strung over it.

Clark rousted the sappers from the back of the truck, and after consulting a few lines on a crumpled piece of paper chose a side alley and led them down it.

The route between the old buildings twisted and turned with every yard. Within a dozen steps they were out of sight of the Morris. Clark called a halt before a three-storey structure that appeared to be part house, part store of some sort. After checking the scrap of paper once more, the corporal rapped twice on the thinly applied black paint of a low doorway set into an angle of the wall.

A shutter at an upstairs window partially opened and a close-cropped head stuck out. The face beneath that vestige of hair was pink, fleshy and sweating. In contrast, the bulbous nose that adorned it was red and peeling. A spittle-stained cigar dangled from rubbery lips, and waggled from side to side as its owner scrutinised his callers. 'Is you guys buying or selling?'

'We're buying.' Ash floated down towards Russell, and he took a pace back to avoid it.

'OK, come on in. Up the stairs on your left.' The repulsive face withdrew.

It was Tatman who was pushed into leading the way into the coolness of the house and who, after prompting from Alf Porter as to which was his left, led the others up a flight of unguarded wooden stairs.

If the lower portion of the building had presented the

interior its external appearance might have led them to expect
– a jumbled mass of broken farm tools and split sacks of
moulding grain – then what they found at the top of the stairs
came as a revelation.

The large room they found themselves in was packed from
floor to ceiling with every description of goods, but all with
one thing in common, their American army origin. Cigarettes,
drink and soap predominated but there were also cases of
motor spares, stacks of clothing, tyres, boxes of razor blades
and chocolate, and in a corner the complete engine from a
jeep.

The body of the individual they had already seen was no
more attractive than his face. As they reached the room
he was shutting a door that led off with one hand, and but-
toning his trousers with the other. The glistening rolls of fat
that his open shirt revealed hung down over his belt.

'I was in the middle of something, so don't keep me long.
What are you after?'

'We want some .45 automatics, with ammunition.' Clark
came straight to the point.

'Now what do you guys want with rods like that? Shit, has
your crummy army run out of everything?'

'We're going into action tonight . . .' Clark's elbow in his
ribs cut short Harris's explanation.

'Well, have you got any?'

'I ain't selling.'

'I asked if you'd got any.' Clark had to move round to stay
in front of the man who had turned away reinforcing the
impression of bored disinterest in his voice.

'And I said I ain't selling. Jesus, you guys get on my tits.
What are you, bloody keen? Buying your own equipment.
Hey, you, leave that stuff alone!'

While the proprietor waddled across to slam back the lid
of a packing case that Tatman had opened to peep inside,
Mike Russell nudged the corporal and nodded towards a
shelf at the back of the room. It was piled high with hand
guns.

'How much do you want for eight, with thirty rounds each?'
As an added inducement to get the bargaining started Clark
took out the roll of notes they had all contributed to.

The American laughed, an ugly sound that displayed alternate black and gold teeth. 'Jesus Christ, you crease me. Shit,
I can get twice that for just one pistol with twenty rounds

35

from any local hood who fancies going into business for himself. Someone else's business, that is.' He laughed at his own joke and waved a Colt automatic that he took from the shelf.

A tall thin Negro climbed the stairs. He didn't even bother to look at the British soldiers, but sat down on a pile of tyres and proceeded to peel an apple.

'Look, we have to have those Colts.'

'Shit, you're boring me. If there ain't nothing else you want then piss off out of here.'

Clark was about to give up, but Pat Reilly had other ideas. He pushed through to the front and thrust his closed fist out towards the American.

'If you won't take money, would you be interested in these?'

'What have you got there?' The black-marketeer was suddenly interested, greed was in his eyes. He stared down at the locked fingers. 'What you got, some gold teeth?'

The Irishman's fist didn't unclench. Instead it zipped straight up towards the man's face. For all his bulk the intended victim was fast enough dodging back to almost avoid the blow. Almost. Missing the multiple chins the knuckles caught the underside of the fleshy nose. There was a loud crack and a spout of blood arced to the floor.

Eyes watering copiously, hands clenched across his face in a vain attempt to staunch the fast flow, the American succumbed to the excruciating pain of the injury and collapsed into a foetal position on the floor.

He failed to snatch it as it was dropped from the fat fingers, but Reilly had the released pistol and was pointing it at the Negro an instant after it hit the floor.

'Not much point in your aiming that thing at me. It ain't got no bullets in it anyhow.' With a complete disregard for his confederate's suffering the black man went on with his eating, pausing occasionally to spit out a pip as he chewed round the core.

'You're not going to stop us. We need those Colts.'

A wide pearly smile was immediately directed at the corporal. 'You're right there. I sure ain't gonna stop you. You just go on right ahead and take what you need.'

The sappers exchanged looks, then; still puzzled by the man's unconcerned attitude, they searched round for what they wanted. There were five Colts and enough ammunition to fill four magazines for each. An empty sack was appropriated from a pile and the items thrown into it. While that was being done the apple-eater made no move to interfere, but even so Reilly loaded one of the pistols and kept it trained on him.

'I wonder what he's got in there?' Harris had kept on eyeing the door they had seen closed when they first came in. 'I think I'll just have a peep.'

Harris licked his lips. He was sure the Yank would have some tasty bit of skirt in there, maybe there'd be time to . . . The door wasn't locked. He enjoyed his growing erection as he anticipated what he'd find.

'Here, Alf, Nobby, come and have a look at this.' His shout brought them running.

Perhaps she was older than she looked, but the girl sprawled naked on the rumpled bed had no vestige of pubic hair and her breasts as yet were no more than tiny bumps that pushed small nipples proud of her smooth chest. She made no move to cover herself, just lay there staring back at the men crowded in the doorway, her big brown eyes quite expressionless.

'The dirty bastard.' Porter whirled round and charged at the still prostrate fat man. It wasn't until the heel of his steel-shod boot had crashed down for the sixth time that the others managed to pull him off.

'She's a kid, just a bloody kid. Dirty bastard,' he kept screaming, still trying to lash out at the crushed and bloody bundle even when he had been hauled well beyond reach.

'Hurry up and get that stuff out of here.' Clark, aided by Harris was having a hard task to restrain Alf Porter from inflicting further damage to the unconscious body.

'Has he killed him?' Almost at random Russell was stuffing pistols and boxes of ammunition into the sack, and anything else that took his fancy.

'How the hell should I know? I'm not touching him. Just get a move on.' The corporal shouted to Tatman to get the girl out.

A minute later she appeared, being pushed by the big sapper, carrying her clothes in a bundle clutched before her, but it seemed more with the intention of retaining her property than protecting her modesty.

'What do I do with her?'

'Oh, Christ. Put her outside and give her a shove. Here, give her this.'

It was the girl who caught the notes, grabbing them out of the air before Tatman had even made ready to. With that she was down the stairs and out of the front door, and gone.

'And what about him? He saw it all.' Reilly called over his shoulder, not taking his eyes off the Negro.

'Heck, don't you fellas worry none about me. I ain't in no position to tell nobody nothing. They might want to know just what I was doing in this Aladdin's cave of goodies; 'specially as my unit are still waiting for me to get back from my last forty-eight hour leave, in March.'

'Come on, let's leave him.' Clark began rounding the others up and herding them towards the stairs. 'We've got enough with having to kill Jerries, without going round bumping off Yank deserters.'

The corporal led the rest of the section in a rush back to their transport. Lucas had the engine running and had already turned the Morris round. He waited only for a shout that told him everyone was on board before crashing into first gear and accelerating out of the village.

The sergeant had anticipated his men having problems and their precipitate return tended to confirm that they had created trouble of some description behind them. Precisely what, he wasn't prepared to speculate.

Saville too had his suspicions that all had not gone smoothly, but he wasn't keen to commence an investigation into what had happened right there and then. Later would do, much later. In fact, if he was quite honest with himself, he thought maybe never would be the best course of all. He called back to Clark to ask if they'd got what they went for. With satisfaction, and without question, he accepted the NCO's immediate affirmative.

Back at the house the phlegmatic Negro popped the last slice of apple into his mouth, stretched languidly and walked over to the still breathing human wreck on the bare boards.

'Well, well, Private First Class Shapiro. That gent sure made a mess of you. But never you mind, I'll take real good care of the business. And I'll sure give you a pretty funeral. Actually there won't be a lot of mourners though, on account of I just don't know anyone who cares whether you're alive or dead. You sure are taking a time to die. I hope you bleed to death before it gets dark. It's gonna be tough enough as it is, dragging your fat carcass out of here to some nice lonely spot, without my having the bother of having to slit your throat first.'

A hefty kick failed to elicit any response from the unconscious form. 'You sure is an ungrateful bugger. It's funny how things can change so fast, ain't it, Fatso? A while back

38

there you were all set to do dirty things to that pretty little girl, and now you're gonna die. My, my, PFC Shapiro, war sure is hell.'

The view from the truck as it bumped over the rough track on the way back to the main highway was an endless succession of neat fields and well tended olive groves. There were hardly any signs of war apart from an occasional wreck of a vehicle, overturned or burned out at the side of the road. The only other indications that war had been this way were the circular scorched patches on distant hillsides or a glimpse of damaged trees in the middle of a plantation, and a sprinkling of jagged sheets of metal catching stray rays of sun that found their way through the overcast, marking the resting places of crashed aircraft.

But as they drew nearer to the highway with increasing frequency they saw the familiar multi-lingual sign boards that warned of mines. Grim stencilled skulls-and-crossbones made the messages abundantly clear even to those who didn't catch the words.

'We are being flagged down, sir.' Lucas slowed the truck and let it coast to a stop by a group of four soldiers who were removing their packs from a jeep that had lost a battle with a large boulder at the edge of the road. One of the men dabbed at a bleeding nose with an already red scrap of grubby rag.

A garbled mixture of Polish and halting English came from the quartet as they clustered about the cab of the Morris.

'They're Poles, sir.'

'Thank you, Sergeant, I'd gathered that for myself.' Saville picked out a craggy-faced veteran whose English was reasonably fluent. 'What do you want?'

The Pole waved at the jeep. 'Bloody no good now. You give us ride to other side of village.' He pointed to a small cluster of buildings that lay about a mile further down the road. 'Or maybe to the big road, yes?'

'Why the other side of the village?'

'Bloody Ruskies there. Mines all over. We not able to walk round bloody Ruskies.'

'I don't know what you're on about. There aren't any Russians within a thousand miles of here.'

The soldier disagreed. 'No, I tell you, bloody Ruskies there.'

'Well, I don't know what you're on about but hop in the back, we'll take you through.'

The Poles wasted no time in slinging their gear into the Morris and scrambling in themselves.

'Better take it slow when we get to the village, Sergeant, just until we find what this is all about.'

At a gentler pace than they'd experienced at Lucas's hands so far the truck was driven towards and into the outskirts of the settlement.

It was somewhat larger than the village they'd visited earlier, but as they drove through it was just as quiet as the other had been, although several shops and a couple of bars were open. Turning a corner brought them into its main square and suddenly the noises and colour of a large crowd greeted them, and the way was instantly blocked by a close-packed throng of Italians.

The Morris could be nudged forward only a couple of yards, and then the press about the vehicle was too close to risk going on. But although they were now effectively trapped, the attention of the people was not on the army lorry in its midst. They were all looking towards a precarious make-shift platform in the centre of the square, from which a fiery little man with a mane of grey hair and apparently lungs of leather was screaming passionate rhetoric at the mob.

'There, don't I tell you? Bloody Ruskies.' The veteran had thrust his head through from the back of the truck and now in a dramatic gesture indicated the pair of red flags adorned with hammers and sickles, that hung limply over the orator.

One of the crowd pressed close to the open window of the cab must have heard and recognised the accent, as instantly a howl went up from the assembly and their mood abruptly changed from indifference towards the soldiers among them to fury.

'Now we've got problems.' Lucas slowly extracted the starting handle from beneath his seat and took a firm grip of it.

Saville suddenly saw his timetable falling apart in the face of the crisis with which they were faced. 'It rather looks, Sergeant, as if our fighting is going to start rather earlier than we'd expected, and this is one battle we just can't win.'

As if by accident the lieutenant let his hand slip down from his lap to rest lightly on a sten gun secured between the seats. The invective from the crowd became more violent, and he took a tighter grip on the sub-machine gun.

At some unnoticed moment the crowd in the immediate

vicinity of the Morris became no longer a cross-section of the local community, but a mass of fist-waving youths and young men. The situation had all the potential of an ugly incident. Already the mood of the Italians had passed the moment when it might have been subdued by reason or argument, and had now reached a pitch where it was doubtful if even a pistol-waving threat would work.

Saville knew that even if the mob contented itself with doing nothing more than screaming abuse and waving its fists, it might take hours for it to run out of steam sufficiently to let them pass. All the time in his mind there was a mental image of the gun emplacement waiting for them.

A couple of Italians close enough to see the action shrank back as far as the press of the crowd would allow when Saville made a show of cradling the sten in his arms, but when he made no further move their confidence returned and they resumed their role in the affair with redoubled vigour.

There was a minor turbulence in the wall of bodies immediately to the front of the truck, and the little man with grey hair climbed onto the vehicle's towing-bar. Perched precariously, swaying backwards and forwards, he went about his rabble-rousing. He was facing the truck and every now and again would raise a howl of appreciation from his audience by making dramatic fist-waving gestures at Lucas and Saville in the cab. He obviously assumed they were all Polish.

'What's going on, Mike?' Tatman had been made to sit on the floor of the truck by the crush, and had from that position a very restricted view of what was happening. He'd been forced by the others to adopt that place of rest as it was generally agreed that by his vacating a seat a space was made sufficient to fit two standard-size bottoms.

'Lot of greasy Wops getting excited and foaming at the mouth. Nothing unusual.' Russell was quite unperturbed by the clamour outside their canvas cocoon.

Corporal Clark had rolled down the back flap of the tilt as soon as the trouble had started. Now he reached out and stopped Harris from lacing it.

'Don't fasten it. We might want to get out in a hurry if one of them thinks of dropping a match down the tank.'

'What are they getting so worked up about out there? We're all on the same side now, aren't we? Or hasn't anybody told this lot?' Porter kept taking peeps out through a slit in the canvas.

'It's not us, it's them.' Clark indicated the four Poles who all sat stiffly alert, each of them with his rifle at the ready.

'Why's that? They're a decent bunch of lads.'

'You're an ignorant sod, Reilly. A lot of the Poles have spent time in Russian prison camps. A load of them died there and others who came through it were bloody wrecks when they got out. They hate the Russians as much as they do the Germans, and I don't bloody blame them. Treacherous bloody sods, the Russians.'

'But what's that got to do with this lot outside?' Reilly stuck his head out for a look and ducked back as a soft wet missile burst on the canvas close by. 'Fuck that. I'm going to get bloody mad in a minute.'

'This lot are Italian communists, red Wops. They're just ruddy puppets, they don't pee unless Moscow tells them to, and Moscow has said have a go at the Poles.'

'And we've driven into the middle of some sort of rally they're holding. I wonder how long it'll take them to work from rotten fruit to half-bricks.' Harris jumped as another object squelched against the canvas by his ear.

'Bloody Ruskies, bloody Wops, all rubbish.' The veteran tapped Corporal Clark on the knee to attract his attention. 'Italy a country to fight in, not fight for. All bloody rubbish!' At the conclusion of the announcement he winked and spat neatly out through a hole in the side of the tilt. He was rewarded with an especially loud howl of rage from an insulted individual outside.

'I don't care if they're red, pink or blue with orange spots, I wish the lieutenant would do something and get us out of here.' Harris started on another nail. The floor below him was already littered with slivers of bone.

It was taking an effort on Lucas's part to resist the temptation to poke the starting handle into a pimply face that mouthed at him through his window. 'We'll have to be getting out of here soon, sir. We've still better than an hour's drive to get back.'

'I am aware of that, Sergeant. Increase the engine speed gradually, will you?'

Lucas didn't query the order. By degrees he eased the pedal down until the six-cylinder engine was nearing maximum revs.

Saville meanwhile had unfastened the one piece fabric roof of the cab and draped it back out of the way. That done he stood on the seat and made an ostentatious show with the sten. After a momentary reaction among the crowd the effect was lost and the scene went on as before, loud and aggressive and becoming more so.

With deliberate slowness Saville brought the weapon to the firing position at his shoulder and aimed it straight at the old man still teetering back and forth on his uncertain perch. The oldster stumbled over a couple of sentences, swallowed deeply so that his large adam's apple bobbed up and down, and then took up his theme again as he became convinced that it was purely a bluff.

'Put it into first, and when I nudge you cut the ignition for a second and slip the clutch enough to make this wagon jump forward a couple of inches, not more.' Having lowered the sten in order to bend down and deliver the message into the sergeant's ear, Saville once more raised the weapon with slow deliberation.

At the moment the sub-machine gun pointed straight at the old man the lieutenant tapped Lucas's thigh with his foot.

The running motor was inaudible above the crowd, and even Lucas only knew it was off for that instant by the shudder as it over-ran. As he switched the ignition on again he snatched his foot from the clutch pedal. The sequence of rapid events blended together with the fluidity of a single action.

As the sten came up the Morris gave an almighty backfire and jerked forward. The loud report instantly silenced the crowd, with one exception. Losing his balance at the unexpected movement of the truck, the old man fell forward, or as far forward as he could. His progress was arrested by his crotch making hard contact with the, by now, boiling-hot radiator cap.

The tormented scream of anguish produced by the oldster went right up the audible scale, and off it. He toppled to one side, his eyes rolling up to reveal only the whites as he did. His impact with the hard paving of the square restored his vocal powers and without appearing to pause for breath he commenced a series of the most appalling yells that made Saville's scalp tingle, and the hair on the back of his neck rise up.

There was already a jam of bodies in the exits from the square before the old man hit the ground. Three seconds after he started howling in earnest there wasn't a living soul to be seen, just a litter of hats and shoes at each egress.

'Russell, Harris, out and move the body!' Lucas was surprised how much he had to raise his voice to be sure of being heard above the fuss the writhing form on the ground was making.

'I hope his old woman likes it well done,' was Mike Russell's cruel comment as they hauled the sufferer aside.

They dropped the Poles as they waited, the last of a line of a dozen vehicles, to turn out onto the main road. Every one of the many nationalities that made up the Allied army was represented among the varied selection of transport that trundled past in a seemingly endless convoy.

A file of American Dodge trucks loaded with grinning Gurkhas was followed by a number of the weird looking Indian armoured carriers, manned by Sikhs, to be followed in their turn by Canadian-built Ford trucks pulling the British six-pounder guns of a New Zealand anti-tank outfit. With scout cars and dispatch riders of the South African contingent, an armoured car of the Free French, and an occasional dashing jeep from one of the Polish divisions the road perfectly illustrated the cosmopolitan Allied Army in Italy.

'Have a last drink, mate.' Porter offered the veteran the bottle that had been going to rounds in the back of the Morris.

In a gnarled fist the bottle was raised high. 'Winston Churchill. Bloody good!'

As he accepted the bottle back Porter sought for some way to reply to the impromptu toast. A name came into his mind, dimly remembered from a lecture they'd had from an officer 'about some of the, eh, other chaps on our, eh, side.'

With a flourish and a silent prayer that he had got it right, Alf lofted the bottle. 'General Anders!' With massive relief he read delight in the Poles' faces. 'Bloody good,' he tacked on for full measure.

As they shouldered their packs the veteran turned back a moment. 'You for Cassino?'

Porter nodded.

'There bloody Germans in our country now, soon I think it bloody Ruskies. Maybe no country for us to go back to when this over, but we do a bloody good job at Cassino.'

As he watched them go Porter muttered under his breath, 'Yeah, we do a bloody good job at Cassino.'

'If this sets in it'll undo all the bleeding work we did on those ruddy approach roads.' Harris craned his neck to look out at the sky from which a light rain had begun to fall.

'Are you hoping they'll call off the attack if it does?' Russell enjoyed goading Harris, and now he had a head start as Slacker had already been made miserable by being given a two-inch mortar and ammunition to carry.

The section had been lucky on happening on a partially completed dug-out that another outfit, more fussy about their comfort than concerned for their safety, had abandoned when the bottom six inches filled with smelly oil-flecked water. With a handful of improvised duckboards wedged above the flood, a few more to roof it over plus the addition of a few crushed oil drums and scraps of camouflage, they had a reasonably weather- and fragment-proof shelter.

But sleep had proved impossible. It wasn't the continuous hammering of the guns, after months of war they might have experienced difficulty sleeping without that background of noise. The rest they needed wouldn't come because each of them in his own way was too keyed up. Their minds were too full of the thousand things there were to do and think of before going into action.

So when they had finished their letters and checked their weapons and packs for the tenth time, there was nothing left to do but squat on the planks, taking turns to start trivial conversation that no one could summon interest in. At intervals one of the men would find the silence too oppressive and would leave the dug-out to take a walk around the area, accepting the slight but real risk of the occasional random shell from the enemy artillery.

In the cab of the truck Lucas and Saville went over the arrangements yet again. It was darker in there now as the Morris was draped with camouflage netting, and festooned with bundles of wild corn and grass.

'There's not as much information as I'd like as to what to expect in the way of enemy wire and mines.' Saville shuffled through the photographs until he found one that showed a portion of the valley floor as well as Monte Cassino and the monastery.

'The main concentrations of German defences in the valley are marked, sir. If we can thread our way between them it'll just be the mines and any isolated machine-gun posts we'll have to watch out for.'

'Yes, once we're across the river and turn right towards the hill we might be able to dodge round the prickliest parts.

But it'll make the job of navigating several times more complicated. At all times we'll have to know where we are pretty precisely. Stay or stray too close to the river and we'll run onto the massive defences and mine fields they've got around the road and rail junction. Too far west and we'll miss the hill altogether and waste a lot of time having to work our way back. It would make life easier if we knew exactly what Jerry wire was going to be cut by the bombardment.'

'You reckon the barrage will do a good job, Lieutenant?'

'Do I detect a shadow of doubt in your mind, Sergeant Lucas?'

He chose his words carefully, though there was nothing in them he'd not heard officers say a hundred times before. 'No, sir. It's just that, well, we've all seen these barrages before. Sometimes they work, but sometimes they miss altogether or don't do as much as was expected, or chew up the ground, slow the advance and give Jerry time to move up reinforcements.'

'I'll admit that has happened in the past but this time the gunners are putting on a really big show. Sixteen hundred guns go into action tonight. If that lot doesn't flatten Hitler's Gustav Line and Monte Cassino in particular, it will at least make his men keep their heads down long enough for our lads to get a firm grip on the far bank.'

'It'd be nice if they stayed down while we tiptoed up the hill as well.'

'I'll drink to that, and talking of drink, Sergeant, I detected a distinct aroma of whisky as we were driving back. My mind was rather full of other things at the time to bother with it then, but as we've got a moment before we attend that briefing you might check to see whether or not my nose was playing me tricks.'

Lucas sought round for something he'd taken the precaution of obtaining and stashing under his seat just in case of such an inquiry. 'I thought you might mention that, sir. So I had a word with Russell and it came to light that we had a bit of change from the, eh, transaction for the pistols. He asked me to give you this, sir, with the lads' compliments.' He handed over a near-full bottle.

Saville smiled. 'It would be ungallant of me to speculate what caused or prompted Russell's uncharacteristic generosity. Convey my thanks to them, Sergeant.'

'I'll just make a final check of the men's packs then, sir.'

'Here, have a swig of this before you go. If it doesn't keep

46

the rain out, at least you won't care about getting wet. It's an abominable way of drinking decent whisky, but if you're not fussy . . .'

Surprised and slightly confused by the unexpected offer of the bottle, Lucas hesitated and then accepted it. Whisky was far from being his favourite tipple, but he had no wish to give offence, and took a good pull at the contents. 'Very nice, sir. Thank you. I'll be off and make those checks then, sir.'

'Very good, Sergeant.' Saville added an afterthought: 'Oh, and once you're satisfied, don't let Corporal Clark keep giving them a lot of nitpicking jobs to do. I know he's keen, but impress on him that rest is of as much value as any minor tasks he has in mind.'

Lucas departed, soon disappearing from sight among the towering heaps of camouflaged stores and ammunition.

Saville watched him go. He felt he was lucky to have a sergeant like that, a good, steady, reliable type who could be trusted to take the weight of the petty details from his shoulders. He tended rather to be over stiff, over formal, but doubtless that was just his way of maintaining some 'distance' between them. Certainly he had no reason to worry about him and perhaps with a bit more time their relationship might mellow.

He took out the sack containing the remaining revolvers and automatics and marvelled again at how Clark had managed to get all of these, and the 'change' as well. Each was considered in turn, and finally his choice was narrowed down to two.

The Luger was a fine weapon, but the five-shot advantage of its thirteen-round magazine tipped the scales in favour of the 9mm Browning automatic. How an American had come into possession of the weapon he couldn't imagine, the Canadian-made pistol had only been issued on a limited scale to British commandos and paratroops.

Having filled three spare magazines for it from his stock of 9mm parabellum cartridges meant for the sten, Saville slumped back in his seat. There was nothing more to do, unless fresh information that came up at the briefing prompted a major change of plan. Everything had been checked and double checked. Fuses, wire cutters, plastic explosive, special ammunition for the mortar; everything was ready.

Now he had time to think. The job was far tougher than any he'd imagined he might get, tougher than anything he had ever tackled before. The sappers he had chosen to go with him were all first-class men in their own way. All very much

47

individuals, and all experts in a different facet of their work, with the exception of Tatman who was in because of brawn, not brain.

What he was doing now had some parallels to when he'd been at school. He'd always led the crosscountry field when they went out of the gate, had always led the charge in a snowball fight and volunteered to have a solo run at British bulldog, even though there was never hope of breaking through the packed ranks that faced him, and the result was certain to be debagging. And now he was out in front again, or would be. But this time it was not just snowballs.

Sleep wouldn't come, though it was more than twenty-four hours since he'd last enjoyed that happy state. In his mind over and over again he went through the arrangements, searching for anything he might have missed. There were such a lot of question-marks hanging over the job.

*　　*　　*　　*　　*　　*

Hauptmann Wolff's pencil tapped lightly against the list of names and reference numbers. There were so many. From the reports sent in by the field engineers it would appear that at least the top five positions listed were in need of rebuilding, not repairing. A direct hit from a heavy-calibre shell or five-hundred-kilo bomb left little of a pill-box or gun pit intact. He sought an entry further down the list, first underlining it, then circling it heavily. That was one he'd have to take a look at, and not just because the emplacement had been built on the Fuehrer's personal orders.

It was inconceivable that several hits from a large siege gun would not have done damage, but Wolff felt irritation all the same. He looked out the report from the stack, seeking the engineer's name. The man was clearly incompetent. His summary of the damage was sketchy and incomplete, altogether highly unsatisfactory. Yes, he would have to go and have a look for himself.

'What do you want?' Gefreiter Henschel answered the summoning bell with a snarl in his voice and cake in his mouth.

'When you have finished displaying how much like a pig you are in habit and appearance, you can get my car.'

For Wolff the words were sharp, but they failed to penetrate the NCO's armour of loutish ignorance.

'Oh good. I fancy a drive. Where to, Rome?'

'I want to inspect some fortifications in the Gustav line.

Now get my car.'

'Into the shitty firing line again,' Henschel muttered under his breath as he stuffed the last crumbs into his mouth and left reluctantly to obey the Hauptmann's orders.

Really the man was insufferable, becoming more impossible each day. Wolff would have loved to have him replaced, but he knew that any slight chance there might have been of that happening had disappeared when he'd refused to carry out the Oberstleutnant's scheme to falsify the records.

He carefully put his glasses away, stood, and straightened the papers on his desk. The telephone was like a magnet for his eyes. It would be easy for him to slip away, simply go out and do his job; but he was supposed to check with Steiner first. Well, he had to talk to him sometime. Might as well get it over with now.

'Hello, this is Hauptmann Wolff Inspect . . . Wolff here. There are some fortifications I must check for myself before authorising work on them. I am going out now, is that in order?'

The tone of voice on the other end of the line was almost honeyed. 'If that is your judgement, Wolff, then that is good enough for me.'

Wolff gained the impression that there was more to come. There was.

'About that matter this morning, Wolff. I think we can forget that now. It was . . . it was a loyalty test. Of course there is no need to mention it to anyone.'

So that was it, the old fox was worried he might report the conversation to Division, or even Army. Perhaps there was a limit to the protection he enjoyed.

'As you wish, Oberstleutnant, as you wish. Oh by the way, I shall not be in again until tomorrow. I intend to visit the Fuehrer's emplacement and as it is under British observation I shall make it my last call and not go there until after dark.'

'Of course, Wolff. No point in coming back here so late. I'll have Koch finish the daily analysis.'

When he replaced the receiver Wolff experienced an immense feeling of satisfaction at the way the conversation had gone. It especially pleased him that Koch, who at every opportunity hived some of his work load off onto him, should for once have to do some of his work. Things were looking a little brighter. Perhaps there was a chance that he might be able to get rid of Henschel. Perhaps – oh lovely thought –.

even dump him back on Koch.

And now he could look forward to an afternoon doing the work he really loved. If there remained in his mind one nagging worry it was what he might find when he eventually reached the twin gun emplacement on the south slope of Monte Cassino; but a confidence he had in his own work and a general feeling of well-being made him think it was likely that the damage was not severe. Certainly it was very hard to credit the truth of that throw away line in the report that said 'a shell has penetrated the right-hand gun compartment'. That reinforced concrete was over two metres thick, three at the base, and faced with thirty-millimetre armour plate. In addition, the whole of the front of the emplacement was piled to the depth of a further metre with broken rock that afforded substantial protection as well as camouflage. No, it was much more likely that the oaf who had skimped the report had been over-impressed by a heap of uncleared rock that had fallen from the roof under the shock of repeated heavy impacts. The roof was the only part of the structure in which he'd ever entertained the slightest doubts, but any fault development would be progressive and there'd be ample time to grout the fissures or take other steps to safeguard the position. Well, before the day was out he'd see for himself.

When Wolff came out of the pockmarked and roofless building Henschel was already installed behind the steering wheel of the Horch. The Gefreiter pretended he didn't see the officer, to avoid having to get out and open the door.

The car's roof had been folded back, although the rain had only just stopped, and from the look of the sky might start again at any time. For a quiet life Wolff decided not to pursue the matter, unless it began to rain once more.

'Have you taking a sudden liking to fresh air, Henschel?' Wolff contented himself with asking.

'Can't stand the stuff. Give me the fug of a beer hall any day. I put this down so I can jump out if I see an Allied fighter-bomber pouncing on us. Gefreiter Lueger and Leutnant Drexer were fried yesterday when their Kubelwagon was shot off the road and burned.'

'I think I met Drexler once. A very tall young man, good looking and rather serious. Was he killed?'

'Done to a crisp. They had to use a crowbar to get him off the metal of the car.'

Wolff could have done without the details. Not that he was squeamish, well, not as much as he used to be. The interior of Russian blockhouses he'd inspected, after Panzer grenadiers had used flame throwers against their occupants, had hardened him to a degree that would have severely shocked his wife. He found that with the bodies of people he had never known he could in a way turn his mind off; it made a sort of detachment possible. What he did find hard to take was the death of people he'd known, however slightly. That was why he'd asked his wife not to tell him the names of people killed in the air raids, not unless it was close family. He found it very difficult to forget that the name mentioned in passing, now a grossly disfigured horror in a shallow grave somewhere, had once been a healthy, living person, a human being. He was very glad that Hilda had now moved permanently into their holiday home in the country.

'Where to first?' The Gefreiter was rattling the gear stick impatiently.

The Hauptmann gave his driver the reference number of a trench and tunnel complex in the village of Sant'Angelo. They had been there several times before and on every occasion, before the repairs were completed, further damage had been done by shells that struck it over and over again. It was like that all the time. The Allied artillery and airforces gave the German defences no respite. When they were not blasting chunks out of the defensive lines, they were pounding the roads, destroying supplies coming forward, damaging machinery, and delaying often by a week or more those vital loads that did get through.

In this seemingly endless cycle of building and breaking, repairing and destroying, Wolff had kept his sanity, carried on coolly and calmly with his work while others about him had taken to the bottle or, unable to find oblivion or solace in that, had reached a stage of frustration where they now simply went through the motions. Like Koch, who did as little as he could, and did that badly.

Wolff had come to treat the war like an extension of his civilian practice, thinking of it as no more than one of those mercifully rare projects on which absolutely everything went wrong: from high accident rates to sub-standard materials. Seen that way he could deal with it. The war did intrude, but most of the time he saw his work as construction, demolition and renovation. There was no aspect of those with which he was not familiar, or could not cope.

As the car drove down the much repaired wreck-flanked road leading to the valley floor he scanned the list once more, and again his eyes came to rest on the boldly circled entry. He brushed a half-formed thought from his mind. No, it was quite inconceivable that the Fuehrer's emplacement could have suffered anything other than the most superficial damage, quite impossible. He leant forward and tapped his driver on the shoulder.

'What is it now?' Henschel's face was no prettier in profile, as he craned round to see what was wanted.

'If you do see a fighter diving to attack us, do let me know. I have no wish for my first knowledge of danger to be the sight of your oversized posterior as you jump out.'

The Gefreiter completely missed the ironic humour in the remark. Wolff gave a little smile, as an outward sign of the inner satisfaction he enjoyed at the slight joke that served the purpose both of pleasing him and demonstrating once more Henschel's moronic level of comprehension.

For the officer the afternoon promised to be busy and interesting; and with his visit to the Fuehrer's emplacement the last of his list of calls, he also had something to look forward to at the end of the day.

*   *   *   *   *   *

... and so to summarise: H-hour is at 23.00. A forty-minute opening bombardment by the mediums and heavies against the known Jerry gun positions will cover the noise of the boats and rafts being carried to the river. At the same time the heavy ack-ack and field artillery will plaster the forward German defences and mortar positions. At 23.40 the boats go in the water, and as they do,' Saville paused to refer to the piece of paper he held, 'and as they do four regiments of mediums and seventeen of field guns will commence a paced barrage of the far bank that will lift a hundred yards every six minutes. We go as soon as there's room on the boats.'

The section had heard it all before. From Saville, from Lucas and from the major who had given the battalion briefing they'd attended. They knew the broad outline of the attack, their own part in it.

All around them other small groups of men who had been under concealment all day were starting to move and coalesce into larger units, as platoons, companies and battalions set about sorting themselves into their battle order.

Troops of tanks took turns at running their engines, so as not to make too much noise at once, to charge their batteries. As dusk started to settle so the activity became greater.

'OK. We move out as soon as our escort gets here.' As Saville might have expected, it was Russell who chimed in with a question.

'What if they don't come, sir?'

'Then we don't go, Russell. Those Colts you're wearing are not magic wands. We're going to need help getting through the Jerry lines.'

Clark was fussing around the men, taking up a strap here, securing an accessory there, until Lucas, sensing that the corporal's attentions were making the men nervous, sent him off on a minor errand to fetch an item from the truck.

With the corporal gone the men settled down again and the note of irritability that had been creeping into the conversation gave way to flippancy and a string of weak jokes that raised laughter above their due. Tatman especially was highly delighted at the reception he got for a selection of very unfunny crudities.

Now more and more of the other groups about them were moving out, and as each did so their banter trailed off, until by the time each line of men had gone twenty yards every face wore an expression of silent determination. Here and there a snatch of whistled tune was briefly audible, failing quickly in its isolation.

Harris cocked his head on one side, and listened. 'Christ. Hasn't it gone bloody quiet!'

At his mentioning it the others became aware of the fact as well. Gradually the guns which for the last six months, almost without respite, had been hammering away round the clock were falling silent. The last echoes rolled back from the hills.

The unnatural silence rapidly became oppressive, weighing down on the men and making them conscious of the least noise they made. With only the occasional jingle of a loose piece of equipment, hurriedly tracked down and eliminated by vigilant NCOs, more of the infantry filed past to disappear into the thickening brown haze.

Clark returned, and he was not alone.

'Bloody hell, look what he's brought with him.' Mike Russell poked Tatman in the ribs to draw his attention to the small group of men trailing casually along behind their corporal.

A burly young sergeant stepped forward and introduced himself with disarming familiarity to Lieutenant Saville.

'I'm Sergeant Murray. Second New Zealand Division. We've come to give you a hand.'

'Is this all of you?' Saville looked past the sergeant to the four men he'd brought with him. 'I've very pleased to have you along, but I was expecting a few more men.'

Murray shook his head. 'No, this is all of us. You know what it's like when you buy the best. You never do get much for your money.' He'd adopted a relaxed stance, casually cradling a Thompson sub-machine gun in his arms.

Three of the others sported similar weapons, and in addition all were festooned with grenades that hung from their belts and webbing.. Each of them was also well equipped with pouches holding spare magazines for their Thompsons.

'Oh, I nearly forgot, we bought you a little present. Thought you might be able to use it. Bring it out here, Kemp.'

The sergeant's shout prompted a tall thin soldier to leave the group and step out in front of Saville. A bulky sacking-draped pack on his back grotesquely exaggerated his outline. With the same easy informality that had characterised his NCO's behaviour he flipped back a corner and allowed a weapon-like contraption, linked by twin hoses to whatever was beneath the sacking, to slip down into his hands. He held it across his chest, his left hand supporting the barrel, his right draped over the body and trigger mechanism.

'Hey, look. The Kiwi's got a flame thrower.'

At Russell's words the sappers crowded forward to examine the weapon more closely.

'Now that's more bloody like it. Now we're in ruddy business.' Reilly lifted the corner of the material to slip his hand beneath it and run it over the cool curved metal of the fuel reservoir.

Even Alf Porter expressed something akin to interest and made quiet noises of satisfaction at this latest addition to their hitting power. But of all of them it was Tatman who demonstrated the most enthusiasm. He kept hopping round Kemp, not bothering about who he stamped on or bumped into, clapping his hands and chanting a little improvised ditty about 'cooked meat for supper', 'cooked meat for supper', until Lucas cuffed him out of the way and into silence, so that the lieutenant could make himself heard.

'What are your orders?'

'Just to join you, and bring this along.' Sergeant Murray indicated the flame projector that Kemp was now slinging back over his shoulder. 'Oh yeah, and to act as your escort

54

on a little hike you're going on.'

'Have you any idea what the job is?'

'We've been briefed, but from what I can gather it looks like a lot of the action will be worked out as we go along. There doesn't seem to be much of a script for this job.'

'Yes, well, the whole mission was rather slung together at the last minute.' Saville was pleased at the intelligence the New Zealander displayed. 'We can discuss such finer points as there are on the way to our forming up area. There should be time after that before we actually move out to enable you to go over it with your chaps.' He checked his watch. 'Sergeant Lucas, you can lead the men out now.'

As they formed up in double file, Reilly found himself alongside the man with the flame thrower. 'Are you any good with that devil's device?'

Kemp took no exception to the tactless question. 'I've been showing other blokes how to use it for the last couple of months. We're all instructors in one thing or another. Why, did you want a go with it?'

'No thanks, I hear those things have a habit of turning round and biting back.'

'No, that's a load of bloody bull. They're as safe as houses if you use a bit of common. You can have a hell of a lot of fun with one of these as well. Last week we filled a spare fuel container with raspberry jam, had to strain the seeds out first, and then hosed down a Wop village where the locals had been lobbing petrol bombs at Polish trucks passing through. You've never seen so many bloody wasps in all your life as swarmed on that place.'

Lieutenant Saville was asking Murray about the flame thrower, but his question was out of more than idle curiosity. 'How close does your chap have to be to fire with effect?'

'So long as we get him within ten or fifteen yards of a target, he'll hit it.'

It was already clear that the Kiwi NCO was not bothered about the finer points of military etiquette, like saluting or saying 'Sir'. Although Saville hadn't had much dealings with New Zealanders before, he knew them by reputation. Their clannishness, their dry, often caustic humour and above all their intense dislike of what they saw as the unnecessary trappings of regimentation were well known. So was their reputation for toughness, which they'd earned the hard way, in the Western Desert.

Lucas led the mixed group along a carefully taped and signposted track that would lead them out of the safety of Monte Trocchio's shadow and into the dark still night of the flat ground before Cassino hill.

Other columns marched near them, infantry, sappers, pioneers, signallers, all moving out to their start lines. A whole army was on the move and every single man in it was counting the minutes to the hour when the barrage would start and the crossing of the Rapido would begin.

Alf Porter looked at his watch. There were just two hours to go. One hundred and twenty more minutes to live through, and then how many more after that? Porter subscribed to the saying that an old soldier is a cautious soldier, that's why he's an old soldier. This was his fifteenth year with the Engineers, it would be sixteen in another couple of weeks. How many attacks had he been in now, was it ten, or fifteen or twenty? He hadn't kept count and really couldn't remember. It was more than he cared to try to.

His pack was heavy. Sixty pounds of demolition charges and another twelve made up of fuses, cord, wire cutters and other bits and pieces. And to think he'd originally plumped for the Engineers because he'd thought it wouldn't be as strenuous as the infantry! It seemed that in this war there were very few soft options. Oh, a few lucky or clever devils wangled jobs as HQ clerks or echelon drivers, but even that was not without its hazards. The German artillery and, more rarely, the Luftwaffe spread the dangers liberally and indiscriminately into the rear areas. And there was another price they had to pay for those seemingly soft jobs, in constant bull sessions to maintain the standards needed to hold onto them under the constant and critical scrutiny of their own and visiting officers.

Here they were, marching along towards the start of another scrap. Every time before he'd come back, and most times some of his mates hadn't. Chalky at Hell-Fire, Pete Hughes at Alamein, and that spotty kid who'd only been with them a week and whose name he couldn't remember, at Salerno.

And there were others, who lived on and were reminders that death wasn't the only way out of the war. Foster and Grimes who'd lost legs on mine lifting, Solly Berman who'd had his spine crushed in that silly accident outside Alex; and little Reggie Pitt who was back in England now, being fitted with a new face because a boobytrap had taken off his own.

It all made him wonder if it was worth it. All the scrimping and scraping he did, putting pay aside against the day he'd get out and start up his own little building business. If he came through this one maybe he'd blow the lot on a few good leaves, but he knew he wouldn't, he'd carry on the same as before.

He looked at the New Zealander keeping pace alongside him. Tough looking bloke, the sort you need on a job like this. The Kiwis had an air about them, something between quiet confidence and arrogance, rather like that adopted by some British paras and commandos. Their masses of weaponry, the definitely non-standard issue camouflage outfits that they wore, all of that added an air of individuality to them that was totally lacking in Porter's section, who could have been any one of a thousand.

At intervals along the track, briskly efficient military police were keeping the groups moving, directing them to their allotted places.

They were directed to a spot close by a bomb-shattered barn and there, amid a litter of broken tiles and shattered brick, they settled down and waited for the show to start.

'OK. So I'll keep one of my blokes out in front as a scout and keep the rest close.' Murray folded the map and handed it back to Saville.

The lieutenant pocketed the thin piece of silk. 'Have you done this sort of thing before?'

'Can't say we have, leastways, not on purpose. Usually we've gone at the buggers head on, but we got cut off a couple of times; for six days once. Doing it on purpose will make a nice change.'

The long ominous silence of the guns was broken at last by a distant battery of British mediums that opened up a slow fire. After a pause of several seconds the first shell exploded with a faint pinprick of light far down the Liri Valley. Later still the echo of its detonation came to them. Nothing else broke the stillness, except Harris.

'All it needs is one star shell now, and the Jerries would be presented with the sort of target every gunner dreams of. Two bloody divisions sat on their arses in plain view at short range.'

'Will you be shutting your bloody gob. This waiting is giving me the bloody nadgers as it is. Oh hell, I've got to go for another leak.' Reilly wandered off a few steps and turned his back on the group, tilting his head to look up at the stars as he relieved himself.

Sergeant Lucas also wanted to go, but he suppressed the urge. He had had a piss not five minutes ago and he didn't want to give the impression he was nervous. He slipped the .45 from its holster and checked it had a full magazine. The American automatic felt heavy and powerful in his hand. It would have been nice to have a Thompson, like their escorts had; the graceless heavy lines of the Tommy guns had a wicked professional look, but he had enough to carry without adding one of those to his load.

If he concentrated for a long time he could just discern the pale hump of land that jutted out into the mouth of the valley, and the jagged white halo of the broken walls that topped it. Their objective was not far from the summit, invisible now, but perhaps when they were closer they might glimpse it by the flash of exploding shells, before the smoke wreathed it.

Monte Trocchio's protective spine was behind them. Ahead lay the river they had to cross before they could wheel right and head for the hill. There were fifty minutes to go, he'd have to have that pee soon. Thinking back it seemed that the day had raced by, it was these last few minutes that were taking a lifetime. It was difficult to say which he preferred. Forty-five minutes, he'd have to go for that leak now.

*   *   *   *   *   *

'Get a move on, Henschel.' Wolff waited impatiently for the Gefreiter to catch up with him.

The afternoon had not been as enjoyable as the Hauptmann had expected it to be. Oh, he'd found the work absorbing, it always was, but they'd had to waste such a lot of time avoiding the deadly attentions of enemy fighters. At one stage they had been forced to lay beneath a hedge for over an hour while relays of American Lightnings had strafed several locations about them. Fortunately the camouflage-painted, mud-spattered Horch had escaped notice, and for that they could at least partially thank Henschel's extreme reluctance to ever clean the car. And when they had been able to move, it was only with extreme care and at a snail's pace, ready to hurl themselves into cover at any instant. Now they could only hope it would be safe, parked at the bottom of the hill to await their return.

'I'm coming, I'm coming. Can't I even stop for a bleeding piss without you going on at me!'

Without waiting for the complaining NCO to catch up Wolff struck out over the last section, a steep stretch of narrow track that led to the entrance to the Fuehrer's emplacement in the back of the ridge that loomed over them.

They were not alone on the path. Files of grey-clad men were passing up and down all the time. Besides the sweating cursing heavily laden columns of pioneers performing the nightly task of replenishment there were other, smaller groups. Reliefs were being carried out and these were the fresh gun and weapons crews making their way to the caves and holes in the rock that it would be their turn to occupy for the next few weeks. Some of the change-overs had already taken place, and the men on the way down received only sour looks in answer to the banter they aimed at the men laboriously ascending.

Apart from a handful of guns in action on the British side, Cassino was quiet. Doubtless the German artillery had been restrained while the reliefs were going on, as any retaliatory shelling in response to a German bombardment would only make the exercise more difficult.

The path curved to pass behind the ridge, and Wolff slowed to pick his way more carefully, placing each footstep with care on the faint ribbon of beaten ground, barely visible against the uniform dark mass of the hillside. A moment's inattention that led to a stumble might result in a fall and a broken limb, or worse the snagging of a trip wire that would detonate a Schu mine.

'Halt!' A soldier wearing the distinctive smock and helmet of a paratrooper stepped out of the pitch darkness that marked a cleft in the steep reverse slope of the ridge, and the entrance to the emplacement.

The sudden and unexpected demand had made Wolff jump, and now to cover his reaction and demonstrate his annoyance at the tip of the MP40 sub-machine gun pointed unwaveringly at his chest he drew himself stiffly erect and dusted the front of his jacket before identifying himself.

'I am Hauptmann Franz Wolff, Inspector of Fortifications, Cassino sector. I insist you let me pass. I have work here.' The paratrooper appeared unimpressed and made no move to comply. Instead he called back over his shoulder, not taking his eyes off the pair for a moment.

A major appeared almost instantly. His eyes flickered

over the officer and NCO, lingering longer on the Hauptmann. 'Who are you? What do you want?'

Wolff repeated what he had told the sentry, adding '. . . and my driver, Gefreiter Henschel. I have come to inspect damage that was reported this morning.'

After a careful scrutiny of their papers the major stepped aside. 'All right, get on with it. But keep out of my way. I am not in the best of moods.'

Henschel for one did not need to be told that. In the few paces from where he'd halted on the sentry's command, to the door of the emplacement several metres inside the fissure that led to it, he made quite a marked improvement in his appearance and bearing. He had immediately summed up the paratroop major as a no-nonsense professional, a man likely to arrest first and think of the list of charges later.

A thick steel door grated open and they passed through into pitch darkness beyond. As the door slammed home behind them a dull red illumination came on. The passageway was little wider than the entrance itself, with the exception of a small alcove hollowed out beside it and fitted with a shuttered loophole for an MG34 that rested on the floor.

For Wolff, in a way, it was almost like being home again. He knew every centimetre of the tunnel that stretched out before them. It had been fashioned from a natural fault in the rock. In places the stone walls bore the marks of pneumatic drills where blasting had been necessary to widen the passage sufficiently. There was no need to stoop, the tapering walls met a metre overhead.

They had to slow to negotiate an artificial dog-leg halfway along the tunnel, almost exactly in the centre of the ridge. Wolff had installed the rough-finished concrete chicane to give a measure of protection against blast, should a bomb or shell land in the cleft and blow in the door. It would also serve as a second line of defence if enemy infantry stormed the door and managed to destroy it, keeping them away from the magazine and guns, and enabling the guns to stay in action.

Just beyond that was the opening that led to the magazine, leading off from the main tunnel. Wolff was very pleased at how he had enlarged the small fault to fashion a shell store that also served as sleeping quarters for the gun crews. A few more metres on, past a shelf scooped out of the side of the tunnel to accommodate the small generator, and then they were in the emplacement proper, the tunnel coming out into the left hand of the two compartments into which the gun room was divided.

The scene that met their eyes was not what either the Hauptmann or Gefreiter had been expecting. An eighty-eight, looking huge in the confined space, dominated the compartment, seeming to fill every inch of it. It was impossible to walk anywhere without having to duck under the barrel or step over the legs of the cruciform platform on which it stood.

There was nothing unusual in that, nor in the racks of rifles and cleaning equipment fastened to the natural rock that formed all but the front face of the room. It was the sixteen men of the gun crews, sitting disconsolately against the concrete of the embrasured front wall who immediately caught their attention and held it.

They all had their hands on their heads and most were in a partial state of undress, possibly explained by the unexpected presence of two well-built Italian women of rough appearance who sat at a little distance from the men, their thick make-up not disguising their sulky expressions.

An enormous paratroop Unteroffizier stood guard over them all, a sub-machine gun looking toy-like in his huge hands.

Empty straw-wrapped Chianti bottles rolled about underfoot and the whole place smelt strongly of cheap perfume and stale food. So strong that it blotted out entirely the stink of grease that Wolff remembered from all his earlier visits.

'Artillerymen.' The major made the word into an obscenity. 'I thought the flak gunners were bad, but these . . .' He paused, words failing him. 'How rubbish like this ever got in the German Army is beyond me. Well, do whatever it is you came to do, Hauptmann. Get on with it, this place is cluttered enough without you hanging about.'

Wolff needed no second bidding. He had no wish by any action of his to cause the major's ire to be directed at him.

As he picked his way forward to examine the front wall he heard the major grab up the field telephone from a table, and bellow down it at some luckless signaller who answered tardily or incorrectly.

A very thorough examination of the concrete revealed no fault apart from some sintering that must have been caused by the shock waves of direct hits that had failed to penetrate. Wolff went over every inch of the front wall, examined the fifty-millimetre-thick armoured shutter over the embrasure and the mechanism that worked it. Everything was in order. He looked up at the bare rock roof. Although the light wasn't good he gained the distinct impression that a few of the cracks had widened a trifle, but not sufficiently for him to feel any concern. Of course he would have to have them grouted now, but the injection of concrete into them should consolidate the rock.

He skirted the thick wall that divided the gun room into two and went into the other compartment. If anything the eighty-eight in there had even less room, one of the legs had been modified for it to fit in.

At first glance everything looked in order. The roof again showed signs of having settled, but not to any alarming degree. It was when he ducked under the long barrel of the gun, and examined the far side of the room that he got the shock.

'Henschel, come and give me a hand.'

The Gefreiter came faster than was normal for him and worked with a will to move aside the pile of sandbags thrown down haphazardly in the corner. His alacrity surprised the Hauptmann until it dawned on him that the paratroop major had struck fear into the NCO.

As the stack diminished it revealed a roughly circular hole where the concrete met the natural rock; a hole so wide that a man could have crawled into it. The loose stone piled against the outside of the wall must have collapsed into the rent after the shell had passed through, blocking the far end of the passage the projectile had bored, and partially filling it.

'Major, could the gun commander come in here?' Wolff kept running his hand round the edge of the hole, having difficulty in believing what it was he was looking at. It was incredible. The emplacement had been designed to withstand virtually anything, and a shell had punched its way in, right in.

'You wanted me, Hauptmann?' The middle-aged Oberleutnant was a pitiful sight. Clad only in his vest and trousers, his face was blotched red where he had been slapped about by the major, and stained by tears that were the product of abject fear. He held his cap in his hands, and was swiftly reducing it to a shapeless mass as he twisted and wrung it in his distraction.

Wolff looked up from where he crouched by the hole. He felt no sympathy for the man, his only interest was the problem presented by what his inspection had revealed. The discovery of the hole had come as a shock to him. While nothing he could do would alter what had happened, perhaps there might be some consolation to be found in an exceptional explanation for its cause. 'What did this?'

The gun commander was bewildered. What could this prim and proper officer really want? With what was going on in the emplacement, surely he couldn't really be interested in the hole. 'The women are refugees, Hauptmann. They must have come down from the monastery, they are not here of our doing. I was going to send them on immediately.' His whole mental horizon was filled with the terror of the predicament he realised he was in. If he could get the Hauptmann to support him . . .

'What did this?'

'The women are refugees, Hauptmann, it is not my fault. I did not bring them here, on my word of honour. If you could explain to the major . . .'

'I am not interested in the slightest in your troubles, Oberleutnant. I wish only to know what caused this, this damage.' Wolff had started to compose his report in his head, and had decided that the word 'hole' was one to avoid.

'It was a shell.'

'Thank you, I had already deduced that for myself.' The man's dullness was irritating Wolff. No wonder the dolt had got himself into such deep trouble. The oaf must have forgotten the reliefs were due, or forgotten about time. 'What sort of shell was it?'

'A very big one, Hauptmann.'

'And where is it?' Wolff decided to cut short the idiotic exchange. A personal examination of the shell was more likely to yield information than this dullard.

A blank stare was his only answer.

Wolff decided to give the man one last chance. He spoke slowly and clearly, as though to a slack-jawed moron. 'I am aware that the . . . damage . . . was done by a big shell. I want to know where it is. It obviously didn't explode on penetration or none of this would be here now.' His arm swept out in a gesture that encompassed the eighty-eight and the whole compartment. 'So where is it now?'

'We carried it out and threw it down the hill. I didn't think anyone would want it. Fahnjunker Jurgen's blood was all over it, and it smelt horrible. He was standing right where you are when it came through.'

Not for any conscious reason Wolff moved away from the spot.

'Hauptmann!'

The bellow from the other half of the gun room broke into Wolff's thoughts and he hurried to obey the major's summons.

Henschel stayed where he was, unwilling to bring himself to the major's notice even by coming within his field of vision. The Oberleutnant trailed disconsolately behind, his face a picture of resignation and fear.

'I have to leave now. I am making you responsible for these prisoners. You will wait here with them until their reliefs come and then escort them down to the road. A section of field police will be waiting for you.'

There was no chance for Wolff to voice any objection or question the order in any way, or even time for him to make up his mind whether or not it would be wise to do so.

As the major spoke he was already rounding up his men and herding them back through the tunnel. 'Remember, you are responsible. I have advised the field police how many prisoners to expect. If any go missing then you and your driver will make up their numbers.'

For Hauptmann Wolff life had instantly become much more complicated and unpleasant. The major's words had wrenched him from his cosy world of make-believe, the little cocoon of detachment that had made it possible for him to tolerate the harsh realities and crudities of army life. From the tunnel echoed the loud metallic crash of the door being opened and closed.

Henschel had taken one of the Mauser rifles from the rack, and now fitted a five-round magazine into it.

'I don't think that will be necessary.'

The gun crews were undecided what the rapid change of events might mean to them. Some kept their hands on their heads, others had taken theirs down, and shifted uneasily as they entwined their fingers, or played with buttons or buckles. One or two were unable to decide on the best or safest course of action and kept their hands hovering between a raised and lowered position, giving the appearance of a session of slow-motion callisthenics.

'Fuck that! If we take our eyes off these cruds for a bloody second they'll be off like bats out of hell. And I don't intend to end up having my neck stretched with piano wire just because some of these sods decide to take a stroll over to the British.' Henschel suited his actions to his words, levelling the rifle at the artillery men.

Wolff checked the time. It was almost 23.00. The relief crews would be there any minute. Then he'd be able to herd these unfortunates down the hill and hand over the unwelcome responsibility to the waiting field police. It could do no harm to take a precaution or two against anything going wrong.

While the Gefreiter made an ostentatious show of guarding the prisoners, every few seconds he would leer at the two whores. They did not seem to be too bothered by what was going on about them, passing the time by preening themselves and adding fresh layers of garish cosmetics to those already caking their faces.

'Bloody good pair of udders that one in green, the older one, eh, Hauptmann?'

'Do you have to be so coarse? Are your only thoughts those of the bed or the beer hall?' Wolff was glad of the distraction. The gun commander had been trying to catch his eye and he had no wish to get involved with the man.

'Nothing else worth thinking about, is there? Maybe you ought to give them a try. A few litres of beer and a bloody good roll with a nice fat juicy tart, do you a world of good.' Henschel was grinning broadly. He was revelling in his sudden importance.

For an instant Wolff was on the verge of replying, but he didn't. What could Henschel understand of how it was with him and his Hilda? He recalled that last night of his last leave. The beautiful supper they had prepared together, the surprise bottle of hock she had produced that must have taken her ages to find; and then afterwards, and she had worn that white silk he had found in Florence. No, what could Henschel understand of that? The lout's finest experience was probably a swift transaction with a whore that he hadn't even remembered the morning after.

'I want to inspect the shutter mechanisms. Douse the lights.'

A threatening pace forward by Henschel and the slow reacting Oberleutnant tripped in his sudden haste to reach the control panel. The dull red illumination dimmed and vanished. It was pitch black. In the dark the sound of a rifle bolt being worked put an end to a growing movement emanating from the direction of the artillerymen.

Wolff's hand closed on the crank that worked the shutter. It was slippery with grease, but despite that evidence of maintenance the mechanism was stiff and he had to use both hands.

With loud protesting groans and creaks the slab of metal hinged upwards, and by contrast with the darkness of the emplacement the starlit sky was bright. Although the night fused the countryside below into a blank black sheet Wolff knew to the last metre and bush the range of vision the position provided and every feature that lay within it. He recalled the words of a staff-officer who had visited the position shortly after its completion. The Oberst had been showing a gaggle of high-ranking Luftwaffe officers over a portion of the Cassino defences.

Accompanied by a grand dramatic gesture the staff-officer had indicated the view through the embrasure. 'That,' he had proclaimed, pointing down into the valley, 'is the gateway to Rome. With these,' he'd slapped the barrel of an eighty-eight, 'when the Allies next attack we shall turn it into the gateway to hell.'

It was very still out there. Wolff looked towards the Allied side of the river. The Rapido was just visible as a thin pale thread winding away from the hill. Satisfied that it was working correctly he made to secure the shutter, when something he saw out of the corner of his eye made him turn back. As he looked it seemed as though every inch of ground beyond the Rapido had burst into dazzling light.

The scream of approaching shells followed almost immediately.

* * * * * *

Only by looking at their watches could the waiting men now know that it was day. The smoke and dust of the barrage, thickening the morning mist and added to the products of hundreds of smoke generators had stretched the night to abnormal length. Nor was the cordite-tainted, dun-coloured half-light the only demonstration of the fog's strength. Matches struck to light cigarettes burnt with only a small pale flame in the particle-laden, oxygen-starved atmosphere.

The section of British Engineers and their New Zealand escort had polarised into two separate groups a few yards apart as they waited for Saville and Murray to return from a reconnaissance of the river bank. They were just two groups among many that had sought the shelter of the sunken road when the German shelling had begun to gain strength. Occasionally a spent bullet or tumbling piece of shell casing would drop down and raise a small fountain of dust, and the men closest to it would huddle deeper into the slit trenches they had scraped in the embankments.

'They're back.' Corporal Mitchell, the Kiwi second in command, shuffled together the scruffy pack of cards he'd been about to deal, and stuffed them into one of his many capacious pockets.

Lieutenant Saville and Sergeant Murray half jumped, half slid down the embankment to rejoin their men. A massive surge of hot air followed them as a mortar bomb blasted the spot they'd occupied a moment earlier.

'Bit rough is it, sir?' Lucas gave his officer a small wad of cotton with which to wipe the blood from a cut on his cheek.

'Yes, it is rather. There's no chance we'll be going yet. Most of the boats have been sunk or swept away, and the couple of rafts that are still working are booked for infantry and anti-tank guns for quite a while yet.'

Murray, without taking his helmet off, was examining by touch two large dents in its brim. Only a shred of the double layer of camouflage netting it had sported earlier remained. 'Looks like the barrage missed a few of the Jerry positions. Either that or they were dug in so deep all they had to do was wait till the worst had passed and then pop up again.'

Another mortar bomb blasted a hole in the crest of the bank and strips of white tape fluttered down. The roadway was littered with such remnants. They were all that was left of the carefully laid out lanes that had guided the men in the night. Now they made rare splashes of white in the uniform grey that the day had become.

'So we just sit here, and let the buggers shell the shit out of us.' Despite his complaining Mitchell prepared to make the most of the situation and brought the cards out again.

'It rather looks like it, Corp.' Murray settled back against the stump of a tree, pulled the brim of his helmet down over his eyes and prepared to sleep. 'But if you feel like taking a stroll down to the Rapido and swimming over, then I ain't stopping you. But just because the smoke's even worse down there don't think that Jerry won't get you. They've got machine guns firing on fixed lines covering most of the likely crossing points, and mortars zeroed on all of the approaches.' He reached up and tapped the two dents. 'These weren't done by no bloody bird shit.'

'Knock it off, Sarge, I weren't volunteering for no solo action. I'll just hang on here till we're all ready to go.'

Gradually the German artillery was recovering from the destruction and disruption caused by the British gunners' efforts during the night, and was now beginning to reply in earnest.

A long line of stretcher bearers filed back along the road,

They took advantage of the shelter offered by the cutting to pause for a rest, and put their charges down. None of the wounded made any noise save for one man whose upper face was hidden beneath a large field dressing; he kept up an ugly wheezing sound that ended every time in a rattling choke. A few accepted cigarettes and exchanged news of the fighting with the men who were waiting to go forward; others lay so still that their shallow breathing hardly raised the blankets that covered them.

An order was passed down and the bearers took up their loads once more. No sooner were they out of sight than another column followed.

Besides the bang and crack of artillery and mortar fire, the continuous rattle of small arms could be heard, interspersed with long bursts of machine-gun fire.

The casualties were mounting.

'Pity it didn't go a bit deeper, then you could have hitched a ride on the next passing stretcher.'

Harris winced as Corporal Clark dabbed with a swab of cottonwool at the side of his head. The lump of stone that had done the damage had started its journey sixty yards away, set in motion by the impact of a German 150mm howitzer shell.

'If it had gone any bloody deeper I wouldn't have needed a stretcher. Oi, take it bloody easy!'

Clark picked through the stained material, poking at small dark specks. 'That's about done it. I reckon I've got it all out. In ten days all you'll have will be a bald spot and a bit of a scratch.'

'How can I pull the birds looking like I've got the ruddy mange? This war makes me sick. When it's not chopping chunks out of you it's ruining your bleeding sex life.'

'I'm surprised you've got one worth ruining. The way you go on about the number of women you've had I wonder you haven't worn it out by now.'

Harris took an aggressive step towards Russell, who immediately stepped behind the lieutenant.

'Cut it out, you lot. This is no time for clowning.' Lucas wandered back and forth around the group, like a patient old sheepdog doing his best to tolerate the idiocies of frisky lambs.

The waiting was always the most difficult time, and the

men had endured almost eighteen hours under constant and growing shell fire. Now that they would shortly be off, the relaxation of tension was expressing itself in horse-play and general buggering about. Lucas knew it was a state that would wear off quickly, but it was none the less irritating while it lasted.

Since the offensive had opened in the last hour of the previous day they had gradually learnt something of what was going on. From stretcher bearers and from the walking wounded of the Bedfords and East Surreys who had passed them, they had pieced together a picture of what was happening. It was not encouraging.

The first wave had crossed the sixty-foot-wide Rapido with few casualties, under the cover of the massive opening bombardment, but almost immediately many of the boats had been swept away by the fast current. During the night the remaining craft had been further reduced in numbers as they were sought and sunk by mortar fire.

Attempts to construct bridges had failed when the alerted enemy had heard the unmistakable sounds of the vehicles that were moving the heavy components and prefabricated sections down to the bridging sites. A torrent of fire from every calibre of weapon had hosed out of the smoke at the slow-moving trucks and many had been hit, burning with their valuable cargoes still on board.

What little information had come back from the far side of the Rapido told a tale of repeated ferocious counter-attacks by small groups of German infantry, which had forced the British assault troops to dig in. They could only hold on, and hope that the next night would see more successful attempts to push armour across to support them.

Throughout the day Monte Cassino had drifted in and out of vision as the smoke pall shrouding it had occasionally thinned, before it could be thickened again by fresh salvoes of smoke shells. The evil brooding influence it held over the battlefield was in no way diminished by the damage the monastery at its summit had suffered, and continued to suffer. Rather, the fact that so much of it was still intact after the pounding it had taken added to its aura of impregnability.

Now, late in the afternoon, the British artillery fire was undergoing a subtle change. An increasing proportion of the rounds that cut through the air above them was landing on the far side of the river – not with the thunderous crash of detonating high explosive but with the thump and instantaneous cough of bursting smoke shells; the screen of rolling grey clouds was being made even denser. Inching their way forward through it were long lines of Leyland and Albion trucks. Each one of them carried girders or panels that when assembled would make a bridge capable of supporting tanks: another attempt was being made.

This time Saville took the lead. With every step the crackle of small-arms fire became more distinct, individual shots and bursts standing out more clearly. They passed the rusting hulks of burned-out trucks, and the smashed hulls of broken boats, wreckage of the American 36th Division's abortive attempt to secure a crossing five months before.

The ground was heavily cratered, all but the most recent pits sprouting and overgrown with wild corn, poppies and a thousand other forms of vegetation. Dust-caked gangs of sappers were wrestling with crudely trimmed lengths of timber and sheets of metal mesh as they laboured to construct the approaches to the bridge being put together further on.

Saville found himself peering at the individuals he could make out amongst them, looking for the other men of his platoon, but he saw none. Beside the neatly taped path lay two jacket-covered bodies.

Every few minutes a shell would come down in their vicinity, and then as one they'd duck, tensing their bodies in expectation of the impact of a scything red-hot fragment, but none came. In places the smoke was so thick that to let the man in front get more than a yard ahead was to risk losing contact with him.

'If we find a gap in the Jerry defences big enough to sneak this lot through, the whole of the bloody army will be able to follow.'

'Keep it to yourself, Slacker.' Reilly's voice came from somewhere towards the rear of the file. 'There might be a bonus in it for us if we do.'

Alf Porter didn't look up when he joined in the exchange, he was busy watching his footing as he clambered down one wall of a gigantic crater and up the far side. 'If we do, it'll mean nice big shares for those of us that get back.'

'None of you will bloody be coming back if you don't buck your bloody ideas up. Close up there, shut your bloody racket.'

'Could you say that a bit louder please, Sergeant Lucas.'

'I said shut your bloody noise. What's up, Tatman, have you gone deaf?'

'No, Sergeant. It's just that I don't think the gunners heard you the first time.'

Tatman delivered the sentence in a tone of perfect innocence, but fortunately a salvo of screaming minnies coming down a couple of hundred yards away drowned out Lucas's rejoinder.

A large white ball of luminescence flashed from the pall to their front, raced by and was gone. Another followed, closer, and they felt the breeze of its passing. The low flat trajectory of the projectiles, and their tracer, marked them as direct fire from a German anti-tank gun.

They halted by an aid post on the order of a military policeman. When a moment later they moved on, it was to run, crouched as low as they could, to the churned hummock of a flood bank that marked the edge of the river.

It was an incredible sight. While infantry waiting to cross squatted by the water, seeking what protection they could from the banks against the storm of incoming mortar bombs and machine-gun fire, parties of sappers and pioneers were frantically working unprotected in the open, man-handling the sections of bridging equipment onto the already prepared seats that were to anchor the structure. Some were bleeding from minor wounds, others worked on with hastily applied dressings on their heads, arms or legs.

Ropes stretched out across the fast flowing water, their far ends as invisible as the distant bank. A few rafts were being worked along the ropes backwards and forwards. Without the assistance of those life-lines the current would have whirled the unwieldy platforms from sight.

As Saville and his men took shelter, a mortar round blew a fresh crater in the bank, near to the bridge seat, throwing up a great shower of mud. For a moment all action froze, then, without uttering a sound, a lance-corporal bolting sections of girder together toppled over backwards and plunged beneath the racing water. The work immediately resumed and another sapper came forward to replace the one who had disappeared into the torrent.

Another wait, but only two hours this time, though it seemed much longer, forced as they were to crouch in the deep mud at the stream's edge, unable to dig any sort of shelter. The belching smoke generators brought night early and the darkness provided at least an illusion of safety.

The men who were working the rafts kept roving up and down the bank, checking the identities and priorities of the

71

units waiting to cross.

'What's this, a private army?' The lance-corporal who gave the lieutenant a hand onto the deck of the raft had a word for everyone, regardless of rank. He wore a field dressing on his right thigh, and that was virtually all, apart from a scrap of cloth about his waist that might once have been his pants. 'All aboard the Skylark, gents. Sorry, I can't take any return bookings, I've been let down by some customers already. Here, what are you Kiwis doing here, you're a bit off your patch, aren't you! Last I heard, your mob were about twenty miles from here, the lucky buggers.'

Prolonged buffeting by the fierce current and damage caused by near misses had cost the raft much of its buoyancy. It spent much of the slow journey submerged several inches.

The ferryman had an answer for that. 'Don't get worried, folks, if you can't see the raft just pretend you're walking on the water. We could all do with a few miracles today.'

The moment the last passenger was off, the raft was shoved off again to return for another load. As it neared mid-stream another of those big balls of tracer zipped over the bank and struck it dead centre. When the huge spout of water raised finally settled it revealed the raft spinning away upside down. Of the lance-corporal and his crew of three there was no sign, just the wild tumbling water.

'Come on. Move yourselves, move yourselves.' Lucas strode about, pushing that man and this, forcing the men to tear their eyes from the spectacle they had witnessed and follow Sergeant Murray, who had found a gap in the bank and was waiting for the rest of them to join him.

In the order they had prearranged they left the river and struck out to the right, towards the positions held by those units that had made the furthest progress towards Monte Cassino.

Barbed wire was everywhere. Although much had been flattened or cut by the barrage, wide swathes remained, forcing many detours and frequent changes of course. Virtually nothing was left growing in the area. Hedges, trees, even the very grass had almost ceased to exist. What little of the countryside was visible through the swirling smoke was now a pock-marked moonscape. The very air was alien, thick with rasping fumes, heavy with the stench of cordite.

The severely churned ground, while difficult to traverse for the men with the heavy loads, offered at least one compensation: as long as they kept to a route that led through the areas most torn about by the shelling, the men knew there was little chance of coming onto mines. Many of the anti-personnel devices with which the terrain was sown must have been detonated by the concussion of landing shells. And the handful that had not succumbed had most likely been deeply buried by the mountains of soil the explosives had excavated.

Dark figures that reeled from the smoke, caused a dozen alarms. Walking wounded, including numbers of unescorted and dazed-looking Germans, tottered past, clutching bulky dressings to massive wounds. Others they passed just sat about, unwilling or unable to move, waiting to be picked up.

All the time as they moved closer to the forward positions the weight of shot and shell and tracer grew more intense, until their progress was reduced to a series of spurts from one crater to another, seeking every inch of cover that they could on the way. It was as they carried out one such dash that they sustained their first casualty.

*   *   *   *   *   *

Wolff's ears still rang with the effects of that first forty minutes of intensive shelling. It was precisely twenty-four hours since he had seen that first blaze of white light. The deluge of explosives that had followed had seemed to strike the emplacement with several monstrous hammerblows every second, and then when it had fallen to a more tolerable five or six a minute, the smoke had started.

For an hour that had been the only sound, and then the field telephone had shrilled. Wolff had taken the call from the observer perched among the ruins of the monastery high above them, and passed on the coordinates he was given to the gun commander.

The Oberleutnant had acted with alacrity, seeing in the change of circumstances the possibility of salvation, the chance to redeem himself. He had made the most of it and both guns had opened up with a maximum rate of fire, adding the stink of cordite to the discomforts they already laboured under.

Not once, out of the fifteen times they had engaged targets during the day, had they seen what it was in the valley that they were firing at. Twice during the afternoon the link with the observer had been broken. The first time it was for only thirty minutes, but the second time the line had gone dead

73

for over an hour. Wolff did not envy the task of the signallers who had to scramble up and down the bare slopes tracing the breaks and repairing them. Early in the evening the line to one of their two protective machine-gun positions had been severed, and shortly after the one to the field exchange in the valley had also been cut. Neither had been restored.

Now their only communication with the outside world was the line to the tiny three-man pill-box at the western end of the ridge, and the single frail wire that snaked between the rocks to the spotter in the monastery.

One of the artillerymen, a veteran of a hundred actions according to his officer, had suddenly gone off his head in the middle of the afternoon. His reason had gone without warning, and it had taken four men to subdue him. Now he sat mindlessly on the floor of the magazine, watching the rounds being fused, gouging grooves with his nails into a rifle butt he had got hold of from somewhere.

After looking at the human wreck a couple of times Wolff had been unable to bring himself to visit the magazine any more. It was not that he was unsympathetic, it was just that, well, there was nothing that he could do, and such a feeling of helplessness made him irritable. The pathetic creature made him think of his sister-in-law's mongol child. He still admitted to himself a slight feeling of guilt at the relief he had felt when he'd heard of the child's sudden death at one of the new state homes.

The guns were quiet at the moment, the crews taking advantage of the lull to clean the barrels of their charges. They had left the shining breeches open to facilitate cooling, and there was a strong aroma of hot metal in the emplacement. It occurred to the Hauptmann that there were several similarities between their circumstances and what it must have been like on the lower gun decks of a ship of the line, back in the days of sail, except that they would not have had women about then. Or did he recall having read an article about women having been present on some of the Spanish ships during the battle of Trafalgar? Well if they had, they would doubtless have been of the same stamp as these two; rough, vulgar specimens, able to hold their own with men at swearing and smoking and talking filth.

He was glad that the woman in green had managed to calm her younger companion. The girl's recurring hysterics during the first three hours had been unnerving, coming on top of everything else. They had, though, served one useful

74

purpose. The state of the girl and the preoccupation of the woman had meant that Henschel's unsubtle advances had met with summary and violent rebuff. There were still out-line finger marks on the Gefreiter's face, hours after the slap that had put them there had made everyone stop what they were doing and look to the dark corner.

'You want some of this?' Henschel pushed an unappetising sausage under Wolff's nose. 'Come on, you must be getting bloody hungry. It won't poison you. I've had some.'

'Yes. I can see your tooth mark on it.'

'Oh, I am sorry. Next time I'll bring it on a silver tray, with a nice white napkin.' Henschel took a huge bite out of the white-marbled pink meat, and spoke through a mouthful, spattering the front of his unbuttoned jacket with specks of food. 'Except, of course, that there won't be any left. The reliefs must have been bringing fresh supplies with them; I suppose they'll be splattered all over the bloody mountain by now. They must have been caught in the open when that lot started last night. Anyway, I've rounded up what was left, and I've hidden it. I ain't going to starve to death just because these greedy bleeding gunners have scoffed every-thing.'

'I don't think we will have to worry about that possibility. As soon as the telephone link to the valley is restored I'll advise HQ of the situation and they'll send up fresh reliefs. Then we can take these men down and hand them over.'

'Shit!' The NCO took a massive bite out of the sausage, his single tooth and ragged gums leaving bizarre patterns on it. 'They're not going to let anyone off this bloody slag heap until this lot is over. They'll be shovelling cannon fodder onto it like bleeding maniacs at the moment. There's no way they'll let this cruddy load of rubbish enjoy nice safe cells while decent blokes are getting their knackers shot off. No, they're staying, and while they stay, we stay.'

On reflection Wolff knew that his driver was right. While the battle raged, remained undecided, they were stuck where they were. There would be a lot for him to do when this was all over. If the Gustav Line held then the list of repair works would be enormous. If it broke and there was a general retreat to the Hitler Line, or even the Caesar Line, then work on them would have to be accelerated dramatically. Neither was as complete as it should be.

'Looks like we're giving the Allies a bloody nose again.' The gun commander exuded an air of optimism. He was building all his hopes on the belief that a brilliant performance during the battle would cancel out his earlier transgression.

Wolff wanted nothing to do with the Oberleutnant, but Henschel was prepared to offer him conversation, of sorts.

'I don't reckon that's any bloody consolation, not if they're tearing our legs off while we do it.'

The Oberleutnant looked to Wolff, expecting him to reprimand his NCO. Perhaps the Engineers' officer was testing him; he had best take the task upon himself. 'I don't want to hear talk like that. We are going to win, like we always have.'

'Funny how we keep winning battles and losing the war, ain't it!'

'We shall not lose the war, we cannot. Hitler himself has said so.'

Henschel spat. Possibly it was by accident that he hit the Oberleutnant's boot. 'Oh shit. You're not another crud who believes in that noisy little sod, are you?'

'How dare you!' The gun commander bristled up to his full if unimpressive height. 'You are not even fit to mention the Fuehrer's name.'

'Balls. You go on spouting rubbish like that and they'll make you a member of the Shit for Hitler Club. From then on all your shit will be stored to build a suitable burial mound for little Adolf.'

The Oberleutnant had been watching Wolff for his reaction. Detecting none as yet, he decided that perhaps he ought to lay it on a bit thicker. He turned to the Hauptmann. 'Won't you speak up for our Fuehrer?'

'It would not be proper of me to reprimand the Gefreiter. He is, of course, a product of Hitler's system. Aren't you, Heinz Henschel?'

Henschel smiled a broad gummy smile. 'Oh certainly. I've been a party member since 1936. I was a second assistant standard bearer at one of the Nueremburg rallies. I stood within spitting distance of old Toothbrush 'tache. My only regret about that day is that I didn't take advantage of the opportunity and put a big green gob right in his ear.' He put his head on one side and rolled spittle round in his open mouth.

'This imbecile should be shot, he's a traitor . . .'

Since he was now involved in the ridiculous conversation Wolff decided that he might as well milk it for what amusement he could.

'Hardly a traitor, Oberleutnant. As I said, the Gefreiter is a product of the system Hitler created. He has the two vital qualities needed to make a first-class Nazi. First he has given up membership of the human race, if he ever belonged to it, which I doubt. And secondly he has had his brain washed. Unfortunately they forgot to put it back again afterwards, but then a brain is hardly an essential requirement for a party member.'

The Oberleutnant looked from the faintly smiling Hauptmann to the dribbling NCO. He didn't know what to make of them, so he gave up, almost, deciding to change tack.

'It wasn't my fault the women were here when the major came. They are refugees, they must have come down from the monastery. If you could back me up . . .'

'Rubbish!' Wolff lost patience with the man. 'The last of the refugees left the building in February, or March at the latest. You, or your men with your connivance, brought the women here. Well, you did it, you pay for it. I have no wish to get involved.'

The gun commander gave up, and went away to shout at his men, a few of whom had not been as fast as they might have been in wiping smiles off their faces when he turned round.

It was a mark of the strain he was under that Wolff had bothered with the man at all.

'Were you really a party member, Henschel?' That piece of information had surprised Wolff.

'Still am, but I don't go round blabbing about it, in case some clever sod decides it makes me the right sort to be with those war-mad bastards in the SS.'

'Then why did you join?'

'For the fights. We had some lovely punch-ups in the early days. And of course once you were in you could get away with bloody murder. If you fancied fingering a fat Jewess then you did, whether she wanted fingering or not.'

There was nothing that surprised Wolff in the answer. Given time to consider the matter he would have come close to guessing the reasons. He cut short the telephone's shrill by snatching up the receiver as the bells began their clamour. It was a long message, and he made notes as it went on.

'Would you all gather round? Oberleutnant, summon the men from the magazine, will you?' Wolff had continued to hold the handset to his ear some time after the caller had rung off. It was merely a tactic to delay doing a job he did not wish to do.

The men gathered in a semi-circle around him. He cleared

his throat, made a pretence of checking his notes first. It would be difficult to make the words sound convincing when they seemed hollow even to him.

'A message has been relayed to us by the monastery. I am told that the Allies have opened an attack on the Gustav Line, and Monte Cassino in particular . . .'

The loud braying noise that broke in at that moment came from Henschel, who was laughing. 'What did those silly arses back at HQ think all the bloody noise was last night? Did they think we'd all been eating beans?'

'Be quiet. As I was saying. It is not yet clear whether they intend to make their main thrust into the Liri valley, or whether the fighting here is merely a feint to draw our attention and our reserves from elsewhere, to cover a break out from the Anzio beachhead.' At that point he hesitated, knowing the men would recognise the next words, as he had. They closely echoed a special order of the day that Hitler had issued late in 'forty-three.

'I am ordered to tell you that there is to be no withdrawal. No position is to be surrendered. The bitterest struggle is expected for every metre.'

As the sentence tailed away the men went back to what they had been doing before, without waiting to be dismissed. The words had not reached them. War had become a habit. They would go on making it because that was all there was to do.

The phone rang again, and within two minutes the eighty-eights were in blazing action once more. Dust fell in curtains from the long cracks radiating out across the rock ceiling, shell cases rattled to the floor at regular intervals.

Wolff went out into the tunnel, in the hope that the noise would be less punishing. He'd meant to install internal doors that could be used to seal off the magazine or gun room in the event of fire, and had ordered them, twice, but each time they'd been victims of enemy air attacks while being delivered.

But even without refinements such as that Wolff realised that he was probably safer in there than anywhere else that far forward. All he had to do was sit it out and wait for the Allies to be beaten back. They still had more than twenty litres of water left, and used carefully that should last them until relieved. They would be hungry by then, but they would be alive. And if the Allies did by some fluke of luck break through into the valley, then they'd have ample notice and be able to make their way back over the narrow mountain tracks to an area still firmly held.

After fifteen rounds each the guns fell silent. The empty cases were gathered up and pushed out of the embrasures to bounce the ten metres or so to the bottom of the cliff.

As he watched the artillerymen tidying the gun room Wolff realised with a start how he had been letting things drift. Perhaps it had been because he'd expected to be out of there soon, but now he had reluctantly to admit that it looked likely he was in for a long stay, perhaps several more days. It was time he took steps to get organised.

'Henschel.'

'Yeah?'

'Bring all the water that we have into here, put it under the telephone table, where everyone can see it but no one can touch it without being seen, and bring in any food as well. And include your own private hoard also.'

'Oh fuck it, why me? Get one of these other cruds to do it.'

'Henschel, you have tried my patience a great deal. I am almost at the state where I believe I can overcome my distaste for the field police and their version of justice. Now be warned.'

For a moment the NCO appeared about to make a reply, but he decided against it and went off to fetch the water.

The Hauptmann felt that his life had just taken a turn for the better. He had bested Henschel, for the moment, and in a while would try to get some sleep. Not on those filthy bunks in the magazine, though. He'd have a bed of sorts rigged up for him in the tunnel. The women were in the magazine, and he wanted as little as possible to do with them.

Not that they had presented any real problem so far. The gunners had been effectively warned off by the fright the major had given them, and Henschel had been put very firmly in place.

But they presented the only problem he could imagine arising, and with a little vigilance he should be able to prevent any trouble developing. And of course the Oberleutnant had a vested interest in keeping things running smoothly, without incident.

On the whole Wolff felt that he had everything fairly well organised. Yes, things were looking decidedly brighter.

*   *   *   *   *   *

The burst of machine-gun fire came out of the darkness to their left. It lasted only a couple of seconds but in that short time the German MG42, instantly recognisable by its distinctive ripping snarl of rapid fire, had loosed off forty rounds.

Alf Porter didn't stop when the New Zealander beside him threw up his arms and pitched forward on to his face. He kept running, willing himself to greater speed. A second, shorter burst cut the air behind him and then he was tumbling into a water-filled crater beside Lieutenant Saville and the others.

'I didn't know you had such a bloody good turn of speed, Alf.' Harris cautiously raised his head to look out at the body that sprawled in the dirt, arms and legs spread-eagled, unmoving.

Reilly as usual had something to add. 'Yeah. You keep that up and they'll have you in the regimental team.'

Lucas overheard. 'No good, he wouldn't put up the same sort of times. They only use blanks in the starting pistols.'

One man remained to cross the stretch of open ground that had already claimed a victim. The face of the New Zealander could just be made out as a paler patch beneath a tangle of barbed wire twenty yards back.

Sergeant Murray took up a position at the lip of the crater and aimed his Tommy gun out into the darkness. 'All right, Mitchell, on the count of three. One, two . . .'

The corporal broke from cover and sprinted for safety. As he did, Murray's sub-machine gun hosed a line of tracer towards the unseen enemy post. His aim must have been good. This time the Germans were not so fast off the mark, and their fire when it did come beat dust from the ground several feet behind the running man. Mitchell made it, hurling himself in as the enemy gunners sought him unsuccessfully with a second even more cautious ripple of fire.

With a last look out towards the body they were leaving behind them, Murray led the group out of the crater. They were using every shred of cover and were constantly forced to seek shelter against the incoming torrent of mortar fire. Progress was very slow, dictated by the slowest speed of the most heavily laden man over the difficult terrain.

'Sounds like a bit of a rough house going on up ahead.' Murray had slipped back to warn Saville. 'Could be the front line. If it is, your blokes haven't got half as far as they'd planned to by this time.'

'Yes, well, you hang on here and I'll nip forward to find out how we stand.'

'That's our job, Lieutenant.' Murray was suspicious of the British officer's reasons for taking over the scouting.

'Quite right, Sergeant. But things have obviously been rather hot around here, and our chaps could be somewhat jumpy and trigger happy by now. They might take one look at that camouflage outfit of yours and think you're a Jerry paratrooper. So just hold on here, I'll not be long if I can help it.'

Murray raised no other objection, and watched as Saville disappeared into the smoke. But he continued to harbour suspicions. Scouting was their work, his responsibility, and having it taken away even temporarily, for whatever reason, rankled. It was like they weren't trusted to do the job. Serve the bugger right if he bought it, cocky sod. He was almost disappointed when Saville returned fifteen minutes later.

'Hell of a shambles out there. No proper line at all, just what's left of our chaps, dug in up to their eyeballs, facing the way they think Jerry is. I found a couple of our bren gunners who pointed out what looks like a possible way through. They're pretty sure it's a gap. Not enough of them left to exploit it, but we might be able to wriggle through before Jerry wakes up and plugs it.'

The wire became thicker, with few gaps, and the weight of mortar fire reduced their rate of travel still further as they were forced to dash in small groups from crater to crater.

'Bloody hell. What have we got that'd make a hole like this?' Reilly was marvelling at the size of the massive crater in which they sheltered.

'Don't be so bloody thick.' Lucas had taken out his Colt, and with his free hand was patting his pockets to check where he'd stowed the spare magazines. 'Jerry blew a bloody great long line of these along here, a couple of months ago, as a tank trap.'

The bren gunners had moved aside at the rim of the crater to allow Murray and Saville room to examine the ground they'd have to traverse. They took it in turns to use the lieutenant's small binoculars, peeping out between the large sods of earth with which the pit had been roughly crenellated.

Thirty yards off, on the far side of ground that had been turned over but not too heavily gouged by shell fire, just visible through eddying smoke, was the smashed remains of a

German pill-box. The octagonal concrete structure had been broken open by the sledgehammer impact of a large-calibre artillery round. All of the roof was gone and most of the walls had been pushed down or pulverised. A small fire still burned inside.

'What do you think?' Saville handed the glasses to the New Zealander.

Murray scrutinised what was left of the structure, then carefully examined every inch of the ground before it. There was a little wire, but not much, most of it having been blown into a large tangled ball out to the right. 'Well, I can't see anything, but that doesn't mean the bastards aren't there. Still, we've got to get through somewhere, and it's as good a place as any. Yeah, I reckon we'll give it a go. If these blokes with the bren can cover our flanks, and you can put down a couple of smoke rounds with that mortar of yours, I'll nip over with Mitchell and Nicolson to check it.'

'Good. Let's get it set up, then.'

The bren gunner unwittingly punctuated the end of the conversation, sending five quick single shots at a dimly-seen target momentarily glimpsed further away.

'Are you any good with that thing?' Mitchell watched Harris setting up the two-inch mortar at the bottom of the crater.

'Only brilliant, that's all.' Harris made a great show of tamping down the loose soil before seating the weapon's small base plate firmly onto it. He stood on tiptoe to glance over the rim of the hole, then adjusted the angle of the barrel until it was within a degree or two of the vertical. 'Ready when you are.' He took out three smoke bombs, laying two beside the weapon and keeping the third in his hand, poised over the tube of the mortar.

'Let's have that smoke.'

On Murray's instruction Harris dropped the first round down the short tube and sent it on its way. Without waiting to see the impact, by which to gauge his accuracy, he sent the other two rounds after it immediately.

The first burst of white phosphorus smoke was ten yards short of the target, the second detonated immediately in front of the shattered structure, scattering much of its contents over the remaining fabric. As the white fire dripped from the pitted surfaces the last bomb ignited right on what was left of a loopholed wall, sending a shower of fiercely burning chemical across the interior of the gutted fortification.

A rapidly thickening and expanding cloud hid the pill-box, and as it disappeared from sight so Murray and his two men broke from cover and ran forward. They had covered half of the distance when a flashing line of tracer whipped out of the smoke in their direction. At once the men hit the ground, and as the bren hammered away in the direction from which it had come, they instantly replied with a flurry of hand grenades.

Close upon one another the steel-wrapped lumps of Baratol burst in, on and about the pill-box. A single New Zealander leapt to his feet and sprinted into the white fog. Moments later a Tommy gun could be heard firing, a long burst that must have emptied its magazine, then there was silence.

To the men lying out in the open, and to those still back at the crater, the wait seemed an age. Then a wraith-like figure appeared at the edge of the smoke and beckoned them on.

An overpowering smell of scorched meat permeated the area of the pill-box. Two badly charred bodies burned with flickering blue flame in one corner, another with limbs contorted into unnatural positions sprawled on a pile of rubble. Nearby lay a badly damaged machine-gun and curled belts of ammunition.

They paused there only a moment, to check that everyone had made it safely, before making their way out the far side and using a partially collapsed communication trench to put distance between themselves and the scene of the action. A bombed-out gun pit offered them a place of comparative safety while Saville consulted his map and compass.

'As close as I can figure it, we have a little over a mile to go before we cross Route 6 and hit the lower slopes of Monastery Hill. Now we don't know what state the rest of the Jerry defences are in, but if what we've just encountered is a fair sample then that mile is going to be a hell of a long one. From now on we go round any opposition. Wire and mines we'll just have to take as they come. I don't want anybody getting impatient and trying to push ahead. The chances are you'll not only blow yourself up, you'll draw attention to the rest of us. Is there anything you want to add, Sergeant Murray?'

'Yeah, if anyone goes down, leave him, even if it's your best mate. Leave him and get to the next bit of cover. We'll sort things out then. You won't help by adding yourself to our casualty list.'

Murray had drilled that into his own men time and time again. He'd seen too many good blokes buy it, cut down when they'd stopped to render assistance in the open. In an attack you kept going, and this situation wasn't much different. They faced all the dangers of an assault, without the compensation of being able to hit back any time they wanted to. These British were an unknown quantity to him, it wouldn't do any harm to spell out the basics to them. The measure of his success in this mission was how many of the heavily laden Engineers he escorted to the target. He had no intention of being made to look some kind of no-hoper, just because they got themselves bumped off.

'Right, on that cheerful note let's get going.' Saville eased the straps that were biting into his shoulders. He ached already, and he was carrying a load twenty pounds lighter than some of his sappers.

Now they were right in among the German defences. Not all of the gun pits, strongpoints, and machine-gun posts were manned. Many were fall-back positions that would be taken up by reinforcements as they were fed in, or by front line troops pushed back by British advances, but it was impossible to tell which were and which weren't. Consequently they had to act as though from any one of the enemy positions might come a burst of fire and shower of grenades, and as a result their progress became pitifully slow.

Wide belts of wire and mine fields laced the gaps between each compact complex of defences. The barrage had ploughed up some of the mines, cut some of the wire, but not all. Every yard was fraught with danger from a dozen sources. Twice in the first hour they had to travel over stretches of furrowed soil on their bellies, in single file, the lead man probing for mines with a carefully wielded knife.

Inviting gaps appeared in broad belts of wire, and were ignored. The openings had been left deliberately, with the intention of channelling attackers into killing grounds in front of machine-gun nests.

A quick ten yards they made using a damaged German trench ended abruptly amid the bodies and smashed weapons of a mortar pit that had suffered an ammunition explosion; then it was back to the nerve-racking process of feeling their way forward inch by inch.

In that first hour they made one hundred yards, in the next they slowed to fifty, then the third hour thought themselves lucky to make all of a hundred and thirty.

Mercifully the smoke stayed thick, and hung low on the ground. And all the time the rain of shells continued, screaming down and filling the air with their razor-sharp bullet-fast fragments. At times they fell at random, indiscriminately gouging holes in the fields and lanes, and then without warning they would fall in massive concentration, pounding a hundred-yard square of crops and hedges into a torn mess of heaped earth, scorched stalks and shredded wood.

The Cassino to Pignataro road was suffering just such punishment as they reached it. It was a major obstacle they had to cross, certain to be covered by dug-in self-propelled guns and tanks as well as the static defences.

Lieutenant Saville peered out from beneath the overturned Krupp six-wheeler under which they'd taken cover while they surveyed the difficulties ahead.

Much of the road surface was invisible, hidden by the debris that had been hurled onto it by the many rounds striking the fields alongside. The red and yellow flashes of the impacting shells made short-lived beacons in the fog.

'Best time to go would be now – ' Murray didn't wait for his advice to be sought, 'before this lot ends and the Jerries stick their heads up again.'

Saville had already made up his mind. 'Send Mitchell over first to establish a collecting point. Then we'll put them across one at a time.'

Mitchell made it safely, and waved an all-clear when he'd found a safe spot close by a gutted mark 4 Panzer.

At ten-second intervals the men made the thirty-yard dash, hurdling what was left of a ditch and hedge, and then running as fast as they could, bent almost double, to join those who had already made it.

The sappers were out in the open precious seconds longer than the more lightly equipped infantry, and a bigger target while they were, their bulky packs working against them in every way.

Corporal Clark was the second to last to go. Saville gave him a slap on the shoulder to send him off. His eyes followed the NCO but his thoughts were only partially on him. What was uppermost in the officer's mind was that he was next. Within half a minute it would be him making that sprint, running the gauntlet of their own artillery. He prepared himself. As soon as Clark made it he would break from the slight but comforting shelter of the wrecked truck, and without waiting for the ten-second gap would pit his life and his speed against his quota of luck.

Clark had just reached the far side of the road when his ran out. A shell crashed down nearby, and when the dust cleared the corporal was flopping about on the road like a fish out of water.

Even before Saville had finished forming the intention to go to his aid another round struck. The power of the shell's explosive charge was multiplied several times by the detonation of the contents of the corporal's pack. When the road was visible once more, Clark had ceased to exist.

Although the morning mist and drifting smoke had extended the night, day had still come too soon. As it had grown lighter and the concealment offered by the smoke had become more erratic and less dependable, they had been compelled to go to ground, literally.

The black mud and decomposing leaves at the bottom of the ditch, when scooped out in handfuls, had provided an excellent natural camouflage. Murray had added the finishing touches to each man's own efforts, then climbed in himself and rolled round and round in the oozing glutinous muck until, laid on his face with his Tommy gun shielded beneath him, like the rest of the assault group he was indistinguishable from the gully in which they lay.

And there they stayed, each man alone with his thoughts and his fears throughout the day. The shelling had come to them as a steady drumming that had kept the ground in trembling motion. Occasionally hot fragments would *plop* into the mud and cool with slow hisses that sent miniature plumes of steam into the air.

For a while, shortly after midday, a nearby hedge had burned and showered them with sparks and embers, until a near-miss cascaded damp soil over the flames and smothered them.

Though they fought it, despite the damp and discomfort of their situation, sleep stole up on all of them at some time. Their awakening was inevitably with a start as their brains took a second to adjust to the nightmare they awoke to.

Twice patrolling tanks growled past their hiding place, and once a heavy self-propelled gun actually crossed the ditch further along. Those awake to see it were able to clearly make out the equipment adorning its shrapnel-scarred camouflage paint scheme, as its threshing tracks bridged the shallow excavation and spun for a moment before it hauled itself clear.

Those incidents apart, there was no other evidence of life in the landscape, aside from the curling smoke and the rising bubbles of flame from impacting ordnance.

The hours of daylight had been shortened at both ends. Saville stiffly pushed his cramped body from the mould it had made for itself at the bottom of the clogged drainage channel a full hour before sunset. His first task was to confer with Murray over their precise position. Their eventual conclusion was not encouraging.

'Then we're only half way to the road, and if we have another night as bad as the last we'll be lucky to reach the hill by first light.' Murray found the slow pace infuriating. 'By the time we get there the bloody battle will be over.'

Saville had more patience with their progress, slow as it was. 'I think not, Sergeant. So much of the German defences remaining in one piece means that the main push behind us is going to be moving just as slowly, perhaps even more so. They can't go round anything, and mopping up the masses of positions all over this area is going to be a mammoth task.'

'So we plod on.'

The lieutenant nodded in agreement. 'We crawl on if we have to. For us the main job is to get there and fix those guns. There's no timetable, we'll just do the best we can. Even getting there late is going to be some help, certainly it's a damned sight better than not getting there at all.'

Lucas watched his officer talking with the New Zealander, as he herded the men together and stopped the less thoughtful among them from gulping down all their water there and then. There was a growing resentment in him at the way the Kiwi got on with Saville. Not that he could do much about it right now. He'd have to keep an eye on the situation and stamp on any attempt by the other sergeant to usurp his position.

Maybe with a bit of luck the Kiwi would go the way Clark had, pity he'd not gone instead. Strange, but that was almost the first thought he'd given it since it happened, none of the men had mentioned it either, or spoken of the Kiwi who'd been chopped down by the machine-gun inside their own bridgehead. It was as though none of them wanted to attract death's attention by speaking of it.

'If you're all ready then, Sergeant Lucas?'

Lucas realised he'd been daydreaming. Shit, that had started the night off on the wrong foot. 'All ready here, Lieutenant.'

Except that there was less barbed wire to contend with, the night was almost a repetition of the previous one. And even that advantage was cancelled out by the fact that their route lay now through territory that had largely escaped the attention of the British gunners so far; what wire there was had hardly been damaged at all. The wire cutters remained in frequent use, and there was the added refinement that some of the strands had been laced to boobytraps. Rather than become involved in lengthy and risky clearance work, they were forced each time they encountered wire so treated to make a detour.

During the day their clothing had gradually become soaked right through, and the night air did nothing to dry them or even the mud that caked them. Moving at such a slow rate they didn't even generate any worthwhile level of body heat; aches and cramps began to affect them all.

The German strongpoints were more widely spaced than those near the Rapido but superbly camouflaged, and within minutes of their starting out that was nearly their undoing. Lulled into a sense of false security, they failed to see the grass-covered low-relief emplacement until they were about to step on it. They froze at the realisation, and the smell of cooking came to them from inside. Gradually, one careful step at a time, they backed off. Nicolson who had been scouting had passed within a couple of yards of the front of the main blockhouse without seeing it, so artfully concealed was it with growing plants and carefully laid debris.

At times the smoke, thickened by the fine dust kept in suspension, was so dense that each man had to hold onto the webbing of the one in front to avoid losing contact. When they crossed the railway line and passed a Nebelwerfer battery concealed in a shallow cutting, even though it was in full screaming action, all that they saw of the huge rockets as they leapt into the air at a prodigious rate was a faint glow from their rapidly-consumed propellants' exhausts.

Here the countryside, what little they saw, was less severely punished by the constant shelling, but even so, every few paces they would pass a tree or hedge that had been scarred or clipped by shell or bomb. And on some of the paths they crossed, near burning or shattered vehicles, there were other, more gruesome signs of the work the explosives and incendiary material were doing.

*   *   *   *   *   *

On the far bank of the Rapido something was burning very fiercely. Wolff could make out the brilliant white centre of the fire and the soft pink-and-blue halo it created in the thick surrounding smokescreen. At times the area of illumination would expand dramatically and a large ball of flame would soar into the air accompanied by the firework effect of burning tracer ammunition that flew upwards with it.

He handed the night-glasses to the gun commander. 'What do you think it is?'

The Oberleutnant studied the conflagration for a while. 'Ammunition trucks, I should think. We must have got lucky and caught a convoy of them bunched up on the approach to a bridge. It's a wonder we're hitting anything, the amount of smoke they're using. I've never seen anything like it.'

'*Bridge?*' Wolff could hardly believe what he'd heard. 'But we've had no word about the Rapido being bridged.'

'Do you seriously imagine for one second that anyone would bother to tell us?' There was bitterness and sarcasm in the Oberleutnant's voice. 'We'll be bloody lucky if they tell us when the hill's surrounded.'

'But a bridge, how can you possibly tell, how can you be sure?'

'I can't. All I know is that nine times in the last six hours our observer up in the monastery has had me shelling the same map reference. Now, as tanks aren't in the habit of hanging about that long when an eighty-eight has found their range and is shovelling shit all over them, then I figure it must be a bridge we're firing at.'

Wolff looked out again at the valley. The shelling was not as intense as it had been but still every second that passed was marked by another explosion somewhere below. Small pockets of red fire marked where vehicles burned, and flames of several hues flickered from blazing gun pits and pill-boxes as guns and men and ammunition were consumed. It was like an aerial view of hell.

He turned away and reached for the crank handle to secure

the shutter, pausing to take one last look before it was fully closed. The scene was as before, a smoky inferno of fire and tracer and exploding shells. He was glad he was not down there.

*   *   *   *   *   *

Apart from a slight tinge of luminescence in the pall over their heads, the only proof they had of the sun's rising was that provided by their watches. The inevitable mist that came with it coated every blade of grass with beads of water, and soaked the men further, settling on their clothes and seeping into the material every time they moved.

Mitchell was out in front edging his way forward with extra care, warned by Saville that they must hit the main highway at any moment. He reached a wide belt of wire that stretched away to right and left without a gap.

'Oh, the bloody hell with it! I ain't going to piss about with any more bloody mystery tours just to get round this lot.' He took out his wire cutters and grabbed the first strand.

Saville's hand clamped down on the New Zealander's wrist as the jaws of the cutters closed on the platted metal. Mitchell, his thinking dulled by tiredness, didn't understand, and then a small grey cylinder attached to a post at the end of the wire caught his eye, and comprehension suddenly dawned. He looked round, and found he was quite alone apart from the British officer, who reached out and held the strand steady while he slowly withdrew the cutters from contact.

Perspiration stood out on both men as with extreme care the wire was allowed to relax back into place. That done, they carefully backed away until they reached where the others lay, and got down to join them.

'How about cutting through this lot? It looks like it's intact for a long way in either direction, could cost us a lot of time trying to work round it. And there's a fair chance there'll be a Jerry machine-gun nest where it ends.'

Murray's suggestion was tempting to the lieutenant. All of the men were tired. Blasting a path through the wire might save an hour or more. The risk that the blasting might draw attention to them had to be balanced against the possibility of their being spotted in the growing light by an alert German sentry as they stumbled about searching for a way round. He made his decision.

'Sergeant Lucas, I've a job for Russell.'

Russell crawled cautiously towards the wire. He'd left his pack with the others, and now his only load was the eight half-pound slabs of explosive and the long length of cord that linked them. He'd turned down the offer of an escort for the job, preferring to do it on his own, with no one watching. This way he could work at his own pace, had only himself to worry about. Lieutenant Saville and the Sarge had made up the charges so he knew they'd be all right. Now it was up to him.

The wire was ahead. It was thickly sown with various types of devices, some attached to the posts, others hanging from the wire, swinging in what little movement of air that there was.

The smoke and mist together created several strange effects. They made estimating distances very difficult, as objects rippled in and out of vision; they washed the colours from the day and even blotted out the disc of the sun, making its light so diffused that it was impossible to locate its exact position.

Placing the first four blocks of explosive presented no problem, but Russell knew that some of the charges had to be set right in amongst the belt to be sure of starting off a chain reaction that would detonate all the boobytraps as well as cut the wire. With extreme care he slid under the outer strands and attached the fourth innocuous-looking wad to a post. He was about to position the sixth when the ground shook to the impact of a heavy shell two hundred yards off. At intervals of a couple of seconds two more of the same calibre followed, each time coming closer. As a fourth came down Russell knew with terrible certainty that the salvo was marching straight for the wire.

He dropped the remaining blocks and began to wriggle back out as fast as he could. Shell number five came hurtling down as he crawled clear, the blast from number six caught him as he began to run. A roaring wall of sound and dust and debris struck him and bowled him over. He could hear the rain of pebbles it created bounce on the wire, and clatter against the posts.

Number seven landed dead centre in the middle of the wire. The thunder of its detonation was instantly followed by a storm of smaller explosions as the demolition charges he'd

91

left and the boobytraps went off.

Russell was just thinking that seven should be his lucky number when a searing pain shot up his leg and made him cry out.

Saville examined the twisted double strand of barbed wire that protruded from the back of the sapper's thigh. It had been driven in a long way.

'We can't fix it here, can you move?'

'I can hop, if it's not too far. It was worse at first. I wasn't expecting it.'

'Good man. I'll have one of the Kiwis help you. Hold on a bit longer and we'll do what we can to patch you up.'

The wire had been the last obstacle before the road. They had reached it, Route 6, the via Cassilina, but that for the moment was as far as they were going. There was no jubilation among the men, with most of them it barely registered, it was just another landmark. Even Saville, who fully realised the achievement, spared only a fleeting moment from his problems to enjoy a brief feeling of satisfaction.

With the mist rapidly lifting, and the smoke coming only in fitful bursts of varying density that could not be relied on for cover, they had no choice but to once more find a place to hide up for the day. They would have to wait for dark before they could cross the broad metalled surface and the patches of alternate rock and cultivated land beyond that gave way to the slopes of Monte Cassino.

The Monastery itself was clearly visible, seeming to float high overhead on a cushion of rolling grey and white, as the British artillery strove frantically to build a bank of cloud about it that would mask its magnificent and deadly field of vision.

'I think we've found just the place.' Murray stuck his head through the foliage of the hedge in the shadow of which the engineers had taken cover. 'It's bloody perfect, even furnished, sort of.'

For a moment Saville was about to ask what he meant by 'furnished' but decided it would be easier to wait and see. The first priority was to get there.

As the Kiwi sergeant led the way, Saville wondered what it was about the man that made his off-hand manner easier to get along with than Sergeant Lucas's somehow stiffly-proper behaviour. Perhaps it was because he sensed in the

New Zealander the same attitude to war that he had. Yes, that might well be it, the fact that he felt he was seeing, in a way, a reflection of himself. For him war was the best thing he could be doing at the moment, so he made the most of it, did it the best he could. The alternative, had another deferment been possible, would have been another three months in his father's plant-hire firm. *The son, Mr Roy*, God how he hated those titles, and worst of all, *Young Mr Saville*. At thirty-one, to be *Young Mr Saville*!

Without the war he'd have gone on being Mr Roy for how long, another twenty years? It was possible, with his father as fit as he was. There'd be no going back to that now, no more steamrollers and cement mixers, no more road lamps and barrows. He could have cried with sheer frustration when he was dumped on the Royal Engineers, and had wasted no time in wangling himself into the line of the Engineers' work that offered the most action, most often. It would be interesting to find out what Murray had done in civvy street, to test his theory.

The furious chatter of machine-gun and small-arms fire that had continued throughout the hours of darkness, giving an indication of the intensity of the battle for the bridgehead going on behind them, had slackened with the coming of daylight. But if the infantry had gone to ground, the artillery had really come to life, commencing in earnest its attempts to dig them up again.

He noticed a slight twitch that his left eyelid gave every time a shell landed within a couple of hundred yards. Was that how battle fatigue started? Was it the first symptom that signalled the gradual onset of that numbed state the mind retreated to when the pressure became too much? The hell with it, he wasn't going to let it get to him. Not until he'd broken that bloody emplacement right in half.

Twenty seconds after they'd left the hedge, he had the tic under control; then the site they'd occupied took a direct hit.

The culvert ran right under Route 6, but its far end had been blocked some time before by a bomb that had struck the edge of the road and caved in several feet of the roof. Water no longer found its way down the crude gutter in the middle of the floor, and the stone had already dried out completely, indicating that the damage had been done at least five or six days previously.

In that time, the Germans had already found a use for the place. Besides a considerable quantity of engineers' stores – coils of barbed wire, stakes, implements and a small concrete mixer – there were five tarpaulined shapes parked in a row against the wall. Handles of tubular steel projected from one end and thick-tyred wire-spoked wheels showed below the fringes of the heavy material.

While Murray set a guard at the entrance and Tatman and Harris helped Mike Russell to a comfortable position against the wall, the lieutenant pulled one of the covers aside to examine what it was the Germans had decided to store there.

As the tarpaulin slid off it revealed a squat, tracked device, resembling a miniature version of a World War One tank, about three feet long.

Reilly had seen the object as well. 'Jesus bloody help us! We're sharing a tomb with a ton of bloody explosive.'

The other four tarpaulins were tugged aside by Lucas, and each in turn came away to expose yet another of the German Goliath demolition tanks, each ready for use complete with its transporter trolley. 'You're wrong, Reilly. There's only about half a ton in the lot of them put together.'

'And is that supposed to make me feel a whole lot better? What if them as owns them decide to come and collect them? I'm telling you, what with them and our packs, this is no bloody place to be in a fire fight.'

'If any Jerries do turn up then Murray and his lot can handle them, that's what they're here for, aren't they?'

'If you say so, Sergeant, if you say so. But I'm telling you, there's other things I'd rather be spending my time in the company of right now.'

Saville had removed a small inspection panel from one of the mobile bombs. He examined the vehicle starter motor that drove it, and the drum of heavy-duty cable that paid out after it supplied its directional instructions and power.

'Sergeant Lucas, I think we can do a decent job of scuppering these by buggering the motors. Do it as unobtrusively as possible. With a slice of luck Jerry won't even twig that they've been got at until he comes to use them. That'll give the blighters a shock.'

Detailing Harris and Reilly to assist the sergeant the lieutenant went over to where Porter was getting their casualty ready for attention.

Now, with the material torn away to expose it, the wound

94

could be seen properly. The plaited strand stood out from the flesh. There was very little damage about the point of entry, just a star-shaped network of short cuts radiating out from the wire. Very gingerly Saville tested the tissue around it with his fingertips, after using part of the torn trouser leg to wipe away most of the blood. The wire was firmly embedded in the thick muscles, but had not penetrated right through, having been stopped by the bone.

'What do you reckon, sir? Pull it out?'

'Do you mind, Alf, that's my bloody leg you're talking about!' Russell couldn't see the examination that was going on behind him as he lay on his face, but he'd heard Porter's words, and they'd alarmed him.

'I don't know.' Saville quickly let go of the metal after a very tentative tug elicited a loud cry of pain from the wounded sapper, which Porter's hastily applied hand had only partially succeeded in stifling. 'I rather think that a couple of barbs have been driven in there. It'd be rather like trying to pull out a well embedded fish hook. There's a big artery near there, somewhere. We might do more harm than good.'

Murray had heard the shout, and came over. 'It ought to come out. You never know what might have been having a Jimmy on that wire.'

'Anything from a Kraut to a polecat.' Russell thought he might as well try to keep his own spirits up with a dash of humour, as it appeared that no one else was going to for him.

'Probably both. You just keep still or I'll whip it out now.' Saville knew that the Kiwi was right, but it was not as clear cut as that. 'Yes, that's what we should do, but I don't know whether we should try mucking about with it, or leave well enough alone. He can still walk on it at the moment.'

Russell was learning to cope with the pain of the wound, but the thought of the inexpert probing he'd be subjected to at the lieutenant's hands terrified him. He'd always had a fear of hospitals, even of visiting them. 'Couldn't you just leave it for now? Just sort of snip it off short, to stop it catching, and put a dressing over it. I'll manage.' He remembered the incredible lengths he'd gone to in a vain attempt to avoid having his jabs for overseas service. And now, now he was faced with the prospect of a bloody amateur poking about inside him with a none-too-clean pen-knife and in a state of abysmal ignorance. 'Look, I'll be OK for a while. It's just that the wire's been wagging about that's bothered me. Once it's cut off short I'll be as right as rain.'

This was the sort of thing no amount of training ever prepared you for. Saville wanted to believe the sapper, though he knew that really the wire should come out. Damn it, he was no surgeon. If it was a bullet in Russell's leg he wouldn't have dreamed of trying to extract it. Maybe it was because, with about six inches of the fragment sticking out, it looked like it should be easy. And even if he did by some miracle remove the barbs without doing more harm than had already been suffered, there was no effective way he could cleanse the wound. Indeed, he might even introduce a source of infection to it.

'Get me some wire cutters.' He knew he was taking the easy way out, and made up his mind to get it over and done with as swiftly as possible. 'Sergeant Murray, will you spread your fingers on the leg around the entry point?'

Porter, very casually, reached forward and let his hands rest on Russell's shoulders. He nodded to the lieutenant.

Mike Russell sensed what was coming, and though he knew it would make it more difficult, couldn't prevent all his muscles from tensing. It was as though he could feel every movement that was made, magnified a thousand times. Though he couldn't see them he knew that the jaws of the snips were in position about the base of the wire.

There was no warning. The wire in his leg moved as the cutters bit into it. The pain was incredible. As the jaws bit deeper the wire twisted once more and a big black pit opened up to swallow him.

Murray slowly and lovingly rolled a cigarette. It was his last Rizla, it would have to be bloody newspaper from now on, unless he could scrounge a few more to tide him over. Not that he'd need too many, because he was down to his last few shreds of Pirate Shag as well. What a bloody time to be running out. In the hurry to get underway when word had come through he'd not had the chance to stock up. The wet lick he gave the edge of the paper served the dual purpose of joining it and slowing the rate of combustion when he lit it.

He looked at the faces of his men. Behind the tiredness that lined their features he could read their frustration at the slow pace of their journey. They'd been in attacks where ground had been covered much more slowly, or where they'd fought bitterly for days, marking time, or even being pushed back, but they had been in action, here they were deliberately avoiding it. For men whose whole training was slanted towards getting to close grips with the enemy it was not an easy situation to adjust to.

And there was another factor weighing the men down. Since they had started out they had been constantly under their own shell fire. That was always especially difficult to bear. It was small consolation that the shells making life so hazardous for them were making it just as unpleasant for the Germans.

The only luck they'd had so far, to his way of thinking, was their low casualty rate, two dead and one wounded; and him more inconveniently than seriously. But then that was what this exercise was all about, getting there. Caution rather than dash, hide rather than seek. Avoiding detection and casualties, making sure every possible ounce of explosive was delivered to the target. But that knowledge didn't make it any more easy for him and his men to stifle the urge to rush on and tackle the job themselves. Not that there would be much point in their doing that. Without the loads the British carried all they'd be able to do would be knock on the door of the emplacement and ask to be let in.

From the direction of the bridgehead came the sounds of the daytime battle as it ebbed and flowed. The rest of the Eighth Army was having a hell of a tough time clawing its way through the Gustav Line. It was one thing for a small group to slip through in isolation, another entirely for a coherent attack to bulldoze its way across the same ground on a broad front.

He allowed himself a couple of sips of water and a nibble of the hard chocolate from his K-ration. Best to make it last, there was no knowing how long it might have to yet. Not that it did him any good to think about it, but a couple of juicy lamb chops would have been nice. Four would be better, and washed down with a pint or two or three of decent beer; not the watered-down muck they got served out here. Oh what the hell, he'd started his gut rumbling now. He might as well try to get a bit of sleep, then it could go on making all the bloody noises it wanted. It wouldn't bother him.

Though he woke suddenly, he did not need to be cautioned to silence. Murray had woken to danger a hundred times

97

before and knew how to react. Instantly awake, he grabbed up his Thompson. It was Saville who'd shaken him.

'One of my men is on watch. He's spotted three Jerries who look like they're heading this way.'

'Where are they now?'

'About seventy yards from the entrance. They go to earth every time a shell comes down within half a mile.'

'OK. Get your men to the back of the tunnel, out of sight. We'll see to it. Take Kemp with you.'

'Here, Sarge, what's up? Ain't I good enough or something?' Kemp objected to being left out of the welcoming committee.

'Just for once, Kempy, do as you're bloody told. I'm not having you buggered and being lumbered with carrying that toaster of yours myself. Now get back.'

Kemp looked like he had more argument to offer, so Murray ended the discussion on the subject by turning him round bodily and giving him an almighty shove.

With Mitchell and Nicolson, Murray hid among the litter of equipment just inside the mouth of the culvert. Crouched down low between the piles, they merged with the clutter into invisibility.

There was shouting outside, the sound of running, and three men burst into the tunnel. Their speed took them several paces inside before they pulled up and stood to regain their breath. As they recovered from their exertions they joked between gasps for air. The individual who had been first inside was singled out as the butt of considerable humour, which he seemed to take in good part, and replied to in kind, as more shells like those that had caused their precipitate arrival impacted in the distance.

Lucas had quietly taken out his Colt. In a moment the Germans, who were all armed, must see the uncovered Goliaths. The one he had just been working was nearest to them, in plain view.

Just as it seemed the New Zealanders were never going to make their move the three silhouetted figures were joined by others that appeared as though out of solid ground.

Arms flailed, a helmet fell with a crash and rolled in the gully. There were several dull thuds and a single strangled cry that was part made of fear and pain, and part of alarm. It came too late, once more there were just the three outlined figures, but these three wore helmets of English outline.

All of the Germans were dead, sprawled in an untidy heap,

mouths gaping, open eyes unseeing.

'A neat job, Sergeant Murray. But you had me worried for a moment. I was wondering when you were going to take them.'

'We've had a bit of practice at it. We'd have stuck them sooner, but I wasn't expecting them to come in at a rate of knots. If you'll ask any more that turn up to come in at a stroll we'll hit them right on cue!' Murray wasn't sure whether the lieutenant was having a dig at him or not. You had to watch some of the beggars. They started to get a bit uppity about not being saluted and all that sort of bloody nonsense. This one had been all right so far, but you could never be sure they wouldn't turn regimental on you all of a sudden. Not that it would do him a lot of bloody good if he did.

'What shall we do with them, *sir*?' Lucas put a particular emphasis on the last word as he indicated the dead Germans. He couldn't understand why Saville was letting the Kiwi get away with so much backchat. He wouldn't have got away with it for a minute.

The trouble was the bloody New Zealand 2nd Division had been told so many times by their own ruddy generals that they were special, and lauded so much by the press, that they'd begun to believe it themselves. It rankled with Lucas. A British division was just one of many, no matter where it served, but the Kiwi outfit was the only one their country had in the Med and consequently got the sort of special consideration that was accorded to the Guards Division. What with that and the way it seemed to be run like a bloody debating society, it made him sick.

Saville had considered moving the bodies to the back of the tunnel and hiding them under the rubble, but he could think of problems that might arise if they were missed and couldn't be found.

'Find a fresh crater. Not too near the entrance, and lay them down round that. If their mates come looking for them they'll think the artillery got them.'

'Oh, now that's clever, sir. That's bloody clever, to be sure.'

'I'm glad you think so, Reilly, because you and Tatman are going to do it. And don't loot the bodies. Anybody coming along might not notice that they've been stabbed, but they will think it's a bit queer if all their buttons and insignia have been cut off.'

Tatman had already taken out a small pair of nail scissors he carried for that purpose and was not made happy by the

99

lieutenant's caution. He regarded souvenirs as a legitimate perk and took a ghoulish delight in rifling any bodies he came across, quite unbothered by the extent of their mutilation or state of decomposition. Frequently as he went through pockets and packs he would hold mock conversations with the dead, usually assuming an appalling mock-German accent for the one-sided exchange.

When the victims of the ambush had been safely dumped at a discreet distance, the guard on the entrance was doubled and those men who were able set about making themselves as comfortable as their temporary quarters would allow. But although their situation was by several degrees more comfortable than the ditch they'd spent the previous day in, rest did not come easily to any of them, with two exceptions. Sergeant Murray had the facility of being able to go to sleep instantly, anywhere. Mike Russell had slipped from his faint into an exhausted slumber.

For the others there had to be a period of winding down. Few of them dropped their packs, preferring the discomfort of their continued wear to the extra seconds' delay that grabbing them up would cause if they had to make a run for it.

There was little conversation. Every ear was constantly alert to the slightest sound outside, straining to distinguish an imagined footfall from the patter of falling debris. And now that they were safe from the shell fire, now that at last there was a dry, flat surface that they could stretch out on, most would gladly have swopped it for the night that was still so many hours away, when once again they would be moving. Even the climb that lay ahead of them was preferable to the unnerving waiting.

The strain showed on their faces and in their subdued behaviour. They would soon have to tap their reserves of inner strength, and as yet their work had hardly begun.

*   *   *   *   *   *

Henschel held out the greasy bundle of notes towards the girl. She had come down to the door where the Gefreiter stood guard to try and get some air. The magazine was stifling, catching none of the slight draught that passed down the tunnel.

'Come on. There's a bloody fortune there. That's every ruddy lira I've got. Come on, drop them, and be quick about it.'

The girl didn't understand the words, though she knew what the money was for. She held back. He was very ugly and the penis he'd crudely exposed, before offering the added inducement, matched the rest of him, big and coarse and dirty.

'What are you waiting for? Oh come on. Here, just stand up against the wall.' He was in a hurry and pulled her forward, increasing the force he used when she tried to hold back. 'Come on. You'll bloody love this big one. I've treated some of the fattest fannies in Italy with this, should be a lovely tight fit on you.'

As he bent his knees to bring his belly down against hers he reached for her skirt and hauled it up. His fingers met hers and there was a struggle between their hands before she wrested the notes from his grasp.

Henschel grunted with satisfaction as he felt the massive rod of his erection slide over her silky underwear. 'Here, that's bloody lovely. A couple more like that and I'll be staining your knickers without going in.'

She felt the dampness that was seeping through the thin material and realised what he was striving for as with exaggerated movements he slid up and down against her. He was so heavy, but she got her hands to the waist of her drawers and tried to push them down. They were her best ones. The wet tip of his penis wiped across the back of her hand and she clenched her teeth to stop from retching. And then the wetness was being prodded into the top of her legs and the moment's resistance she was able to offer to its probings was rammed aside.

'Bloody hell. I needed that.' Henschel felt relief surge through him as he came. He hadn't even got it in but the second he'd felt those hot thighs clamped either side of him and that thick black hair grinding into him he couldn't hold it any longer.

'I'll want another one later for that much money. You hear me?'

With practised distaste the girl was wiping the mess off her legs. The words meant nothing, though their tone conveyed the message. She shrugged, a gesture that could be taken to mean anything. But she'd not be caught by this one again, not if she could help it. For the once the money was good, for twice it was not enough.

'What is going on here? You, go back to the magazine.' Wolff had seen the raised skirt the girl had not been fast

101

enough to drop, and read the leer on Henschel's inflamed features.

The girl tossed a piece of cloth into a corner, smoothed her clothes and with hips swaying went back down the tunnel.

Hauptmann Wolff made a point of looking elsewhere as she deliberately flaunted her breasts at him as she squeezed past, taking unnecessarily long to do so.

'I told you to stay away from the women.'

'Don't bloody go on at me, it's not my fault. She came to me. Must be 'cause I'm so lovely.'

Wolff found the vision that came to his mind, of what must have been going on before his arrival, quite revolting. The thought of that great lout with his ill-proportioned smelly body against that young flesh . . . it was disgusting.

A girl like that should be with young men, far away from this horror, still unsullied by experience, still fresh and clean and vital. She shouldn't already be a lined whore while still in her twenties. Prey for any ugly monster like Henschel.

'I don't want to know about it. Just stay away from her, and the other one.'

'If you think I'm going to hang about here for God knows how long, with nothing to do except build up a bloody thirst and feel my stomach shrink to the size of a bleeding walnut, and resist the temptation to poke the arse off two very presentable bits of skirt then you're in for a bloody big disappointment, Herr Hauptmann.'

There was nothing for it but to back-track over ground he'd already covered. Not that he expected it to have any better impact on repetition.

'Just stay away from them. Just stay away, that's all.'

'All right, just to please you. I promise to be a good boy and eat my greens and not go diddling any of the . . . ladies. How's that? Is that what you want?'

'At the moment I want you to do the job you're supposed to be doing, and keep a lookout.' Wolff sought a way to conclude the unpleasant exchange. 'Now get on with it.'

'Whatever you say, Herr Hauptmann. Pity you weren't here a bit sooner. You'd have had a good view from there.' Henschel called after the officer as he left. 'But if you want a nice souvenir,' he looked at the stiffening piece of material on the floor, 'I've got a couple of thousand little Heinz Henschels going cold down here.'

The last few words thrown at him as he traversed the blast-wall were indistinct and Wolff was grateful for that.

He'd had quite enough of the Gefreiter for now and could do without any more of the uncouth ideas his brutish words conjured into his mind to sully it.

When he was alone again Henschel took out a cigarette, from one of three packs he'd managed to steal from the gunners, and blew a neat smoke ring at the small vision port.

He'd thought when they stuck him there that they were doing it just to shunt him out of the way. Well maybe they had, but he'd turned it to his advantage. There was no way he'd have had a good fuck in the gun room or magazine. He'd have to try and get back here when it got dark.

The next time he'd bend her over and try it that way, or maybe he'd make her go down on her knees. Yeah that'd be good, it was ages since he'd had that, not since he'd got his old landlady drunk. He remembered how her gums had felt funny ، ، . Oh yeah, he was looking forward to the night.

*   *   *   *   *   *

There could be no mistake. The noise that was growing louder and more distinct every moment was that of approaching tank tracks.

'It can't be looking for us, can it?' Harris cautiously stuck his head up over the side of the road and looked in the direction from which the sound was coming. The smoke thickening the dusk had brought the visibility down to about forty yards and as yet there was no sign of the Panzer.

Saville listened to the growing rumble of the powerful engine, and the racket made by the Panzer's tracks as they clanked over the return rollers and ground on the hard surface of the road. 'Just a routine patrol, I should think, or possibly it's moving up to reinforce the Germans holding the town. Our Brigade of Guards must be giving them a hell of a rough time by now.'

From the swirling smoke came first the snout of a long-barrelled 75mm gun and then the massive squat superstructure of a slab-fronted Sturmgeschutz self-propelled anti-tank gun. The armour and tracks of the tank-like vehicle were almost totally concealed behind sheets of steel that flanked the hull and spare lengths of track that were draped over it everywhere else. All of the hatches were shut, and it carried on straight past where Saville's men crouched tight against the slight embankment on which the road ran. Without any sign

103

of having seen them, it went on its way to be lost in the gloom.

The men with the heaviest packs all needed help to get up onto the road, so did Russell, whose pack had been divided among the other men, amid muttered comments from Harris and Porter about 'bloody pack-mules'. Tatman had not helped soothe their frame of mind by doing one of his famous donkey imitations. The impromptu variety act had coincided precisely with a short lull in the shelling; his full-volume bray had been incredibly loud.

When Lucas had taken him to task over the amount of noise he was making Tatman had attempted to talk his way out of trouble by insisting that since all donkeys sounded alike the Germans couldn't possibly have known it was an English donkey he was imitating.

Reilly had capped that by assuring Sergeant Lucas that he wouldn't let Tatty make a donkey out of him.

Fortunately for the pair of them the lieutenant had called Lucas away before he could commence the retribution he considered was called for.

As they crossed and moved away from the road the *crump* of smoke shells landing gave way to the more frequent and much louder crash of harrassing rounds of high-explosive aimed at the tracks leading from it. The British artillery intended to make it costly, if not impossible, for the Germans to re-supply their troops during the hours of darkness.

In the entrance to a farm, at the end of a rough cart track, they passed a burned-out Horch car, and near it a Krupp personnel carrier riddled by shell fragments. The larger vehicle listed to one side, several of its tyres flayed and deflated.

Close by the Krupp lay the bodies of five German field police. The corpses were grossly disfigured by the explosion that had cut them down, and all had been charred extensively by showers of phosphorus from smoke rounds.

Tatman only had time to snatch a polished steel gorget and chain from one body as he passed. After a moment's consideration he hung it around his own neck. As he walked he squinted down at it and burnished it with his sleeve.

The last few scrubby patches of cultivation scraped from the lower slopes of Monte Cassino almost instantly gave way to steeply rising ground composed of alternate layers of bare rock and gorse-dotted expanses of scree, that slid away from underfoot with much rattling of stone and raising of dust.

In places the loose material had been welded together by a white crust, the residue of fierce chemical fires that British shells had delivered.

Progress became slower and slower. The need for silence, to keep close together and to detour around suspected strongpoints or impassable wire obstacles – all combined with the sometimes near-vertical climb to make the pace they had maintained in the valley look like a gallop by comparison.

In desperation, in the hope of making better time, they risked taking a narrow path that appeared to head in approximately the direction they wanted to go. It ended abruptly in a massive crater filled to waist depth with powdered rock.

Now the loads the sappers were carrying really began to tell and despite breaks every hour, each of them at some time had to have the assistance of one of the more lightly burdened New Zealanders, when the going became almost impossible.

As they climbed the view of the battlefield behind and below them became more panoramic, but few of them dared risk letting go a hold for even a brief look.

As dawn broke they found a shallow cave and Saville and the two sergeants tried to work out an accurate estimate of just how high they had climbed.

The monastery was at one thousand seven hundred feet, the emplacement at a little over fourteen hundred. At the closest they could reckon it, they still had five hundred feet to go.

Saville looked out at the amount of smoke already wreathing the slopes about them, but even before he looked he'd known that his mind was made up. 'Thirty minutes' break, and then we're going on.'

No one argued, muttered or dissented in any way. If anyone harboured private doubts about the wisdom of continuing they must have evaporated within five minutes of resuming the journey, when they ran into an obstacle that, had they encountered it in the night, would have cost them massive casualties before they'd have managed to extricate themselves.

There was no alternative to going through the ravine. To either side were wire and gorse so thick it would have meant staying in the open for hours to cut through, and among the natural and artificial thorns were familiar looking cylindrical grey objects.

It was Private Nicolson who, making up for an earlier

mistake in not spotting a blockhouse down in the valley, was the first to see the thin filaments of wire that crisscrossed the track running between the walls of rock.

On Saville's instructions Harris put the little mortar on a flat slab of stone and set it to lob a bomb to the far end of the section of path that was trip-wired.

'Take your time.' That was the only other thing the lieutenant said to him. Harris was a natural with the weapon. On the range where he'd been trained for a special task on Monte Camino he'd quickly bettered the performance of most of the instructors.

Now the sapper took out a fishing-reel-like attachment and clipped it to the mortar barrel then, after securing the loose end of line to the special round, carefully loaded it.

The shot was a tricky one, a fraction to right or left and the harpoon-like projectile would be lost among the litter of jagged boulders flanking either side of the path at the end of the gorge.

Harris made a fractional correction to the aim and fired. After the initial report of the round leaving the barrel there was nothing for several seconds, and then there was a puff of dust in the middle of the path right at the end of the ravine.

When Lucas, from behind the shelter of a rock ledge, began to pull the line in he felt resistance with less than a yard of the wire gathered in his hand. A gentle tug produced the loud crack of an anti-personnel mine going off. Before all of the line lay coiled at his feet Lucas had felt that slight resistance eight more times, and eight times the narrow confines of the pathway were lashed by a lethal hail of steel particles.

'Not far now.' Saville gave Russell encouragement as he limped past, but he knew that if the sapper went any slower then they would be forced to leave him behind. They would have to leave him somewhere reasonably safe in the hope of collecting him after the job was done or picking him up on the way back down.

For the last hour, since midday, the lieutenant had been aware of a new noise in the battle. It came from above them, and he had stopped frequently to scan the higher slopes in the hope of finding its source. So far the smoke had hid it from him, but there could be no mistaking what it was. It

106

came again, the bark of an eighty-eight.

After slipping in and out of vision all morning the monastery was now well shrouded by the smoke, and they were travelling if not faster, at least with more confidence now that it was out of sight. Every man had felt quite naked, totally exposed to the hidden eyes that watched from the black pock-marks of the windows that dotted the ragged façade of the cream-coloured walls.

But as the lieutenant once more quartered the hill, it was another structure, much closer to hand, that suddenly took all of his attention. It was barely visible, little more than a plain slab of concrete cowering beneath a jutting overhang, at the top of a small cliff. The concrete was pierced by two rectangular openings and the bottom of it was hidden by a jumble of piled stone that rested on a narrow artificial ledge. As he looked the blistered grey snout of a cannon barrel vomited fire and a tongue of flame leapt out from an embrasure.

It was as they rounded a spur and came into clear view of the face of the emplacement that a burst of machine-gun fire sent them scrambling for cover. The bullets came from a compact loopholed square of concrete nestling among the remains of splintered trees at the end of the ridge. Positioned where it was, it completely dominated their route and the ground to either side.

Murray and Saville compressed themselves into as small a space as possible in order that they might both shelter behind the stump of an olive tree. As they did so the German machine-gunner sent a long burst at them, which chewed slivers from the wood and showered them with splinters.

'Can you and your men take out that pill-box?' Saville spat shreds of bark.

'Not starting from here. I'll have to draw them back first, get sorted out, and I might need one of your blokes, if you can spare a bit of what's in one of those packs as well. You're sticking to the plan to tackle the emplacement from the back?'

Saville didn't have to pause to give the question consideration. His first glance at the front of the emplacement had confirmed his plan for him. 'Yes, we've no choice. Even if we could climb that sheer face, and it must be all of thirty feet, and hung every ounce of explosive on the face of it, I doubt if we'd do anything more than give the gun crews a headache. So it's the back door or nothing.'

107

The sharp-eyed German in the pill-box made the withdrawal far from easy, chasing every movement he saw with long bursts that must have had him changing the overheating barrels every couple of minutes. Ripples of tracer bounced after them as they edged out of his field of fire.

'As soon as the smoke thickens up a touch we'll be off.' Murray watched the ribbons of white fumes the breeze was wafting by the space between the two boulders where they all sheltered.

There was a growing whistling noise and a shell came screaming down. Every man squeezed himself into the smallest space possible and waited for the impact. It came with a muted thump, instead of the devastating bang they'd been anticipating.

Instantly every breath they took was agony, causing a searing pain in their chests as dense volumes of smoke filled the air about them. Their eyes streamed and there was no part of their bodies that did not prickle and itch.

'This thick enough for you?' Lucas rasped out the words.

Murray was squashed tight against one of the boulders, when he opened his eyes to blink away the stinging water that filled them he couldn't even see the rock an inch in front of his nose.

'I reckon this might just be overdoing it a touch.'

* * * * * *

The gun room trapped and amplified the thunder of the eighty-eights as they kept up a steady fire. Able to stand it no longer, and finding no respite in the tunnel, Wolff was forced to seek the sanctuary of the magazine.

He felt dirty, was sure he must smell. Their tiny ration of water did not stretch to allowing them to indulge in such luxuries as washing or shaving. It was the first time he'd ever had more than a day's growth of beard on his face since he'd started shaving at seventeen. The stubble had an unfamiliar feel, and itched.

It came as a surprise to him that the women had managed to keep the room so neat, its irregular shape and uneven floor not lending it to that condition.

The throbbing in his temples gradually passed and he sat at a low table on a chair improvised from the same unlikely source, ammunition boxes. With his headache easing he took out his notebook. It was almost full, every page filled with his small scrunched-up writing, and the end covers littered with miniature diagrams of improvements and modifications he'd carry out on the emplacement if he ever got the chance. It had been invaluable in helping him pass the time, and a useful mental exercise.

'What are you drawing?'

The woman's words came as a shock. He hadn't realized she spoke German, having until now only heard her in conversation with her companion, in Italian. She'd had nothing to do with the men.

'It's . . . it's a plan, of this roôm.' He waved his stub of pencil in a gesture that took in all the magazine. Not that he had any wish to offer her encouragement, but it was not in him to use her position in life as an excuse not to obey the common courtesies. Even so, he kept his answer brief.

She came round behind him and peered over his shoulder at the sketch he was doing. 'It is good. You draw me, yes?'

The woman pranced and flounced in front of him, swirling her skirt to make it rise above her knees. She succeeded in revealing both of the fleshy dimpled joints, and something of the wide pale thighs above them. 'You never seen a woman before?'

'I'm sorry, I didn't mean to . . .' Wolff mumbled the embarrassed apology. But how stupid of him to feel that he had to say he was sorry to a . . . a greasy overblown whore. A prostitute, and not even a good one at that or she'd be making her money in Rome and not in this dangerous and dreary place.

'Does your friend speak German also?' He had no wish to prolong the conversation, but he wanted the previous exchange buried as quickly as possible. Not, of course that he had been staring at her limbs; after all, if she was going to do that right in front of him then there was hardly anywhere else he could look. Actually, her body had a suggestion of the fullness of Hilda's. No, he mustn't even think that, comparing in any way his darling wife with this, this . . .

'Why you want to know? You make her an offer? We both charge the same. She a little younger, I have the better body, yes?' As she said it she put her hands on her waist, her fingers going white as she pinched it in, while she took a deep breath and held it to make her breasts pull tight the thin material of her top.

109

Wolff pretended not to notice, burying himself in his note-book, until it was snatched from him.

'Give it back, please. I have work to do.' He tried to keep his dignity in the ludicrous situation.

'You have it back when you promise to make a picture of me. You sign it "love to Gina". That is me.'

He sensed that the others in the room were watching; the girl, the two men setting fuses. Even the shell-shock case, still clutching his rifle butt, was staring mindlessly in his direction. Perhaps the easiest way out would be to go along with her, but he made one last appeal to reason.

'Really, I am not an artist. Please, my notepad.' In a way he resented saying that. There had been a time long ago when he'd harboured certain fanciful notions of becoming a painter. But the discomforts of the bohemian life had not attracted him and instead he had opted for the no less satisfying and infinitely more lucrative and secure field of architecture.

The woman arrayed herself in what she imagined to be an alluring pose, displaying much in the way of breast and teeth. 'I know you can. Please, do my picture.'

He accepted his notebook back, but was reluctant to comply with the condition imposed. He stalled for time. 'Your German is quite good. Where did you learn it; have you ever been to Germany?'

'I learn it from a crazy old man I live with two years. He teach me German and English and French. Every day he talk a different language. I do better than you, eh?'

'Yes, I only speak a little French . . .'

'Did she give you a good one then?'

The Hauptmann looked up to see Henschel lounging in the doorway. The ugly lout was making a crude gesture with his circled fingers and rolling his eyes in simulation of his idea of ecstasy.

Wolff jumped to his feet, dropping the pad and pencil, knocking the table askew. 'Get out, get out!' As he shouted his hand whipped to his holster. He checked the action as his fingers went to wrench his pistol out.

By the reaction he had shocked himself. Not once since he had been issued with the Walther P38 automatic had he even drawn it from its mirror-burnished resting place. In all honesty he couldn't even remember if it was loaded. And for a moment he had been quite prepared to use it, and for no greater reason than an obscene insult. What was happening to him?

Gefreiter Henschel had vanished as the Hauptmann's hand had touched the leather of his holster.

Shame flooded through Wolff. How could he possibly have let that animal get to him in such a way? For a brief instant he had nearly slipped to the same level, the level of instinct, of unthinking reaction to the most basic of stimuli.

The guns had fallen silent again. The ringing of the telephone was briefly audible. As he picked up his notepad and pencil, avoiding the woman's eyes, Henschel was suddenly at the doorway again.

'Thought you might like to know. The British are on the mountain.'

'That's not possible.'

'Well, we've had a report that they've been seen not two hundred metres from here, and coming this way.'

'I can hardly believe it. Who saw them?'

Henschel had forgotten his fright of a few minutes before. 'It was the poor sods in the machine-gun post at the west end of the ridge. They let them get within spitting distance before they opened fire because some of them were wearing camouflage smocks. They thought they were bleeding paratroops bringing up supplies. I bet they got the shock of their shitty lives when they realised who it really was.'

'Did they get them?'

'They're claiming they did, but I reckon that's just to cheer themselves up. I bet they were too busy pissing down their legs to shoot straight.'

The gun commander came rushing in, barging past Henschel. 'Can they get in here?'

'Into this emplacement? No, certainly not.' Wolff thought it only proper to qualify the statement. 'Certainly not through the front.'

'What about the entrance then, how tough is that?' The Oberleutnant was suddenly very professional, snapping his question at Wolff.

'It should prove more than adequate, but surely they will not be able to get that close. The machine-gun positions on the ridge, and by the entrance . . .'

'Shit, just because you built this place doesn't mean it can't be knocked down. They've already managed to stuff a bleeding great shell in here and smear an officer cadet all over the

111

floor. Maybe they've got other new tricks they can deliver by hand.'

Wolff bristled, and rose to the defence of his work. 'They will not get in. There are only one or two points to defend; surely you can manage that.'

'God in heaven, someone save me from Headquarters Staff. Listen, Hauptmann Whatever-your-name-is, you may have rank over me, doubtless won by virtue of outstanding bravery in the conquest of paperwork, but I've been fighting this lost cause with real bullets for the last two years, and I've learnt to be a realist. All I've got is a handful of shit-scared artillerymen, thirty rifles, a hundred and fifty stick grenades and a pair of knackered MG34s with only three spare barrels between them. And why?' He thumped the precarious table with his fist and brought it to the point of disintegration.

'I'll tell you for bloody why.' The Oberleutnant took it upon himself to answer his own question. 'Because the so-called bloody élite divisions, like those glassy-eyed cruds in the Hermann Goering paratroops get first call on anything that's going round here. First and best and most, that's how they get their bloody supplies. Me, I have to go down on my fucking knees and lick twenty pairs of boots before I get so much as a back copy of *Signal* to wipe my arse on.'

'I prefer *Stars and Stripes* myself.' Henschel immediately had cause to regret his weak witticism.

'I'm not having this shitty oaf loafing about while my men are waiting to have their heads blown off. Piss off and clean the barrel on number two gun.'

Henschel threw a look of mute appeal to Wolff, who replied with a thin smile.

'Do as the Oberleutnant says.' The Hauptmann was rapidly altering his opinion of the artillery officer. He envied the definite edge of menace he could inject into his voice. It would have been most useful in dealing with Henschel.

When they'd first come the Oberleutnant must have been in a state of shock, as Wolff had to admit he'd have been if he'd been caught in that sort of situation. Doubtless the paratroop major had put on an overpowering display of indignation and rage, and terrified him with various threats.

The men of the Hermann Goering Division were insufferable at the best of times. Given a genuine reason to feel superior they would be absolutely unbearable, and very frightening.

Now, though, the gun commander had regained much of

his self-confidence. Certainly he would never have been here at all if he and his men had not been a crack team. One never knew what might get back to Hitler, and no Oberst of artillery was going to put a second-rate crew into a position that owed its very existence to a direct order of the Fuehrer's.

'If the British get this far, surely we can hold out?' Seeds of doubt had been sown in the military engineer's mind.

'It'll be a tough nut for them to crack, but if a man can make it, another can break it.'

'But all we have to do is phone the monastery, have them send out a patrol to cover us, and in the meantime we can close the shutters and sit tight. What can they do? This emplacement is built on the soundest principles of modern fortification.'

The Oberleutnant was unimpressed. 'That's fine if a battle's fought with slide-rules, but it's not. Point number one, the link with the monastery went over an hour ago. Point number two, we can't close down. If we're to defend this place I need to know what's going on outside. The front's no problem. Unless they can fly they'll not get in that way. It's the entrance that's the problem.'

'We have the machine-gun port.'

'So we have, but it's situated at the end of a narrow cleft that restricts its fire to a small arc that won't prevent some sneaky bastard getting within three or four metres of the door, and slinging a demolition charge at us around the corner.'

'The structure will resist any attempt made on it. I carried out the work here to the best of my ability. I have absolute faith in the emplacement's integrity. It will withstand anything that is tried against it.'

'We shall soon see, Herr Architect.' The Oberleutnant shrugged. 'We shall soon see.'

*   *   *   *   *   *

This was more like it. Reilly was enjoying himself now. Over to his right he could see Kemp edging forward with his flame thrower at the ready. From the far side of the pill-box he could hear the furious battle raging between its occupants and the rest of the New Zealanders who were drawing its fire.

The pack was heavy in his hand. He'd undone the flap of his holster and checked that the big automatic slid in and out easily. Oh yes. This was very much more to his liking,

113

much more like real fighting. He'd put in that request for a transfer to the infantry when he got back. Patrick Reilly would be mending no more roads if he could help it.

Another cautious move took him even closer to the rear of the German position, and he could make out a wall of sorts that must mark the location of the entrance to the pill-box.

Kemp held his hand up to signal that he was as close as he needed to be. Reilly nodded back and immediately a hissing, roaring wail broke out and a tight spout of liquid flame arced out and flattened against an angle of the concrete. A second followed and found one of the loopholes, and pressure-driven boiling fire splashed in through the opening.

From behind the short section of wall a figure in field grey appeared and sent a spray of machine-gun bullets towards the boulder behind which Kemp had ducked after firing. Getting no response, the German paused to fit a fresh magazine. As he did another fountain of fire reached out and engulfed him. When the short-lived scream of the flame died, it was replaced by those of the fiery human torch that was staggering back and forth beside the pill-box, beating the air with flame-dripping fingers.

A fourth spurt was hosed over the wall, and Reilly took that as his cue. He broke from cover and raced for the position, setting the short fuse as he hurdled a twisting, mewing, burnt black body.

'It's a present from Pat Reilly, with his compliments.' He threw the pack as he shouted, took out his pistol, pushed it in through one of the loopholes and sent three fast shots bouncing about the interior of the little structure. He turned and ran, just making it to cover as the demolition charge detonated.

It went off inside the entrance to the pill-box. The massive thirty-pound charge lifted the roof in one huge piece, and it rose up on a black-flecked, orange ball of flame, accompanied by flaring masses of multi-hued tracer, as all of the ammunition was consumed.

Still intact the great slab of concrete fell back, crushing an angle of the still standing walls as it did, and breaking in half, revealing the intricate patterns of the reinforcing bars within it.

As the column followed the path each man in turn looked into the gutted interior of the pill-box, and at the blackened corpse laid near it. Irregular chunks of stained concrete were strewn about it, many of them linked together, like ancient chain-shot, by twisted lengths of reinforcing rod.

'Smells like overdone pork.' Harris wrinkled his nose as he came to the dead German.

Tatman toed the body over to see if there was anything on it still worth removing.

'Turn it back, you bloody ghoul.' Alf Porter gave the big man a shove. 'Turn it back, it looks bloody revolting.'

It did, too. The facial muscles had contracted in the heat, pulling the mouth open to let the partially melted dentures flow out.

'Getting bloody fussy all of a sudden, aren't you?' All the same Tatman put his boot to it once more and sent it tumbling down the slope. The cloud of dust its progress raised quickly hid it.

'Do you know, Tatty, you're lucky and unlucky, both at the same time.'

Tatman caught up to Harris. 'How do you reckon that? I can't be both, can I?'

'Of course you can. You're lucky that you're so bleeding dim you don't realise how horrible life is; and unlucky that you're so bleeding horrible yourself.'

As Tatman turned his inadequate thought processes to trying to work out if there was an insult in there somewhere, the file of men rounded the end of the ridge.

The path began to dip slightly as it hugged the steep-sided reverse slope. In places falls of rock partially or completely blocked the way, forcing the men to climb over the precariously balanced piles. Not one of them was willing to stray from it and risk the possibility of mines.

A sudden signal to halt was made by Sergeant Murray in the lead, and without waiting to be told the men squatted down on the path, glad of the extra safety from shell fragments that position afforded, and of the chance to ease the straps of their packs.

'How far inside the cleft is the actual door of the emplacement?'

Murray considered the lieutenant's question. 'Twelve, maybe fifteen feet, not more.'

'And you're sure about the machine-gun?'

115

'Certain. The concrete surround is a bit wider on the right, and there's a loop-hole in it. Presents you with a few problems, doesn't it?'

'It does rather. We can't get at the door from above, the slope's too steep and crumbly to climb, and if we did succeed in lowering a charge down, that rock lip you describe above the door would stop it making a good contact. To work, our charges have got to be right up against it; nothing else will do.'

'So use the flame thrower and then take a run at it.' Murray contemplated the rough sketch he'd made in the dust.

Saville took the twig the NCO had used to draw it, and dragged the tip of the wood through the dust between the lines that represented the rock walls of the opening. 'That's our only avenue of approach and that Jerry machine-gun covers every inch of it. Now I don't know how long it might take Kemp to step out, brace himself, fire, and dodge back, but it can't be less than a couple of seconds and he'll make an awfully big target during that time.'

Kemp had been listening, and now butted in. 'It wouldn't be so ruddy bad if the door were out in the open, with the jerry gunner having to keep a watch on three sides, but stuck down there and looking out towards the light he'll have me in perfect silhouette from the word go.'

'If we could just blind him for a moment . . .' Saville had an idea, he called Harris over. 'Have you got any illuminating rounds for the two-inch?'

'Just the one, Lieutenant.'

'That'll be enough.' Saville scuffed out the plan with flicks of the stick. 'It's three hours to sunset, and it'll be dark a bit sooner with all this muck in the air. We'll find a comfortable hole to rest up in until then. After the time it's taken us to get here I don't think another couple of hours will make much difference.'

Scouting round for a suitable cave, turning the column about and getting to it, and then checking it for mines and boobytraps took forty-five minutes. Two minutes after setting foot inside, the man detailed to guard the entrance was listening to the snores of the others.

Lieutenant Saville found that sleep wouldn't come that easily to him. Oh, he needed it just as much, after the tensions and exertions of that gruelling climb he needed it very much. Every bone and sinew in his body ached, his legs in particular. He couldn't begin to imagine what Russell must have gone

116

through in keeping up with them as he had, though perhaps he'd have made the effort as well if he'd been in danger of being left behind.

His water bottle had gone empty several hours earlier and his throat felt like cracked parchment that had been gathering dust for a thousand years. When he ran his tongue over his lips it brought no moisture to them. It was as if his whole body was drying up, withering like an autumn leaf.

He thought of Corporal Clark. Could that have been avoided? No, they'd been lucky to have so few casualties. Considering the obstacles they had crossed, and what they would cost the men that followed them, it was a small price; though too high for those who'd had to pay it.

Clark's death meant another letter to write, a task he hated. Not because he found it too emotional, but because he didn't. None of the deaths ever touched him; not those of the men under his command, nor of his fellow company commanders. Not that he was careless of lives – he always did a job in the way that would cause least casualties – but the fact that he'd dragged others into that situation in the first place, that never bothered him.

The killing didn't bother him either. As yet he'd never directly killed a man; never shot or bayoneted anybody. He could be quite certain that charges he had personally set must have killed a dozen or more Germans, but he'd never seen them, they were just anonymous bodies inside lumps of concrete that stood in his way. And afterwards, when he examined his work, the mutilated forms seemed to have nothing to do with him, they were just more dead.

It wasn't that the war had drained all the humanity out of him; rather, he wondered whether he'd ever had any. Was it natural to be untouched by all this? There had to be some degree of hardening, mental armour, or the result would be insanity, but he hadn't ever been aware of the process taking place inside him; it was as though he'd possessed it from the start. Perhaps it waited for a face-to-face killing situation; if so, it could be soon.

It crossed his mind to wonder what the Germans in the emplacement were doing right now. What sort of men would they be? Fanatical paratroops who would go down fighting; trigger-happy, barely trained conscripts; war-weary veterans who would surrender at the first opportunity? Well they'd know, soon.

Much of what happened when the attack began would rest

117

on the state of mind of the officer in charge of the emplacement. There must be a tunnel connecting the entrance with
the guns at the front of the ridge, a clever man would cause
them casualties before they passed through it, a determined
one might stop them altogether.

Saville closed his eyes, seeking the state of unconsciousness
that his body craved. When it came it was very sudden, and
he never knew the moment.

Kemp checked the ignition cartridges for the flame thrower.
'I've got it. Harris bounces a flare off the door. As soon as it
burns out Porter and Reilly slap a charge against it. When
the muck stops flying I step out and give it two bursts.'

'That's about it.' Saville had been bothered by Kemp's air
of bored amusement with the whole proceedings, and he was
rather surprised at his being fully conversant with the planned
sequence of events. 'Right, so just remember, we're not using
too big a parcel because I don't want to bring the rock down
and just seal them in there. They'll just go on banging away
at our blokes in the valley and dig themselves out when
we've got tired of playing and gone away. Watch the effect
of your first go. If the flame spreads it'll mean the door's
still intact, don't waste another burst on it. We might need
the fuel you've got left.'

'Yeah, OK.'

While he felt happier now that he knew Kemp was properly
briefed, still the man's air of casual confidence grated on
him.

The others were all ready. Murray and the two New
Zealanders with him, who would rush the narrow entrance
if all went according to plan, stood a little to one side of
the variously armed and equipped little group that crowded
about the opening in the rock, just far enough back to be out
of the line of vision of any German who might be on guard.

They were later getting started than they'd planned. An
artillery barrage had swept down as they were about to leave
the cave and kept them pinned there for almost an hour.
Now it was quite dark and any vestige of advantage the
Germans might have possessed with regard to observation was
cancelled out.

For what seemed an age Harris fiddled with the mortar,
having trouble aligning it for a shot at an angle the designers
had never intended it to be capable of. At last he was satis-

fied, loaded it very carefully so as not to disturb the setting, and fired.

A puff of orange light came from the almost horizontal tube. Instantly the rocks echoed to the sound of the bomb it had launched smashing into the rock face inside the cleft. Fractions of a second later there was an equally loud crack as the flare in its head burst into dazzling white light.

'Fifteen, sixteen . . . go!' It had burned out faster than Saville had expected, perhaps because of damage it had received in striking the unyielding material of the ridge. Whatever the reason, it almost caught him by surprise and he sent Porter and Reilly on their way a second after its illumination had died to a faint glow.

The space between the walls of rock was saturated with the pungent smell of the fires that had raged there. As the two men reached the door they flung themselves down, and their hands flew through the sequence needed to set and activate the charges. Leaving the two packs against the base of the bolt-studded warm steel they leapt to their feet and ran back the way they'd come.

As they hurled themselves to either side on reaching the end of the cleft a colossal surge of air followed them, and as though coming from the mouth of a monstrous cannon, pieces of rock and a huge fast moving cloud of dust blasted out.

Even as the last of it passed, Kemp leapt out, braced himself in anticipation of the weapon's surging recoil and hosed a pulse of yellow flame towards the end of the cleft. The spurt of fire cut a hole in the gloom of dust and smoke and then unexpectedly spread out in a mushroom of boiling fire that rapidly turned into a cascade as it dripped from every vertical surface.

'That sure is one hell of a tough bastard. I hope your boss has got something left in his bag of tricks.'

Reilly rose to Nicolson's bait. 'Now don't you be fretting yourself. We've never been beaten yet. We took out a place on Monte Camino that was as bad as this. Blew it clean off the damned mountain.'

Tatman giggled. 'Blew the top off the mountain! Bits of Jerry flying all over, bloody lovely!'

'All right, you warped horror.' Sergeant Lucas came over and put an end to the potentially acrimonious exchange. 'We're going to use that hump on your back for a little job,'

Tatman, his face registering sullen resentment, began to slide the straps from his shoulders in order to drop the heavy beehive-shaped charge.

'You might as well keep it on. It'll be easier to carry down to the door like that.'

The revelation that he was about to play a more active part in the proceedings brought a look of imbecilic glee to Tatman's broad features. 'I thought it was about time. Make way for the expert there, make way for the great expert.'

If Saville hadn't grabbed him, he'd have gone marching down to the door there and then.

'Not yet, you damned oaf, not yet.'

'You going to use that on the door?' Murray examined Tatman's load.

'No. From what Reilly and Porter have told me it would appear to be made up of a sandwich of plates bolted together, and the fact that it just shrugged off a pretty hefty charge suggests that it actually sits against the surround. All we've done so far is to push it harder against it. If I use this thing against the door then the best we'll achieve is to melt a hole through it. That won't do anyone standing behind it a lot of good; but it won't let us in either, so this time we're going to try to smash down the concrete beside it, just below that weapon slit.'

'OK, you're the expert. Just so long as you're sure it'll make a big enough hole. I don't fancy getting stuck with my arse outside and my head in a nest of stirred-up Jerries.'

'If I'm setting it you'll be able to drive a bus through afterwards, sideways,' Tatman butted in.

Murray and Saville ignored him.

It wanted just one minute to midnight when they moved into position again. Saville had to keep one hand on Tatman's belt, to stop him from rushing forward in his eagerness. Kemp stood quietly beside them, stroking the barrel of the flamegun.

Murray felt the tightness in his chest that he always experienced at moments of particular tension. He knew it would pass as soon as the action started. And there was the familiar extra dryness in his mouth that he knew even a sip from the little left in his water bottle would not slake. Hell, he could almost fancy one of those bloody apples out of his father's orchard, and he'd thought when he'd left Nelson that he never wanted to see another one as long as he lived. He heard the lieutenant urging the big man to keep back, and then his whispered check with Kemp.

Everything was as ready as it could be. Saville unfastened his holster and did a mental countdown. The numbers ticked through his mind . . . *four* . . . *three* . . . *two* . . . *Go!*

*   *   *   *   *   *

The Oberleutnant looked down the tunnel from the gun room to where two of his men lay on the floor at the anti-blast wall, manning their precious remaining machine-gun.

'They must be having another attempt soon, if they haven't been chopped into little pieces by their own artillery yet. Are you certain that door will take another knock like the last time?'

Wolff answered confidently. 'Oh yes, quite certain. It's constructed of three plates of thirty-millimetre face-hardened armour steel, with two centimetres of concrete between each layer. And there are five hinges, any two will hold it. The attempt they made earlier broke one bolt and distorted one hinge. Oh yes, I'm quite sure it will hold.'

'So all we have to do is sit tight, just like you said. You will have to build a house for me after the war. One that will keep my wife's mother out.'

It was a weak joke, of a sort that Wolff had never really seen humour in, but for the sake of politeness he tried to look amused, contriving to make a noise that might have been a chuckle or a cough.

The first assault had been half expected, after the discovery had been made that the link with the pill-box had been broken. It might just have been that the cable had been severed by a shell, but . . . none of them really believed that.

So they had been expecting something, but it had still come as a shock to Wolff, rudely tearing down the wall of abstraction he had erected about himself. He had been costing and making an estimate of the time involved in grouting the ceilings throughout the emplacement. The constant concussion of the guns firing had caused further widening of some fissures and it was clear that the job would have to be treated as a priority.

The first they had known of the attack was when the man who'd been on guard at the entrance had reeled back down the tunnel, shouting that he was blinded. His vision was

121

already returning as an explosion outside the door had bowed in the multiple slabs of metal and pounded scabs from the concrete surround that had skimmed into the blast-wall with the speed of bullets, breaking up into flying granules that coated the floor with a fine white powder. Some had struck the machine-gun, distorting the barrel and irreparably damaging the feed mechanism.

It was Wolff who had taken the long lonely walk to the scorched and rubble-strewn position to examine the extent of the damage. His first move had been to close the circular shutter over the gun-port. The metal had still been hot, smelling strongly of petrol, and stained with soot from the flames that had streamed in after the explosion. If the flame thrower had been used again at that moment, with the same degree of accuracy . . . it was a ghastly thought, and he was grateful that his imagination was not up to the task of conjuring it in its every detail. The relief he'd felt when he'd checked the door and the fabric of the surround and found them both intact had been tremendous. Optimism had flooded in to replace his fear.

'Where's my Gefreiter, have you seen him?' The Hauptmann remembered the girl, and was instantly made suspicious. Usually if Henschel was around you could hear, see and smell him. 'Henschel!' Wolff's summons rang through the emplacement.

Henschel appeared from the other gun compartment. He looked dusty and guilty. 'I've been helping the artillerymen tidy up a bit, no bloody harm in that, is there?'

Wolff knew from experience that his driver never offered an explanation in advance of one being demanded unless he was up to no good. With both the women safe in the magazine Wolff couldn't imagine what he could have been up to in the other gun compartment, but doubtless he'd find out soon enough, without pursuing the matter.

The lights flickered. They would not have their dim but welcome illumination much longer. The little generator was sucking up the damp rust in the bottom of its fuel tank now, soon it would fail. His bowels churned. His hunger had forced him to try a little of the sausage, biscuit and marmalade that was the only food they had left. He'd regretted it immediately afterwards. The flatulence it had caused had made him suffer agonies of embarrassment when he used the bucket behind the screen in the magazine.

'Well, what did you want then?'

The Hauptmann had quite forgotten that Henschel was still standing there. 'Oh, nothing, nothing. I was just wondering where you were.'

'You wouldn't like me to give you a shout every now and again, would you? Just to let you know where I am, and what I'm doing. I'll do it if it'll help.' He cupped his hands to his mouth and shouted, 'Hauptmann Wolff, I'm having a shit! Hauptmann Wolff, I'm having a fu . . .' He reeled back in surprise as the officer's hand cracked into the side of his face.

'Get out of my sight.' Wolff was trembling with rage. 'If I hear one more word out of you, one more obscenity, one more belch then I shall, I shall . . .' Wolff sought a threat he knew Henschel would believe and fear. '. . . I shall inform Army HQ that you are a party member and recommend you for a transfer to the Waffen SS.'

The Gefreiter's mouth fell open, but for once no sound came out. A rapid sequence of conflicting emotions chased across his face. He'd been struck, in front of all those grinning bloody gunners. The cruddy little mouse had hit him. No one had ever done that before and still been on their feet a couple of seconds later. And the creep had threatened him. God, he felt he could kill the bastard. And after all he'd done for him, even going along with that silly bit of make-believe earlier, when Wolff had pretended to go for his gun. But did he mean it about the SS?

He looked at the Hauptmann and read the loathing in his face, saw the anger in his eyes, and he knew the threat was real. It took an effort, but he calmed himself down, unclenched his big gnarled fists. The stumps of his nails had left deep crescent marks in his palms. But having backed down that far, he'd be damned if he'd go any further. He'd go to the SS willingly before he'd compound his humiliation by being the one to walk away.

His dilemma was resolved for him. A shout came from the machine-gun crew in the tunnel. With Wolff and the Oberleutnant he raced to see what the trouble was.

As they reached the blast wall and looked round it, long fingers of flame were licking through gaps around the door and past the ill-fitting shutter on the machine-gun port.

'Everyone down. Take cover.' Wolff hurled himself behind the wall and onto his face in the dust, clamping his hands tight over his ears and opening his mouth wide. He didn't know what it was that prompted his violent warning, an intuition perhaps, but whatever it was it saved him.

It was like the end of the world. A huge scab of concrete flew down the tunnel and thundered into the blast wall. Propelling it was a solid shaft of white-hot gasses that brought with it beads of molten metal from vapourised reinforcing bars.

The concrete chicane held, and round the side of it swept a surging, buffeting mass of stifling gas. At the first whiff of the poisonous mixture their throats constricted, reacting automatically in an attempt to keep out the fumes.

Despite the violence of the explosion Wolff was not conscious of it having made any noise, and his hearing was still functioning. From the magazine only a few metres behind him he could hear a girl's hysterical screams, plainly audible even though he kept his palms tight to the side of his head.

Beside him the Oberleutnant had brought the MG34 into action. Wolff tried to move away from the rain of hot cartridge cases pouring over him, and found that he couldn't. The body of one of the artillerymen was laid across him, and he could see a bright blue face hanging down by his own.

The Hauptmann twisted and turned, trying to extricate himself. For the first time ever he knew panic. He redoubled his efforts, threshing about to try and release himself of the encumbrance. One arm came free and that was all.

In short sharp bursts the Oberleutnant kept hosing tracer blindly down the tunnel. The first four brought no reply. As a fifth finished clattering a ball of yellow flame rushed out of the smoke towards them. It stopped short, but they felt its heat and heard its hissing wailing roar.

A moment more and the flame thrower would reach out again, and this time Wolff knew it would reach them. With his free hand he tore at the body preventing his escape, clawing at it, prepared to rip it apart – anything, so long as he got it off. His fingers caught in its mouth and he gripped its lower jaw tight and put all his strength into a final desperate effort to haul himself clear.

The weight was suddenly gone, and Wolff felt himself being lifted. Before he could identify his rescuer he was grabbed and hustled down the tunnel into the gun room.

'Come on, you useless heaps of shit, help me.' Henschel swept all of the equipment off of the table. Assisted by some of the artillerymen he up-ended it and wedged it into the tunnel opening.

Everything that was movable was stacked against the improvised door and the last item had just been frantically pushed into place when the howl of the flame-thrower was heard again. As it ended a blackened hand was thrust through a crack between the edge of the table and the wall, and clawed at the barricade. The cuff behind it was swiftly charring away. It succeeded in getting a hold on a prop that held the table in place, and tugged at it.

With every ounce of his strength Wolff smashed a rifle butt down on the questing hand. 'Get out, you'll kill us all.' Through the gap he had caught a glimpse of the Oberleutnant's face, now hideously disfigured by the burning petrol that had caught him. Another crashing blow and the hand retreated.

'What do we do?' Wolff's mind was numbed by the horror of what he had just done, and by the prospect of his meeting the same fate.

'I don't know about you, but I'm getting out. Stick around if you want to, but I don't reckon those murdering shits are going to take much notice of a white flag.'

From the other side of the barricade came three close-spaced shots that ended in a woman's piercing scream. Until that moment Wolff had forgotten the two prostitutes and the shell-shock case who'd been left with them. But there was nothing he could do for them now.

'How do we get out?'

The Gefreiter didn't answer. He wasn't there to do so. When Wolff looked round they had all gone. There was only one place they could be and when he rushed into the other gun compartment he saw a huddle of men against the wall on the far side of the eighty-eight. Henschel was overseeing the removal of the rubble from the hole of the British shell had made.

'Don't stand there bloody gawping, give us a hand.'

Mechanically Wolff did as his driver told him and began throwing aside the chunks of rock that were handed to him.

Henschel was urging everyone to work faster, but it seemed that the more of the loose material they shifted the more collapsed in to replace it.

At the moment the legs of the artilleryman working in the shell-created exit disappeared from sight, there was a loud explosion in the other compartment. There was a mad scramble for who should be next to go.

For a second time Wolff felt himself moving without any effort being made on his part, as Henschel's big paws fastened on his lapels and propelled him head first into the hole.

The Hauptmann found himself on his hands and knees peering into the irregular opening, and then a heavy boot connected with his backside. As he began to crawl there came the sounds of a fight from behind him, as Henschel contested his right to be next. A large close-cropped head butted the Hauptmann's posterior.

'Move, you fucking dozy snail, move.'

Without taking any note of the damage he did to himself on the knife-sharp steel and concrete Wolff scrambled his way to the outside. He knew he was through when it was no longer rough sintered concrete beneath him but broken stone. He began to slip, and there was nothing to hold onto.

Amid a shower of stone and dust he began to fall. The rock face whirled past him as he tumbled and there was no time for his mind to scream as the ground below rushed up to meet him.

*   *   *   *   *   *

The table and the hastily piled equipment behind it were flung aside by the one-pound charge that the lieutenant had set on it, and as the last of the splintered wood skittered to a stop on the gunroom floor Murray and his men left the safety of the magazine and charged into the gun room.

Smoke and dust filled the room, rendering the big gun almost invisible. As the New Zealanders fanned out to check every corner, two shots cracked out at them, coming from beyond a thick wall which partially screened a second eighty-eight from their sight.

A draught swept a clearing in the fog obscuring the interior of the other compartment, and Mitchell, who was nearest, made out a knot of struggling men in a far corner, where the concrete of the emplacement front met the natural rock wall. The corporal brought his Thompson to his shoulder and emptied the whole thirty rounds it contained towards the group. The grenade he sent tumbling in after it was unnecessary.

With the echoes of the grenade's detonation dying away, and the last of the considerable fall of debris it brought down settling on the guns and floor, it was all over.

Murray shook the ringing sensation from his ears, and with the return of his normal hearing he became aware of a new sound, the groaning of a badly wounded man, and it came from behind him.

Nicolson had been hit in the right eye by a ricochet of one of the only two shots the Germans had got off at their attackers. Along with four members of the garrison, all of them badly wounded, he had been removed to the magazine while the sappers set about their task of wiring the guns for demolition.

The New Zealander was unconscious but every few minutes his body would arch in a severe spasm that it would hold for some seconds before subsiding again. A scrap of cloth had been put over his face; frequent contortions kept dislodging it.

There was a sixth prone figure in the room, the girl. She was a distressing sight, her face grimacing with the pain of the large wound in her lower abdomen.

'I didn't see the girl, sir. I only saw the Jerry, honest.' Tatman indicated the dead German at his feet. The corpse still clutched a gouged rifle butt across its chest. A neat hole, drilled by a .45 bullet, had been added to its other damage. It was an indication of the state of Tatman's mind that he had not yet pillaged the body.

'I didn't know it was a girl, I didn't see her.' Tatman continued to dog the lieutenant's every step, as he had done since the moment he'd realised the result of his wild shooting.

'Yes, Tatman, all right. There's nothing to be done about it now.' Saville was finally forced to spare time from his discussions with Murray to try and calm the sapper. 'It's all right. You weren't to know the Jerries had women up here. I'd probably have done the same myself if I'd been the one who spotted them hiding behind that screen. Now go and see if any help is needed in rigging the eighty-eights.'

The wounded New Zealander presented them with a problem. A head wound was the most dangerous of cases to move under any conditions, and those prevailing at the moment were not conducive to giving the injured man a smooth passage down the hillside. And there was another complication, Sapper Russell. He'd made valiant efforts to keep up, and was now trying just as hard to hide the fact that he could hardly walk any longer. He was making a show of hopping about the gun compartments but it was quite obvious that every step he took was causing him agony.

One way out would be to move all of the wounded and the women to a cave nearby while the guns were blown and leave someone with them in the hope of picking them up later.

Of course it was possible that the seriously wounded Kiwi would be dead before the time came to make the decision. If that happened then he might decide to try to take Russell with them, and dump the women and the Germans in a safe place, and leave them for their own to take care of.

He knew it was taking the easy way out, but he wouldn't broach the subject to the New Zealand NCO just yet, not until they were ready to go.

There was one job he felt he couldn't really put off, though he wished he could. He went over to where the woman in green was trying to comfort her younger companion, and failing utterly to get through to her, past the distraction of her pain.

'You speak English?' It was a faint hope, but worth a try. The answer came as a surprise.

'A little. What you want, shoot her again?'

'Can you tell her . . . we're sorry. But in the dark . . . you understand?'

'Sure you sorry. She sorry too. Look what you do to her, you ruin her business.' The woman drew aside the blood-soaked material of the skirt.

Saville didn't need to look, he knew what the impact of a .45 bullet did. He backed away, reading the hostility in her eyes.

Tatman's hand was at his sleeve. 'What is it now?'

It was obvious that the sapper didn't know quite how to phrase his question. 'Has she, you know? Has she, is it true that, well Alf said that, that she'd got it in the, you know, sort of underneath?'

'She's been hit low down, yes. Now just get out will you, you're not doing any good moping about here. Tell Sergeant Lucas I want him.'

The lieutenant looked again at the wounded Germans while he waited. There was nothing they could do for any of them. All were multiple-wounded, two with massive stomach wounds in addition to broken limbs and smashed jaws. Their prospects were little better than Nicolson's.

'You wanted me, sir.'

'How soon will we be ready to go?'

'The guns are finished, sir. Porter's just going to run the

wires in here so we can do the shell racks as well.'

'Good, give me a shout when you've finished in here. I'll be checking the charges on the eighty-eights.'

The small generator they had found had refused to function, and so the only illumination in the gun room was that of the candles and torches they had found in a box beside it.

As the sappers trooped out to commence work in the magazine, Saville took Reilly's torch from him, and then extinguished the two candles they'd left behind before going over to open one of the embrasure shutters. Opening it allowed the last of the smoke to clear, though the smell remained. Perhaps it was as well that it did, it partially masked the stench from a pile of torn bodies in the next compartment.

He switched off his torch and looked out. It hardly seemed possible: they had done it. He couldn't make out any details of the ground in the valley that would have enabled him to get some idea of their present elevation, but the pinpricks of light that he knew must be large shells detonating gave him an indication.

Lucas stepped up beside him. 'That's what I call a field of fire, sir. No wonder the brass wanted this place knocked out. It's a pity a few of the Jerry gun crews scarpered, but I don't think we missed more than half a dozen at the most.'

'They must have got out through that shell hole next door.'

'Looks like it, sir. But it's a good drop out there. Any that landed in one piece will still be running now after the fright we gave them. We'll not see them again.'

'I hope not, Sergeant, I hope not.'

* * * * * *

Finding the cave had taken almost as much luck as reaching it in one piece. Wolff's fall from the emplacement had been broken part by the mass of settling rocks on which he'd landed, and part by the body of an artilleryman that he'd found beneath him when he began to get his wind back. Henschel's impact had been heavier, but had resulted more in cuts than breaks. If any others got out, then they didn't see them.

Now they sat on the floor of the cavern, gulping in air and taking in their changed surroundings.

The place was being used as an aid station by a medical team that had been caught on the slopes when the barrage started. Since that time they had done a steady if erratic business, patching together the unfortunates who had not been near good cover when the attack commenced. Those men who had been treated first, laid out near the back of the cave, had dressings on their wounds; those who had come in later, positioned about the middle of the floor, had an assortment of bandages, culled from many different sources; those coming off the rock ledge that served as an operating table now, had newspaper on theirs.

'I know you.'

Wolff looked up. The hoarse voice came from the packed ranks of the wounded. There was no one there he could recognise.

'I know you. The Inspector of Fortifications, isn't it?'

Now the Hauptmann realised the words came from an almost mummified form near the back of the cave. A camouflage smock draped over it carried the insignia of a major of the Hermann Goering Division.

'What are you doing here. Have you been relieved?'

The words had an eerie quality, as though they were being produced by mechanical means, and every one was followed by a wheezing sound like a piano accordion being inexpertly handled.

'No, the position has been taken.' Wolff heard Henschel's groan, and realised immediately that he had said the wrong thing. A simple 'yes' and the exchange might have ended there and then. As it was, it had only just started.

With a spastic jerk the major rose to a sitting position, the stump of an arm was thrust towards Wolff. 'What? What are you telling me? My men are dying all over this heap of Italian rubble, fighting from bare trenches, shallows in the rock, and you sit there . . . Stand up when I talk to you . . . you stand there and tell me as calmly as if you were giving the weather forecast that you've given up your position! Two metres of concrete, God knows how many metres of rock . . . I'll have you shot.' He broke off to call towards the entrance. 'Kroger, Unteroffizier Kroger, in here!' He turned back to Wolff. 'How many attacked you? How many?'

'I'm not sure, Major.' Wolff looked round for inspiration from Henschel and found his driver was edging away from him. 'It might have been twenty.' He read the look on the major's face, what of it was visible between swathes of bandage, and added, '. . . but they had flame throwers, and heavy demolition charges.'

130

'I don't care if there were twenty thousand of them and they had a hundred Shermans, you should have held out.'

A paratroop Unteroffizier appeared. Wolff recognised the young giant who had been in the emplacement, guarding the artillerymen.

'Where the hell have you been?' The major cut short the answer. 'Don't bother, I haven't the time. These two pieces of shit have given up the Fuehrer's emplacement without a struggle.'

Two rapid changes of expression flickered over Henschel's features. The first from detached nonchalance to pure terror as he realised that the major had seen him, and was including him in any charges he was cooking up for the Hauptmann, and the second from that to sheer frustration as he resisted the urge to kick the balls off of the bandaged form, if it still had any. *Without so much as a bloody struggle!* All right, well maybe he hadn't, but a few of the gunners had had a go, and suffered for it. Lousy cocksure gits, the bleeding paratroops thought they were the only ones who could ruddy fight.

'Take them out and shoot them.'

Unteroffizier Kroger stepped forward to herd the pair out. He did it without hesitation, without change of expression. Either it was with him a matter of routine, or he'd been drilled to the point of blind obedience.

'No, wait.' The major waved the stump at Wolff. 'You know that place well?'

'I built it, Major.'

'I helped.' Henschel was swift to see an advantage.

'Kroger, cancel that order.' He said it in the same way he might have ordered a machine to be switched off. 'Round up ten, no twelve good men, poach them if you have to, and anyone else you think might be of use, pioneers, signallers, anybody. Before you go give me the telephone.'

While the Unteroffizier snatched the set from out a doctor's hands as he was using it, the major addressed himself to Wolff again.

'I have a job for you. If it is done in a satisfactory manner I shall reconsider your position; if it is not, you will be dealt with.'

The major didn't wait for an acknowledgement. He shook the hand-set he was given, as though by that he might terrify the static off the line, then bellowed his requirements to the distant operator.

Wolff noticed that the hand he held it with was minus a finger. He jumped as the major fired another question at him.

'How long ago did you abandon the emplacement?'

'We did not abandon it, Major, we were driven out by . . .' He realised the utter futility of trying to justify his actions, or correct the major's interpretation of them. 'It would be not more than twenty minutes.'

At that moment the major's call came through, and he made no comment. 'I want the battery commander. No, not his second in command, not his bloody whore nor his boot cleaner, I want him, now.' There was a pause. 'Yes, of course, I bloody wanted you.' The wheezing coming in between the words gave the major's speech a weird singsong quality. 'You know who I am? Good, I have a target for you. You have the map reference for the Fuehrer's emplacement, on the south face of . . . Yes, that's it. Well, as of now I want a maximum-effort barrage all around it. I want it isolated. I don't give a fuck what target Division have allotted you. Listen, you snivelling dolt! My men, the few that are left, are mad as hell at the pathetic effort the artillery have been putting up ever since this show started. If I don't get this barrage, until further notice, then I'll spare two of my best men to come and pay you a visit. Oh good, you'll do it. I'll expect the first rounds to pass overhead in thirty seconds.'

Kroger took the hand-set as the major collapsed back, fighting for breath. He was as white as a sheet, and blood trickled from the corner of his mouth.

Wolff took a tentative step towards the officer of paratroops. 'I'm sorry, Major. I don't understand, what am I to do?'

The words came out as a croak, and Wolff had to strain to catch them.

'You are going to retake the emplacement. For six weeks I've wanted to use it as a command post and communication centre. I was told no, because it was thought the extra activity in its area might give its existence away, and now you have given it away instead.' The major seemed to draw fresh strength from his anger. 'And now I want it back, and I want the men who took it dead. They will be bottled up in there, waiting for you.' He listened to a low whine from outside that gradually grew to a screaming crescendo as the first salvo of Nebelwerfer rockets delivered their loads of high explosive.

'They're late. Make a note, Kroger. Give these two some work, until you are ready to go.'

Henschel and Wolff were glad to get out of range of the major's baleful glare. Kroger told them to assist the doctor, and then left, leaving a man behind to make sure they stayed.

The doctor was scathing of the pair's offer of assistance. 'Unless you've bought morphia or dressings you're no bloody good to me. I've just got this butcher's shop organised. I don't want a couple of amateurs fainting all over me.' He stood back while two orderlies removed a patient from in front of him, and after a moment replaced it with another.

'Look at this. What am I supposed to do with this, where do I start? It would take an hour and a battalion's supply of dressings to fill the worst holes. Take him away, bring me something I stand a chance with.' There was pause while the dying man was removed and the two overworked orderlies sought a fresh subject.

'If you two want to do something really useful, that'll make a real contribution to the war, that might even help shorten it, loosen the major's dressings, just enough to start him haemorrhaging.'

'Has he had a go at you as well?' Henschel knew the answer before he asked.

'Had a go?' The doctor surveyed a fresh bloody bundle dumped unceremoniously in front of him. 'He's got me on eight charges already. The only thing he hasn't got me for so far is buggery, and I'm afraid to lean too far over my patients in case he has me for that as well.' He indicated parts of the body in front of him. 'Look at this, it'll have to come off, and that's no good to him any more.' He poked at a flap of tissue. 'And what's that doing there? Some of these are in such a bloody state. I don't know where to start, or even which end is which. I thought I'd done a good job of saving the nose of one bearded soldier, then found I'd given him two nostrils in his penis. If you want to help, move this muck out of the way, or I'll have rats in here helping with the amputations in a minute.'

Wolff gagged as he bent down to get handfuls of the soiled clothing, stained dressings and pieces of flesh. 'I can't.'

Henschel pushed him aside. 'I'll tell you a secret. If you've got a shitty job to do, get it done quick. You'll still be just as ill, but not for so long.' He took up a load and stood there with the dripping remnants hanging down through his fingers. 'I had a dog once, kept puking all over the place. Horrible stuff, sort of green slime. Pig of a job to get off the stairs.'

The relevance of the story was not immediately obvious to Wolff. 'So what did you do?'

'Drowned the bloody thing, of course.'

As he didn't understand it Wolff found the sad tale of little assistance in helping him overcome his nausea.

Kroger reappeared as they finished the repugnant task. 'The major wants to see you again.' He held his MP40 sub-machine-gun in a manner that suggested any tardiness in complying would meet with immediate and severe punishment.

The major was in a very weakened condition, but his mind was still alert and though his voice was lower than it had been the words were clear and carried determination and menace.

'There is something I wish you both to understand. As of this moment you lose your rank, the protection of army regulations, and if you should waver in any way, your lives. Unteroffizier Kroger is familiar with the way I work and conduct myself in battle. You will obey his every order as though it were from me. Exceptional circumstances call for exceptional measures. Kroger is now your judge, your jury, and if he does not get the most enthusiastic cooperation, your executioner. I see I am understood. It is as simple as this, Herr Inspector of Fortifications, you either get my men into that ugly great lump of concrete, or you do not come back.'

A weak movement of his remaining fingers was as close as the major could get to returning Kroger's salute.

The twelve paratroopers who waited outside were all young, all with the same air of tough professionalism about them, an aura that was heightened by the belts of machine-gun ammunition with which they were festooned, and the masses of weaponry that they carried.

There were other men there, from an assortment of units, but their lined faces didn't wear the same expression of self-assurance. They carried an assortment of weapons and equipment, including drums of field-telephone cable, sacks of grenades and in one case a cumbersome Panzerschreck rocket launcher.

Henschel had an MG42 machine-gun slung into his arms and at the same time three long belts of mixed tracer and armour piercing rounds for it were draped around his neck. Wolff

134

was luckier, receiving only an MP38 sub-machine-gun and a case of bombs for the launcher.

'Look at this bloody lot.' Henschel displayed his burden to Wolff. 'That sodding major must be stark staring mad. We need more than these pea-shooters to break back into that ruddy place. How the hell are we ever going to do it with nothing more powerful than these?'

'I don't know.' Wolff answered in the same manner he had been spoken to; quietly, when Kroger wasn't looking. 'But I do know that if we are to stay alive, then I shall have to find some way to do it.'

*　*　*　*　*　*

Lieutenant Saville had been about to organise the removal of the wounded from the magazine when the first of the rockets plunged down and bracketed the emplacement.

As a hail of rock had clattered into the cleft outside, Sergeant Murray and Kemp had ducked back in through the gaping hole beside the jammed door. Both of them had suffered minor injuries.

The NCO had lost his helmet and for the first time displayed an extensive bald patch. He immediately replaced his protective headgear with a close fitting woolly cap.

'We'll have to keep watch from in here.' As he spoke Murray dabbed at his split lips with his sleeve. 'There's not enough cover at the end of the cleft.'

Kemp had been hit in the face by a stone as well, and was spitting out small pieces of tooth and filling. 'Yeah, the buggers won't be able to get at us in here.'

'I don't think they'll want to, not yet.' Saville listened to the regular detonations. 'My guess would be that those rockets are intended to keep us in here, to stop us from blowing the place.'

'What about the wounded, sir?' Lucas was hovering, uncertain if the job he'd been about to do still had to be done.

'Leave them where they are for the moment. Sergeant Murray, I don't know how long this lot is going on for, but when it does end I should imagine we can expect visitors; so if you'll set your men to work putting up some sort of defences here at the entrance and at the blast wall, I'll get my sappers to work on wrecking the eighty-eights by hand and boobytrapping the shell racks.'

The work began immediately.

'It's funny not having Mad Mike around all the time. Anyone know how he is?' Harris chewed on a corner of the block of chocolate from his K-ration.

'Why don't you get off your arse and go and find out?' Porter was experimenting with one of the slabs of German biscuit, shaving and chipping flakes from it with the edge of his knife in an attempt to find out if it was really edible.

'What, and be given a bloody job, nursing those Jerries? No fear. Tatty, you go and see how he is.'

Tatman shifted uneasily and avoided looking at any of the others. 'No. No, I ain't going in there.'

'What's up, Tatty my lad? Are you bothered about that tart you shot?' Reilly guessed the reason for the big man's reluctance. 'I wouldn't let it bother you. The lads in the bombers are killing women all the time, only they never see what they hit.'

'Just shut up about it. I just don't fancy going in there, that's all.'

'It won't be because you plugged her in the fanny, and you're mad at yourself for buggering up a good bit of screwing material, would it?' Harris's voice displayed malice and ill-concealed relish.

'I said shut up about it.' With that Tatman left the group and moved to the other side of the gun compartment to finish his food.

Lucas came in, and picked up the small square of biscuit and a slice of suspect smelling sausage that was his share.

'How are Mike Russell and the Kiwi, Sarge?' Porter gave up with his piece of biscuit and put it in his pocket, to try again later.

'Nicolson's holding on. He's skinny, but he must be tougher than he looks. That sergeant of theirs seems to know a bit about these things. He reckons the bullet must have been lodged against a nerve or something, and that was causing the spasms; but with all the jumping about he's done it's moved, and that's why he's easier now. Russell's not too good though. His leg's blowing up, and he's like a ruddy furnace. I reckon he might lose it.'

His attention was drawn to Tatman, who was making horrible noises as he worked up enough saliva to spit at the gorget he still wore, in order to polish it. 'Did you send him over there because of his eating habits, or has he still got some of that goat on him?'

'We were just talking about the girl and he went off in a huff.'

'Knowing you, Harris, you probably provoked him into it. I'll admit, though, I'm surprised at the way he's taken that. I thought nothing ever got through to him.'

'That one in green's a nice bit of stuff though, Sarge, ain't she?' Harris winked and gave Reilly a nudge in the ribs.

'A bit rough maybe, but a lot of woman there. Not that any of you lot need go getting ideas. She's out of bounds. We're even moving the bucket in here, and providing her with her own, so as of now you won't even have to go in there and be tempted, will you?'

'I don't know why you bloody bother. There's nothing so ruddy special about women.' The conversation was irritating Porter.

'You speak for yourself.' Harris was quick to join any discussion on his favourite subject, almost his only one. 'I reckon they're all bloody lovely. Whatever the shape or shade; me, I love 'em all.'

'And that goes for me an' all. Women are lovely. Can you tell me any part of a woman that isn't just perfect, just made for loving?' Reilly delivered the words as a challenge.

Porter accepted it. 'Of course I bloody can. For a start women are bloody ugly underneath.'

'Where?' Only Lucas queried the statement. The others appeared lost for words.

'Underneath. You know, down there. Well, they are, aren't they?'

Harris gave the question deep consideration. 'I can't say I've ever given it any thought, but then unlike the Yanks I don't spend much time with me face down there.'

Lucas hesitated before adding a further contribution, not wishing to become too familiar with the men of his section. 'Can't say I've ever really looked, but before I were married I knew a girl who didn't like balls. I always had to keep me pants on until I was in bed and put them on again before I got out. She said they were ugly.'

'Maybe she meant just yours, Sarge.'

'No, it weren't that.' Lucas decided to let Harris get away with that one. 'Actually she weren't all that keen on it anyway. Last I heard she was living in Tooting with a conductress off the sixty-six route.'

'Lot of funny things happen in Tooting.' Harris remembered some of the strange messages he'd read carved into the doors of the gents' lavatories on Tooting Broadway.

Alf Porter ignored the digressions, and warmed to his theme. 'You give it a bit of thought, and be honest, tell me if any bird you've ever been with apart from those you've paid has ever been as good as you'd hoped.' He went on, without giving them a chance to break in.

'And you know why they never come up to your expectations, don't you? Because you've been bloody conditioned by what you've seen at the cinema. You think every woman wakes up in the morning with her hair all nice, her make-up on and wearing a yard-wide inviting smile. So when the real thing comes along and it's not like that, you get narked, don't you?'

'I get fed up with my old woman wearing a bloody cardigan in bed. Not that her bloody nighties are all that ruddy marvellous, but bloody hell, that damned woolly don't half put me off.' The remarks had struck a cord in Harris.

And Reilly as well. 'What I don't like is those bloody headaches in the middle of the month. Every bloody time. It's getting so I'm thinking of changing me faith, just so I can make use of that marvellous invention, the Durex. Makes you wonder why we bloody bother.'

'Well why did you?'

'Get married? I'll tell you, Slacker. It was because of my dear wife's big family.'

'What's that got to do with it?'

'Well, her father were bloody big, and she had seven big brothers. It was me own bloody fault, though. I should have realised that coming from a good Catholic family with a record of fertility like that she'd fall the first time. I wouldn't have minded, but all I'd bloody done was poke around outside.'

'You'll have to see if you can get a new washer fitted to it before you go back.'

At that moment Murray put in an appearance. He beckoned to Lucas.

'The lieutenant wants you. He's in the magazine.'

Lucas was building up a considerable dislike of the New Zealand sergeant. He felt the younger man was trying to lord it over him. If he was doing so because he reckoned that Kiwi infantry were superior to the Royal Engineers he was likely to be put right in the very near future. While Lucas knew from experience that if he had to he could do an infantryman's job, he was pretty sure that Murray didn't know a pencil fuse from his short arm.

Saville was busy sorting through the pile of weapons the German gunners had left behind. It was not an impressive array, the only really useful and serviceable items being some Mauser rifles. He indicated to Lucas a stack of the best ones that he had put on the side.

'Now that we've wrecked the guns, unless we still get a chance to blow this magazine our specialist role is just about at an end. From now on we're infantry, so you can distribute these. Work out a rota for sharing the watches with Murray's men.'

'We're holding on then, sir. Until the advance reaches here.'

'Well, certainly until this stonk ends. Then it'll rather be up to Jerry. If he comes at us hard we may be forced to stay. If they don't then I'd still like to have some idea of how the fighting in the valley is going before we make a move.'

'The fighting is still on Jerry's side of the river, that's a good sign.' Murray came in.

The lieutenant agreed. 'But it may be some time before our advance reaches the road. If we pull out too early all we'll meet up with will be a lot of very trigger-happy square-heads.'

'And if we don't get out as soon as we can, and the advance is stopped and held, then we'll be bottled up here, inside Jerry territory. They'll be able to mop us up when they like, and we'll be bloody lucky to make it to a POW compound.'

Saville fully appreciated the point. He had already given it a great deal of thought, but he felt that while the situation was still fluid, or until they had a more precise idea of what was going on in the battle for the Liri valley, their actions should be cautious.

'Will you be talking to the men, sir?'

Whether it was intentional or not, Saville was grateful to his sergeant for the change of subject. 'Yes, I'll have a word with them in a moment.'

While Murray and the lieutenant discussed some minor point about the stock of stick grenades they had discovered in the magazine, Lucas took a look at Nicolson.

The Kiwi was very still. Apart from the blood that stained his face and collar, and the wad of dressing taped over half his face, he might just have been sleeping. But there was a pallor about him, even in the poor light from the single candle burning in the doorway.

Russell couldn't get comfortable. The lightest of pressures anywhere on his injured leg was more than he could bear. Lucas let his hand casually, seemingly by accident, brush the back of the sapper's. He was boiling hot.

'Looks like I get a ride down the hill, Sarge.'

'It does at that. Try and rest, and we'll have you in the field hospital in no time.' Lucas hoped the words didn't sound as hollow as he knew they were. If the battle ended that very moment, and they set out immediately it would be more than five hours, at least, before they got him to a place where effective measures could be taken. From painful experience he knew that if a penetrating wound went untreated for more than twelve hours, then suppuration was inevitable.

Russell would be lucky if he kept the leg, and there was no chance of that if gangrene set in.

'I can't hang around here chatting with lazy perishers like you, lying in bed while the rest of us are working. Take it easy.'

'I'll give you a hand with those, Sergeant Lucas.' Saville picked up two of the rifles.

Murray followed them out of the room.

Russell tried to rest his leg more comfortably, but succeeded only in causing himself pain. Christ but it hurt. It felt as though a red-hot poker had been shoved into his thigh, and some rotten sod was continually twisting it about. He looked about the dimly-lit magazine. It would have been a grim enough place without the broken bodies that filled it. An incongruous touch was added by the shell cases catching the flickering candle light. The curved brass surfaces filled the walls, floor and ceiling with dancing motes of white and yellow that were never still for a moment.

The girl had passed out again. She had lost so much blood that the make-up on her face stood out starkly against the white flesh. Her lips were startlingly red and her eyes dark-ringed, deep sockets.

'He's lying. The Sarge never could lie convincingly.' The sapper tried to make conversation with the woman. In an ordinary situation he would have had to have a few drinks inside him to find her attractive, as she was such a lot older than him. She must have been thirty-eight, or even forty. But now he was lonely, and a bit scared, and she grew more attractive by the minute.

'Why you say that?' She had intended to ignore him as she had all the others, but she could not bring herself to.

'Because if they make a run for it, they'll not get far carrying me. And if we wait for Monte Cassino to be taken it'll be too late.'

'Too late?' She left what she was doing and went to his side.

'For this.' Mike Russell indicated his leg. 'Could you fancy a bloke with only one pin? Wouldn't it put you off?'

'I go with men who have worse.' She did not understand all his words, but the meaning was clear. 'Are you frightened?'

'No.' The word came to his lips too fast, and he knew that it wasn't the truth. 'Well, a bit, maybe. I suppose I'll get used to it. There won't be any more football on a Saturday morning on Fair Green, and there won't be much point in going up Streatham on a Saturday night, but I'll manage.'

'Is there anything I can do?'

He almost came out with a crudity, but checked himself. 'Yeah, will you sit with me, and hold me hand for a while.' He felt choked up inside. Stupid, like he wanted to cry.

Gina Vallechi, the Italian whore, sat down beside the wounded sapper. 'Tell me about yourself.'

It didn't feel as though he'd been asleep for three whole hours, when Saville was woken a few minutes after dawn. He had to struggle for a moment to remember where he was, and when it was. They were in Italy, it was May, springtime in this part of the world. Not that there was much in his immediate surroundings suggestive of that attractive month in this lovely country. In fact when he opened his eyes fully and took in what was around him, the scene rather resembled one of those frightening paintings of the after-life so cleverly portrayed by medieval artists.

Was there anything he had to do straight away, apart from visit the bucket? He couldn't think of anything. Such defences as were possible they'd constructed. A sandbag wall at the entrance and a rough barricade of bits and pieces at the dog-leg halfway down the tunnel; oh yes, and they'd rigged up simple locks on the shutter mechanisms in the gun compartments and blocked the shell hole the Germans had used to escape with heavy chunks of metal that they'd stripped from the already pillaged eighty-eights. Even if the enemy did sprout wings, there was no way they'd get in through the front of the emplacement.

The last few sips of water had been set aside for the

wounded, and a bucket had been fashioned for the woman's use from an old petrol can. The latter was a job that had been done with a surprising amount of skill and an incredible amount of noise by Corporal Mitchell. On questioning the New Zealander had admitted to being a tinsmith in civilian life.

Now it was just wait and see. Incredibly the barrage still continued. He listened to the metronome-like delivery of explosive. How remarkably thorough the Germans were. To think that at that moment, someone was standing with a stop-watch, timing the firing of those rockets. Was it his imagination or the last dregs of sleep that made him think there was suddenly a slackening of the regularity with which they were arriving?

Kemp came in, in a hurry. 'Sergeant Murray says will you get your . . . will you join him at the entrance. There are three Krauts coming down the hill, and they're carrying a white flag.'

*   *   *   *   *   *

It was insanity. One-hundred-per-cent, twenty-four-carat insanity. And yet he was doing it. With Kroger on one side of him and another stolid, equally large paratrooper on the other he was walking down the hill towards the entrance to the emplacement carrying an improvised white flag lashed to a damaged machine-gun barrel. Wolff heard Kroger's voice coming from the side, though the Unteroffizier kept looking straight ahead, as he had ordered Wolff to do.

'You will remember to leave the talking to me. You are included because you still wear an officer's uniform. The only purpose you serve is to carry that flag. You are sure the woman will be able to translate? I have only a little English.'

'Yes, at least she told me she could. I do not know if she still lives. I told you, I heard a scream . . .'

There was less than a hundred metres to go. Wolff felt all his muscles tense as he half expected a crackle of fire to come from the hole beside the blackened doorway.

Although the sun was invisible there was enough light to show the details of the cleft's rock walls quite clearly. The smoke was thin as yet, the enemy artillery had not, so far, delivered enough to the slopes to compensate for the dispersant effect of the dawn breezes.

Precisely on time the last of the Nebelwerfer missiles impacted on the ridge.

Now there was only fifty metres to go and the Hauptmann could see the exact dimensions of the hole the British had made in the concrete: it was massive. He recalled the details of the specification he had laid down for that part of the work. Deliberately he had designed it in such a way that damage would be localised, and somehow they had blown a gaping hole in it. What sort of explosives had they employed? It was incredible.

Thirty metres now and they had to slow to pick their way more carefully as the rock became more broken. Now he could make out a sandbag wall just inside the hole. Behind it was only the darkness of the interior. The barrels of two rifles rested on top of the jute-wrapped defences, directed unwaveringly at the centre of Wolff's chest. He felt his eyes being drawn irresistibly towards the two weapons trained on him. Kroger had to snatch at his arm to catch him as he missed his footing and almost went down.

'Act like an officer! Pull yourself together!' The paratroop NCO hissed the words out of the corner of his mouth.

'I don't understand. Why are we doing this?' Wolff pulled his jacket straight and ran his hand down its front, to check that the buttons he had left were fastened.

'Because this is what the major would do. That is all you have to know. It does not matter whether you understand. Now be quiet.'

The rifles tracked them to the mouth of the cleft, and stayed locked on them when they stopped there. Kroger took a smart step forward and saluted the unseen men within the emplacement.

'We will speak with an officer. We are unarmed.' The Unteroffizier spread his arms wide to illustrate his statement, which was delivered with a near-incomprehensible thick accent.

He had no way of knowing how the terse announcement was greeted inside the position but Wolff, who though he didn't comprehend the words understood the gesture, was suddenly filled with a fear greater than any he had experienced so far. His heart was pounding and a lump formed in his throat. The Walther at his hip was suddenly very heavy.

Before they had started down the hill the paratroops had only thought to take his sub-machine-gun from him, when they handed him the flag. It was an indicator of how little

143

regard they held for him that they had only bothered to remove his outward display of weaponry. He was thankful the flap of the holster covered the butt of the P38 completely, and prayed that no one would notice how well filled out the leather was.

Smoke shells were falling regularly now, renewing the stench of their chemical fires, scorching the rocks and consuming more of the fragment-stripped tree trunks.

Wolff, alone of the waiting trio, couldn't help involuntarily flinching as each projectile struck, though none came down within two hundred metres of them. No sound came from the emplacement. Whatever reaction their visit had caused, there was no sign to be seen or heard. The only evidence of the place's occupation was the two rifles, and their stillness was unreal.

After five minutes the Hauptmann had almost convinced himself that the men who had taken the emplacement were gone, that somehow they had slipped away despite the barrage, and that there was no one behind those unmoving weapons. And then, sounding strangely distant and hollow, from deep within the tunnel, he heard the woman's voice.

* * * * * *

Murray looked at his watch. 'They'll be back in five minutes.'

There had never been the slightest possibility of his reversing the immediate refusal with which he had met the first German demand for their surrender, but Saville had agreed to the hour's truce, to 'reconsider', simply to buy time.

He had the most severe misgivings about trying to get back down the hill until they were quite sure that the Allied advance had it surrounded and its defences beaten. If they hung on where they were and waited for that, then every hour that passed was an hour nearer to it.

The lieutenant had heard stories of the old-fashioned, almost chivalrous manner in which the Hermann Goering paratroops conducted themselves in battle, but this was the first time he'd experienced it himself. It had about it an air of unreality, a dreamlike quality. But there lingered in his mind the thought that at times it served the Germans a purpose besides that of promoting simple humanity. Their visit to the emplacement had given them a look at the defences, such as they were, and also an opportunity to gauge the attitude of the defenders. Even though they might not gain an easy victory by securing

144

capitulation, they came out of the affair with some advantage in the form of additional knowledge.

'Have you decided about the wounded, and the women, sir?' Lucas hoped by the manner in which he couched the question to crush in advance any likelihood of the Kiwi sergeant starting a debate on the matter.

'We'll see if they'll take their own wounded. That'll buy a bit more time, while they round up stretchers and bearers. I think we'll try and get them to take the women as well. No point in them being at risk when the bullets start to fly. They might be able to do something for the girl, and they'll probably let the woman go.'

'Shall I get her?'

'Yes; get the wounded ready to move, and then send her in, I'll explain what's happening.'

Lucas had only been gone a moment when from the magazine the lieutenant heard a female voice raised in anger. It grew louder, and then suddenly the woman in green was coming straight at him.

'What you think you doing?' The change from a torrent of passionate Italian to shouted English slowed the flood of words, but caused no reduction in the volume at which they were uttered or any softening of the strident tone. 'You think because you lift our skirts you push us around. What you think we are, animals?'

Taking advantage of a temporary lull while the woman paused for a much needed breath, Saville tried to explain. 'There will be fighting here.' He waved at a circle of floor about them. 'In here, a lot of fighting. We are sending you out. The Germans will take you to a safe place. Your friend will get proper treatment.'

'No, I stay here, with British.'

'The Jerries are back, Lieutenant.' Reilly put in an appearance at the end of the tunnel.

'All right. We'll be along in a moment.'

'Do you want me to carry her out?'

The woman crossed her arms, tossed back her long hair and glowered at Murray, defying him to lay a hand on her.

'We can't force her to go. The Jerries wouldn't take her anyway if she looked like giving them a lot of trouble. I'll give it one last try.'

Saville felt like kicking himself. He should have thought of this earlier, tried to get her used to the idea. It was his own fault, until now he'd simply regarded her as an object, to be moved about at will, with no volition of her own. Well, she'd shown him otherwise, and it had come as a shock. He didn't really believe that he could persuade her to change her mind, and in any event he only had a few seconds in which to try, but he had to make the effort, for her sake.

'Gina.' He was surprised at how readily her name came to his mind. 'You have to leave. The Germans want this place back. There will be a lot of fighting. It is better that you go now.'

'I stay. I not go with the Nazis.'

'What about your friend? We can do nothing for her here. The Germans will have doctors. She'll be able to get treatment.'

'She not need a doctor.'

'Of course she does . . .' The implication of the words struck him forcibly. They hadn't registered at first.

'She is dead. I stay with you, please.' That last word was spoken quietly, but carried more conviction than had all the shouting that had gone before.

Saville looked into the magazine as he passed it on the way to the entrance. Nicolson was still defying the odds, still hanging on. Russell was awake but quiet, his face glistening with perspiration. His hands were roaming over the blanket that partially covered him as he fought the pain, as though he did not know what to do with them. And there was another blanket-covered form in there, beside the row of Germans. The coarse material of an army blanket had been pulled up to conceal the face, and by so doing had exposed the girl's feet and lower legs. Both limbs were speckled with dried blood and a blanched white colour, as though every drop of fluid had been drained from them.

He paused and stepped into the room, crossed to the body and after a moment's hesitation pulled back the blanket. What he saw came as a shock. With her hair arranged, make-up applied and her face set in a faint smile the girl looked as if she were only asleep. The lieutenant almost bent down to take her pulse, to make quite sure.

'It was the last thing she ask. She wanted to be pretty one last time. That how she look when I first know her.' The woman covered the face again.

'She looks very . . . peaceful.' The word he sought eluded him and he had to settle for something trite.

Murray's woolly cap bobbed into view. 'The Jerries are getting impatient.'

Because it seemed the natural thing to do, Saville took the woman's hand as he led her out of the magazine. He let go of it the moment they were in the tunnel. For a moment it had reminded him of how he had led his sister-in-law from the graveside after his brother's funeral.

The same three Germans waited outside again. The two smock-clad paratroopers dwarfed the thin officer who stood between them.

Saville watched their reactions as the woman translated his reply to the repetition of the demand they had made earlier. The only indication of any feeling was from the slightly built Hauptmann in the middle. He gripped the improvised flagstaff he carried a little tighter and held it more in front of him, as though it were a potent talisman that would protect him in any exchange of fire.

Again it was the German Unteroffizier who did all the talking, never bothering to confer with the officer, as if the only function of that member of the trio was to carry the flag of truce. And the lieutenant also noted the Hauptmann's bearing, his drawn expression and drooping shoulders, all giving the impression of a man who had been forced into a menial position to which he was unused and of which he was ashamed.

The final outcome, after some haggling, was that they would return in another hour to collect the German wounded held by the British.

The woman did not wait for any thanks for the part she had played, going straight back down the tunnel to the magazine. There was something she had forgotten to do earlier. She had done all the girl had asked, but before her body was thrown out there was one last thing, that pretty sapphire ring. At least the girl had always sworn it was real, and protected it as though it were, never taking it off, never losing an opportunity to flaunt it.

Well, real or not, it looked expensive, and the dead had no need of such ornaments. It should fit her quite well, her hands were really rather slim, and among all those free-spending Americans in Naples it would help her image.

Perhaps with the right dress she would be able to work the hotels instead of the streets; have officers for customers instead of the common soldiers who always tried to cheat her. Yes, if all went well she would be able to up her price, and maybe come out of the war with enough saved to get an apartment in Rome. Anything was possible. Maybe she could

147

do what the most expensive girls did, have just a small circle of very rich clients, who would bring her presents as well. That would be good, never to know poverty again.

'There they go.' Harris, from where he knelt down behind the sandbag wall, watched the stretcher bearers as they struggled with their heavy loads up the hill. Over their heads he could just make out the broken outline of the monastery walls. Air-bursts were punching black circles of smoke into the sky above it.

'I wonder how much longer they'll leave us alone now?' Porter received a swift answer.

As the last of the German bearers disappeared from sight around a hummock of broken rock, so a long burst of machine-gun fire swept down into the cleft from higher up the hill. The bullets zipped from the stone walls at wild angles, flattened themselves against the warped door and its concrete surround, and then with a fractional adjustment in aim found the opening.

Harris and Porter dived down and sought the cover of the loose-packed jute as it was pounded and ripped by the stream of bullets. As though from nowhere a wood handled stick grenade curled in towards the entrance, spinning lazily end over end. The grey cylindrical head of the grenade thumped into the bottom layer of interlocking sacks.

Seven ounces of TNT burst with a sharp crack that dislodged the top layer of the wall and pushed it down onto the two men. Scraps of the thick-woven sacking smouldered, adding pungent brown smoke to that of the explosive.

It was the moment it took him to push one of the sacks off his back that saved Harris, as another long burst cut across the top of the partially demolished wall. This time the fire came from much closer to hand and the sapper recognised the rattle of a German sub-machine-gun. As he jumped up he snapped off two fast shots with his rifle into the dense smoke filling the cleft, then threw it down, took out his Colt and pumped the contents of the magazine out through the opening, firing blind.

A huge figure reared up in front of him and Harris grabbed the first thing that came to hand to ward it off. With all the force he could put behind it he hurled the jagged lump of concrete at the face of the German. The giant reeled under the impact but stayed upright. The sapper could only watch as the man began to raise his MP40, and then there was a blast of noise and light by his head as a Tommy-gun thundered into life beside him.

At the massive impacts the German was thrown back. The big bullets chased him, making the cloth of his camouflage smock buck as they plunged into it.

Several shakes of his head were needed before Harris was able to restore some degree of vision, and even then that of his right eye, about which the skin of cheek and brow were scorched by the muzzle blast of Mitchell's Tommy-gun, was still blurred and fuzzy.

'Come on, Alf, you can stop hiding now.' Harris gave the partially burst sack on Porter's back a nudge with his boot. Stones and trickles of dust fell in a miniature cascade to the floor, but that was the only movement. He had to wait for Mitchell and Murray to push past to take over the manning of the post before he could reach out to the sapper.

'Come on, Alf. Stop pissing about, get up.' Harris felt a hand on his shoulder. Lucas and the lieutenant were beside him.

'Get yourself back to the magazine. See if the woman can do something for your face, you're cut.'

Until Lucas had mentioned it Harris hadn't been conscious of the warm blood that ran down from his temple, even though he'd several times had to wipe it from his eyes, an automatic action that had not registered. He felt hands turning him round and pushing him away, down the tunnel.

'What about Alf?' He kept looking back over his shoulder to the still body, its head and shoulders buried beneath the tumbled rock and gently smouldering sacking, its backside stuck absurdly into the air.

'It's all right, we'll take care of him.'

Harris resisted the less than gentle shove that his sergeant gave him. 'I ain't going, stop pushing.' He broke free from hands that attempted to stop him and bent over Alf Porter. 'Here, come on mate, don't bugger us about.' He reached out to the unmoving man and tugged at him.

Very slowly the heavy form responded to the force applied to it and as more was exerted at last toppled sideways. The side of its head was gone.

Lucas adopted a brisk manner. 'Right, come on, Harris. Off you go and get yourself fixed up.'

This time the shocked sapper allowed himself to be turned around and guided back down the passageway. Lucas left him at the entrance to the magazine.

Russell broke off from talking to the woman when he read the expression on Harris's face. 'Who was it?'

Dazed, Harris took a couple of faltering steps into the room, and then just stood there, blood running down the side of his face and dripping off his chin. Mike Russell had to ask twice more before he got an answer.

'It was the old boy, Porter. I didn't know he was hit. We both ducked and he didn't get up again. I thought he were indestructible, like he was going on for ever. I kept shouting at him, I just kept shouting, and he were dead.'

Gina led him to a low stack of ammunition boxes and made him sit down while she wiped the blood away and examined the injury. He gave no indication of feeling it when she touched the burned areas with a wad of cottonwool. 'Is not so bad. You hold this against it, until it stop bleeding, then I bandage it.'

It was the first time Harris had been near the woman. He'd tried several times, but always been headed off by an alert Lucas. And now she was nursing him. The side of his face was beginning to smart, but it was bearable. At least he could feel, that was more than Alf could do now.

First Corporal Clark, and now Porter; and there was that Kiwi, Nicolson was it? He was hanging on by a thread, and Mike Russell likely to lose his leg.

Harris could see the ironic humour in the decision he'd made a year before to opt for an assault engineer outfit, because with all the special courses, like demolitions and boobytraps, it had meant less time swinging a pick. Right now a year's road-making or bridge-building seemed like a very desirable alternative.

From behind a screen in a dark far corner of the room he heard the sound of running water, and for a moment he thought the woman must have found a supply that had escaped the earlier searches, then he realised what she was doing, and the old thoughts began to stir.

*   *   *   *   *   *

'We put three hundred rounds of incendiary and armour piercing into it, bombed it, and I still lost one of my best men and got precisely nowhere.' Kroger jabbed a sausage of a finger into Wolff's jacket front and poked hard. 'Now I want you to tell me how I get in there and carry out the major's

150

orders to retake your precious bloody emplacement.'

'I did warn you that a direct assault was unlikely to succeed. It was done against my advice.' Wolff was stung by the Unteroffizier's tone of accusation and aggressive attitude, and refused to be made a scapegoat for the abortive attack.

'Don't be bloody clever with me. Just tell me what I have to do to get in there.'

'As I've pointed out, with the weapons you have sited to cover the back and front of the emplacement, there is no way the British can get out.'

Again the horn-hard digit tried to punch a hole in Wolff's breastbone. 'Listen, you miserable slide-rule soldier, my orders are to take the position, not piddle about outside it. I have four men and two valuable machine-guns tied up watching that place, they could be used a bugger sight better elsewhere. There's other fighting going on around here, you know. On the other side of the monastery the Poles are throwing themselves like maniacs against our men. Down in the valley Allied armour and infantry are carving great lumps out of our defences. The Gustav Line is crumbling and I do not intend to spend the whole of the battle trying to winkle a handful of men out of the shell you built for them. I'll give you one hour to come up with something. After that I may be tempted to use you and that driver of yours as human shields in another attempt.'

Wolff, glad to get away, retreated to the far side of the cellar. A solid shaft of light streamed in through the small window by which they had gained access to the monastery. It picked out every detail of the ruin that war had brought to the fine old building. Torn vestments and altar furniture were strewn all over the floor. They had been tossed from the chests and cupboards lining one wall, and been replaced with the bodies of now mummifying German machine gunners, whose mangled MG34 was near the window. One of the cupboards had swung open and a crinkled grey hand hung out, its colour almost indistinguishable from the faded sleeve above it.

From behind a partially collapsed doorway that led into the heart of the building came the sickly-sweet smell of putrefaction, and a constant squeaking, scurrying noise.

Henschel was sitting by the row of wounded. Kruger had appointed him medical orderly. The extent of the Gefreiter's attentions to each was a single rough blanket thrown over them, and a boiled sweet pushed into their parched mouths, even the unconscious men.

'What does that great gorilla want now?'

Coming from a man who in so many ways closely resembled that member of the animal kingdom himself, Wolff
would normally have found a grain of humour in such a
remark from his NCO, but now he was too tired, too frightened to find light relief in anything.

'I have one hour to come up with a way of getting into the
Fuehrer's emplacement.'

'And if you can't?'

It was not like Wolff to be theatrical, but it saved words,
and he was so tired: he made a cutting motion with his finger
across his throat.

'Then, for fuck's sake, come up with something.' Henschel
looked about to see if they could be overheard. 'And if you
can't, why don't you figure out a way that's sure to get all
these bloody warmongers killed. If they get bumped off we
can hide up here until it's safe to come out with our hands
up. I tell you, at the moment I'd surrender to a blind goat
with a pea-shooter if it was carrying a water bottle.'

When he held his head between his hands Wolff felt it was
hot, and the throbbing of the veins very fast. He was no
longer jumping every time a shell came down nearby, at least
not visibly, not on the outside. The shaking that he felt was
inside himself, and he couldn't control it. With a shard of
shell casing that he picked up from the floor he scratched a
plan of the emplacement's layout on the wall. Without thinking he added those little touches that mattered to his trained
eye, but that to anyone else would just add a confusing clutter
to a drawing already made indistinct by the roughness of
the surface and the crudity of the implement.

He sat there, looking at it. The paratroopers were cleaning
and reloading their weapons. Henschel was squatting morose
and short-tempered beside him, alternately picking his nose
and growling at any of the wounded who were unable to
suppress a groan, or begged for water.

After ten minutes the Hauptmann found his mind was
wandering in circles over and over the same profitless ideas.
He closed his eyes and concentrated, trying to wipe the old
thoughts away, hopefully to make room for fresh ones.

'Here, don't you go to bloody sleep. You can do that after
you've come up with an idea. I don't want a hole in my
head just because you bleeding well nodded off.'

'I was not going to sleep. I was thinking.'

'Oh yeah. I suppose that being an officer, an ex-officer – ' Henschel enjoyed adding the rider, 'you expect to be believed. Well, let me give you a bit of advice. You're a bloody nothing now, same as me. A zero, a nobody; an *un-person* as the Commies call the poor cruds they've got it in for. If they stuck you on a pair of scales against a pat of cow shit you'd only come out more valuable because dead you'd produce more compost. So don't try any smart-arse answers like that with Kroger. Better to grovel at his feet and beg forgiveness. That won't do any good either, but at least in that position you make a smaller target for his boots.'

'Is that really how you see life?'

'No, that's how life really is. However high you go there's always some lousy crud over you. Have you forgotten Oberst-leutnant Steiger so soon? Well, now we're right at the bottom of the heap, so just you remember that, it's the only way you're going to stay alive.'

'Why should you be so concerned whether I live or die? You got me out of the emplacement, saved my life. Why did you do that? Until recent events overtook us I was certain that you had made discomforting me virtually your life's work.' They were questions that had flickered in and out of Wolff's mind, and only now had he strung them together.

'Christ, couldn't you figure that out for yourself? I made sure you got out because I had an idea there'd be trouble over that place being taken, and I figured with an officer around you'd catch all the shit and no one would bother with me.'

He couldn't help it. Wolff simply had to admire the man's practicality, harsh though it was. Everything the Gefreiter did was towards one aim, the survival of Heinz Henschel.

'Do you think we will survive this battle, survive the war?'

Henschel's sole molar was displayed prominently as he grinned broadly for a brief moment. 'I will.'

*   *   *   *   *   *

The barricade had been rebuilt and strengthened, and Porter's body dragged to one side. They were running out of places to put the dead, and those who had been in that condition longest were beginning to smell. One in particular, that of a badly burned Oberleutnant, was giving rise to foul odours that forced the men to hold their breaths as they passed to and fro to change the watch at the entrance.

Any careless movement at the entrance would bring a burst of fire that would beat dust from the sandbags, or ricochet off the ragged concrete.

Just outside lay the body of the German killed by Harris and Mitchell during the attack. The blood soaking the ground beneath it was attracting a growing number of flies.

'Can't we push them out through the front gun ports?' Reilly was trying to scrape brown filth off his boots. He had slipped in a growing puddle of something highly unpleasant that was seeping from one of the bodies.

'We intend to.' Saville had already answered the same question from others. 'But we'll have to wait for dark. The front of the emplacement is covered by another Jerry nest further down the hill. I don't want us to sustain any more casualties just for the sake of having fresh air a few hours sooner than we might.'

Kemp overheard. 'Hell, I thought you were from Ireland. That's farming country ain't it? Don't you know the pong of rotting manure is good for you.'

Reilly wasn't going to have any of that. No bloody smart-arse Kiwi was going to poke fun at him. 'There's other bloody things in Ireland besides bloody farms you know. I'm from Belfast, and we've got more bloody ship yards and factories there than you have in the whole of those two scrubby islands of yours. Our city council counts for more than your ruddy government.'

The note of triumph with which Reilly concluded his retort vanished, like his smile, abruptly, when Kemp's fist made hard contact with his jaw. As realisation dawned the look of surprise on Reilly's face was replaced by rage. He scrambled to his feet, only to run straight into Lucas, who intercepted him.

'Quit it, you two.' The sergeant had his work cut out to hold back the Irishman who made continued attempts to get at Kemp, who stood his ground waiting for him, grinding his right fist into his left palm.

'OK, Kemp, that's enough.' Murray judged honours to be about even and chose that moment to step in. 'Go and find yourself something to do in the magazine. Not the woman.' He watched until his man had gone out, then smiled at Reilly. 'You were unlucky there. Any bloke in my company might have taken a poke at you for that crack, but with Kempy it was damn well guaranteed. He's from Auckland. They breed some stroppy bastards up there, very highly developed

154

sense of national pride. If you really want a scrap just say something about One Tree Hill, or any other Auckland land-mark.'

'Let's leave it at that, shall we?' Saville was glad it had been no worse. A flare up had been on the cards for some time. Perhaps now there'd been one, things would go off the boil, but they'd bear watching those two, and the others.

Murray had been anticipating trouble as well. Hell, he was fed up himself. He'd prefer to get out, get back into the fight that way, rather than wait for the Germans to bring the fight to them. He remembered an earlier Cassino battle, when they'd been trying to take the town. For all the security they enjoyed in their strongly constructed positions, he wouldn't have changed places with the Krauts for anything, preferring the freedom of the attacker to the restrictions of the defender. No matter what the dangers were of getting back down the hill, anything must be better than being sealed up in this mausoleum.

The air in the magazine was stifling, and when Russell fell into a fitful sleep Gina stopped fanning him and went out into the passageway to catch what movement of air there was.

Saville was examining the improvements that had been made to the defensive potential of the artificial kink in the tunnel. 'How are they?'

She shrugged. 'Now they are alive, later who knows? Why you not give up when the Germans ask?'

He hesitated before answering, cancelling unspoken the first glib words that had sprung to mind. 'For the same reason you wanted to stay, because it would be a silly thing to do while we think we can win. You want to go to Naples, we want to stay free. We both thought our best chance of doing what we wanted lay in staying here.'

The woman nodded. She stretched out the top of her blouse to let in a short-lived cool draught, and after its passing flapped the material back and forth to prolong the sensation.

Despite himself the lieutenant felt an urge to close his hand round one of her large breasts. He was beginning to find her attractive, in a rough, tarty sort of fashion. Her face was puffy beneath the over-done make-up, and she was definitely overweight, which was something he had always disliked in women; but he sensed a growing desire inside him that unless quelled was going to add an intolerable extra burden to the long list of tensions he already laboured under.

He tried to rationalise what it was that he felt, and came to the conclusion that it must be the same species of lust that came over men when they went into hospital and came into contact with nurses.

She went back to the magazine and he followed her as far as its entrance, when she heard his footsteps behind her she turned and looked at him.

Saville paused, trying to read what was in her face. Resignation? Invitation? He couldn't tell, he'd never been with a prostitute, never had to pay a woman. What would she be like? Like a piece of wood? Or would she join in, do everything she was asked? Would she play the sort of games he'd always been afraid to ask of those girls he'd been with? One thing was certain, she wouldn't be like them, cool and pretending sophistication, or nervous or frightened or inexperienced. What would it be like to lift that skirt? Was she clean, would he catch something, the major reason he had never been with her sort, although he'd had opportunities. What would happen if he were to reach for her now, pull her to him?

A call came, muffled, from the barricade. It was Corporal Mitchell's voice, full of urgency. 'They're bloody up to something.'

As the officer raced out into the tunnel there was a brief crackle of rifle fire, the sound of running feet, and then the sharp crack of an explosion at the entrance.

* * * * * *

The long tail of flame and smoke from the rear of the Panzerschreck had caught Wolff unprepared and filled his lungs with biting fumes and his eyes with flying dust.

Kroger was swearing as he examined the entrance to the emplacement through a small pair of binoculars. 'The muck down there is taking an age to settle. Are you sure this is going to work?'

Wolff felt the tears running down his cheeks as his eyes watered copiously in an attempt to dislodge the grit blown into them by the backwash of the rocket's exhaust. He couldn't see at all, and his throat was on fire, as though he had just swallowed a spoonful of cayenne pepper. It was agonising to cough but he had to before he could croak out the words.

156

'Yes, yes, it should work.'

'It had better. Here, move out of the way!'

The NCO pushed him aside and slid another rocket into the launching tube, then slapped the operator on the shoulder to signal that it was loaded. The paratrooper aiming the weapon settled it more comfortably on his shoulder, and then supported it with just one hand as he reached over the blast shield and wiped the thick coating of dust from the small square of perspex set in it through which he lined up the front sight. Having done that he gripped it properly again, made a fractional adjustment to its angle of declination, and fired.

This time the Hauptmann was ready, and at the moment the electric impulse from the magneto, actuated by the trigger, ignited the propellant in the missile, he ducked and held his breath.

As the fin-guided bomb arced down to its target Kroger tracked its progress. He saw it impact dead centre on the door, and then once more everything was hidden from sight by the swirling dust and smoke its detonation created. He thrust the binoculars at Wolff.

'Here, you look. Are they going in the right place?'

Cautiously raising his head over the modest parapet of hastily placed lumps of rock, Wolff examined the entrance, now coming into view as the smoke lifted. It was still intact, but a corner of the door had gone, along with part of the surround, and lower down there was what appeared to be a hole right through it.

'Your man will have to aim more for its edges. If we are to bounce these bombs along the tunnel we have to create a bigger opening for them to get through. The door will fall eventually, and that should be sufficient.'

'Eventually.' There was mixed sarcasm and contempt in the Unteroffizier's voice. 'I've got just twenty-five rounds for this stove-pipe. Your *eventually* had better come before they run out.'

Wolff took another of the bombs from its carrying case and pushed it home. He only just moved aside in time to avoid the tongue of flame and red-hot gas that leapt out at his hand.

The grunt that Kroger made after completing another survey conveyed nothing, neither satisfaction nor annoyance. He signalled for the firing to continue.

A gentle breeze that had been evident since mid-morning

died to a whisper and then to nothing, so that between each firing there was a longer and longer wait for the dust cloud to clear so that aim could be taken again.

Hauptmann Wolff fervently wished himself back in the cellar with Henschel. Even that obnoxious company was preferable to being out on these bare slopes, with only a shallow dip scooped from the hard ground for shelter. It was scarcely credible, but the enemy artillery was still dropping a steady rain of smoke shells on to the hill. Most appeared to be intended for the monastery and the observation posts there, but enough of them were falling short for him to be able to see one or two bursting, away to either side of him, every time he looked up. He couldn't begin to estimate how many hundreds of tons of them had been expended so far. The enemy stock must have been enormous at the start if now, on the sixth day of the battle, its fifth full day, it appeared that they were still drawing on an inexhaustible supply.

Since those first five shots there had been no fire from the emplacement, but that was hardly surprising. After the first two or three of the hollow-charge warheads had impacted on the door and its surround, sending their white-hot shafts of molten explosive and lethal gas into the tunnel beyond, no one who had stayed to contest the assault would still be alive. Although not as efficient in this situation as they would be against the armoured vehicles they'd been designed to destroy, the rocket bombs were still a highly effective way of delivering a lot of punch with a little force.

After the tenth round Kroger called a halt. 'Now let's see if we are ready yet to send our bombs right down the tunnel.' He took a long time over a detailed examination of the target, then thrust the binoculars at Wolff. Very well, Herr Genius, explain what we do now. It would seem that someone down there has brains more than a match for yours.'

Not knowing what to expect, or quite what to look for, Wolff accepted the glasses. Kroger was at his shoulder as he used them.

'You said that once the door was down the bombs would go right into the tunnel, tear down the blast wall and set off the magazine. You said there was not the material in there to make an effective barricade against our bombs. So what do you make of that?'

Wolff frantically twisted the focus and at last the entrance swam into view. At first he could not make out what the NCO was on about. The powerful warheads had done exactly what he had predicted. Adding their cumulative destructive powers to the results of the Britishers' method of gaining entry, the door and its surround had been flattened. Instead of just the gap that the original attack had created, barely wide enough to admit one man at a time, now the whole of the tunnel mouth was exposed. The sandbag wall had completely disappeared. The door, holed and warped, lay beneath hunks of scorched concrete amid a web of deformed steel rods.

But there was something else. Smoke was persisting around the opening. A fractional adjustment to the focus produced an improvement in vision that brought a stomach-wrenching sight he had to look away from.

'You didn't think of that, did you, Herr Engineer?' Kroger took back the binoculars for another look. 'Very clever. Very, very clever.'

'Clever? You call that clever. What sort of animals would do that?'

'Not animals, men. Men who wanted to live. Do you blame them for that? Should they lay down and die because to use a means of defence available to them would offend your notion of decency? There is much you don't understand about war.'

'I am learning.'

'Yes, Herr Engineer, I think at last you are.' The Unteroffizier took a last look at the tunnel mouth. The fire just inside it was producing oily black smoke that found its way in puffs from the entrance. As each black ball rolled out it created a draught that caused the flames at its source to spurt a little higher. By their light he could make out the rampart of bodies on which they grew. 'Come on, back to the monastery. We're not doing any good here.'

High explosive began to fall in their vicinity as they neared the towering walls. The paratrooper carrying the Panzerschreck was struck down by a razor-sharp fragment as he toiled up the slope beside Wolff.

'Get up. Get up!' Kroger stood over the man and shouted at him in his loudest voice, a bellow that carried as far as had the piece of casing that had done the damage.

The paratrooper put his palms to the ground and tried to push himself to his feet, attempted to articulate and failed, then spewed a mass of dark red blood and pink bubbles and collapsed back onto his face.

Thinking the Unteroffizier was going to turn the man over to confirm that he was dead before leaving him, Wolff step-

159

ped forward to help. But that wasn't the NCO's purpose. He stripped the shell's victim of weapons and ammunition, adding the launcher to the Hauptmann's load.

As they made it to their sanctuary a barrage of the area began in earnest. Even inside the cellar the danger was not over. Red-hot chunks of metal and lumps of stone travelling with the velocity of bullets would occasionally find the window and come whining in to smash holes in the cupboards and gouge plaster from the walls.

It was as Wolff huddled against the back wall of the basement that one of those small tumbling pieces of Italy came in through the opening, grazed past Henschel and struck him in the back.

Wolff felt the impact, and for a moment thought no more about it; he'd been struck by at least ten spent fragments in the last day. Then he became aware of something warm trickling sluggishly down his back. He twisted to see and touch the spot, and as he did a terrible pain seared through him.

As his brain swam back to consciousness Wolff couldn't feel any pain, though the moment a glimmer of understanding returned he tensed himself in expectation of it.

'I'm not dead. I'm not dead.'

Henschel's ugly face loomed over him. He thought his vision must have been affected, then he realised it was dark outside. He must have been unconscious for some time.

'Full marks, you're not dead. You're carrying a chunk of Italy around with you from now on, but you're not dead.'

Carefully, one limb at a time, Wolff explored the functioning of his body, then raised himself cautiously to a sitting position. He noticed immediately that the room was empty of paratroopers. 'Where are Kroger and his men?'

'They've gone to attack the emplacement. The major telephoned to see why they hadn't reported it taken yet. He must have torn the balls off Kroger. They spent the twenty minutes before they left sharpening their knives. I wouldn't like to be those poor sods inside the place if they get in, they'll be carved to pieces.'

'First they have to get in. You didn't see what I saw. The British are not prepared to give in easily.' Wolff thought of the rampart of human flesh used to defeat the rockets.

'Yeah, well you didn't see Kroger when he left. He's got

160

hold of another four blokes from somewhere and they're armed to the bloody teeth. If one of them gets hit in the ammo he's carrying he'll go up with a bang that'll take all the others with him, with a bit of luck.'

Wolff enjoyed a feeling of relief. In a little while he would be out of all this, well behind the lines in a nice comfortable hospital bed. Oh, it would be so good to feel clean again, to brush his teeth, to know the luxury of lavatory paper, white sheets, fresh-laundered underwear. A fact about the cellar suddenly struck him.

'Where are the artillerymen? Have they been evacuated already? When did they go, why didn't I go with them?'

'You can go with them if you like. You can either blow your brains out or go for a stroll outside and let the British gunners do it for you.'

The Hauptmann immediately understood Henschel's meaning. 'But how? They were all alive a few hours ago.'

'How the hell should I know, I'm not a fucking doctor! I never asked for the job of nursemaiding them. I shoved the last one outside only a few minutes ago. The rats were beginning to get interested. They don't seem to fancy the meat that's drying in the cupboards, like it better moist. It's a good job they hadn't all turned their toes up before Kroger left, or I'd have been dragged along. You'd have been left for the rats, I told him you were as good as dead. Looks like I was wrong.'

It would be as well, Wolff thought, if he got proper medical attention as soon as possible. 'How soon will I be carried down?' Henschel's laugh made him jump.

'Oh, that's a good one. When will he be carried down? Oh, that's a good one.'

As he didn't see the humour in his question, and as the burbling oaf neglected to answer it, Wolff put it again. 'I wish to know. How soon will I be transported to an aid station?'

Making an effort to control himself, Henschel wiped tears from his eyes. 'Oh Christ, you really are a laugh a minute. I'll let you into a little secret. As you've still got your eyes and legs any moving you do is going to be under your own steam, you're walking.'

'Walking! But I have a fragment in my back. It might do untold damage. I could bleed to death.'

'No you won't.'

Henschel's cocksure attitude angered Wolff. 'How do you know, how can you tell? As you said, you're no doctor.'

161

'Oh, I'm not talking about your condition. I just said you won't bleed to death on the walk down the hill.'

'Why not?'

'Because we're not going. Kroger said if either of us skipped and the guns didn't get us, he would. That bastard knows every inch of this shitty hump of rock. I believe him.'

So the nightmare went on. For a short while Wolff had almost been glad of his wound. Even the prospect of that perilous trip down to the road had not diminished the feeling of elation he'd experienced at the thought of getting away from Monte Cassino. And now the hope that had been held out to him had been dashed away. The absence of pain came as a very great relief to him. He did not think he would be able to stand much, and he was grateful he was not yet to be put to that trial.

The only sensation he could attribute to the fragment lodged in his back was a slight twinge in his left shoulder, that became more acute as he made any exertion with his left arm. It felt like a pair of pliers had been inserted in the muscle, and were giving a progressively tighter nip the more he moved.

Only his wound, and Henschel's hopefully incorrect diagnosis had saved him from the Unteroffizier's immediate attention earlier. Now he would have to hope that the paratroopers would be successful in their attempts to take the emplacement during the night. If they were not, and the NCO survived to return, then Hauptmann Franz Wolff had reason to fear the coming of the dawn. There was the very real possibility that it would be his last.

* * * * * *

It was the waiting that was the worst part. When the initiative rested so completely with the enemy then one of his most effective weapons was the fear and uncertainty that his inactivity could build in the mind of his opponent. Lieutenant Saville knew that uncertainty now. Since the abortive attempt with the bazooka to bomb them out, the Germans had left them completely alone, with the exception of occasional reminders of their presence from the machine-guns positioned to cover their every possible escape route. As though to relieve their own boredom the enemy crews would send bullets rattling off the steel shutters or down the cleft at irregular intervals.

There was nothing further they could do to improve their

162

defences, and the only occupation left to them was to speculate on when and how an attack might come.

Saville held the piece of cloth to his face and inhaled deeply. A heavy cloying scent of violets washed the stench of the bodies from his nostrils. Sickly strong though the perfume was, anything was preferable to the abominable smell from the charred corpses in the tunnel. Like all of the men he was grateful to the woman for the petticoat she had sacrificed and the scent she'd used to make the cloths.

Tatman's rare brainwave, to use the bodies to prevent the bombs from skidding down the tunnel, had been quite brilliant, especially coming from him. As each rocket had bounced into the wall of tissue it had harmlessly ·expended its force and energy against the yielding obstacle. The corpses had dissipated the intense heat the warheads generated in much the same way that the projectiles had been nullified by the sandbag defences added to the frontal armour of Allied tanks.

But there was a price to pay for the big man's flash of genius in the form of the foul odours the burnt flesh gave off. The mound had been fused by the heat into a near-solid lump that had resisted their efforts to completely clear it.

Despite Murray's vehement objections Saville had insisted that during the hours of daylight they pull back to the blast wall as their first line of defence. With the entrance now wide open there was hardly any cover there for a man keeping watch, and carrying out reliefs or reinforcements would have proved lethal to everyone involved.

But now with darkness settling once more they would try to set up a post at the entrance to the cleft, where a better field of vision would with luck give them more warning of an impending attack.

Kemp and Tatman, who would be the first to go out, were getting ready, arming themselves with an assortment of weapons and grenades.

While they made their final arrangements the lieutenant went into the magazine to check on Russell. In the last hour the sapper's temperature had soared still higher, and he'd become delirious. His leg was now bloated to enormous size, and about the entry point of the wire, now almost hidden by swollen tissue, the skin was hard and shiny, with a green tinge.

Perhaps he should have taken the wire out when it would have been a comparatively simple job. Now it was possible that Russell would lose more than his leg. The poison was

163

spreading through his whole body.

Murray came over. He'd been with Nicolson, who was coming round by degrees. 'How's your bloke, then?'

'Not so good. Yours?'

'Not making too much sense, but holding on. One thing though, I think he's lost the sight of the other eye as well, but he doesn't realise it yet.' Murray leant over to look at the sapper's leg. 'Nasty, that. I saw one of our medics deal with a case like this, when we'd been cut off for a few days and a lot of the wounds were going off. Horrible messy job it were, but it let a lot of the muck out.'

'Did it work?'

'We got pulled out before I could see, but the medic seemed to think it would.'

'Would you have a go with Russell here?'

There was a long hesitation before the New Zealander replied. 'Yeah, all right, I'll have a go. But I don't want your blokes blaming me if he don't make it.'

'There won't be any question of that. Unless something is done I think his chances are very slim.'

'All right, I'll need some blokes to hold him down. He may be off his head, but he'll know about it when I start.'

'Well that's about it.' Murray held the offending length of wire. 'I don't know what's best now, sew him up,' he looked at the small needle and fine thread soaking in a half-inch of petrol in a mess tin beside him, 'or leave it open and let the bleeding wash more of the muck away.'

The needle and thread were from Gina's handbag, the petrol had been found in the bottom of the carburettor float-chamber on the generator.

'Leave it open.' Lucas injected a note of knowledgeable authority into his voice. He'd decided that the Kiwi had been making the running long enough. 'That's what they're doing at all the dressing stations now. I think it's called delayed primary suture.' He knew full well that the New Zealander could not argue with that source.

For a while now the lieutenant had felt the growing animosity between the two sergeants; he acted to prevent further friction.

'Well, do that then, just put a dressing over it. Time we were getting that post built, Sergeant Lucas.'

As they went out they could hear, from behind the screen,

the woman still unable to control the retching she had commenced when the pus had welled out of Russell's leg. It had taken a strong physical effort on the part of all the men involved not to react the same way.

It was jet black outside, save for distant localised pinpricks of white light as shells impacted. While Saville and Lucas covered them with rifles from the entrance, Tatman and Kemp took it in turns to make short sharp rushes out to the end of the cleft and dump the materials that were to be used to make the post.

Six trips were made without prompting any response from the unseen enemy machine-gunner. Eight trips, nine and then the last and Tatman sprawled headlong in his hurry to regain the entrance.

'Why don't we make a run for it now? If they were out there they must have heard us.'

'Give it a rest, Kemp, and just do the job you've been given.' Lucas had had enough free advice and comment from the Kiwis to last him a lifetime. 'Maybe that's just what they'd like us to do. We'd make a nice easy target once we were all out, slowed down by two stretchers.'

For once Kemp didn't come back with an answer, instead he ran crouched low, followed a pace or two behind by Tatman, to where they had dropped the materials.

From the end of the cleft the two men had a far broader view of the hillside rising above them than was enjoyed from the derelict entrance, but they caught only glimpses of it as they worked.

The assortment of stuff that they had did not lend itself easily to the purpose for which it was intended and it took the labour of thirty minutes, the first ten of which were employed in picking up early attempts that failed, to construct a low-walled enclosure that would accommodate the two men without its falling down every time one of them moved. An additional handicap was the need to work as quietly as possible.

Although they did their best, Lucas, who was watching, winced each time a section of the work collapsed. Always it seemed with a clatter of settling stones that went on and on for ever. When at last it was finished he saw them duck down inside and then pull over their heads as a roof the large irregular-shaped slab of cast steel that had previously been an essential part of one of the eighty-eights.

With a few hastily added stones to a side that appeared in imminent danger of disintegration the result was a compact two-man gun post with an adequate partial roof that offered a degree of cover against small-arms fire and grenade fragments.

Tatman and Kemp were an unlikely pair to put together, but if there was one thing that Lucas really prided himself on, it was what he considered his natural skill and ability to pick the right men for a job. Taken all round they were a pretty good bunch, plenty of skills, not too many weaknesses, and if he could have had them all for a week without Murray around he knew he'd have ended up with one of the best damned sections in the whole of the Eighth Army. Maybe the best.

All the Kiwis needed was a few hours on the parade ground. Tatman needed his ideas bucking up and Harris and Porter . . .

He'd forgotten. Porter, dead. It just hadn't clicked yet, it was taking a time to sink in. Porter, dead. The section, the platoon, wouldn't be the same without him. He'd been a stabilising influence. Maybe a bit too ready to pull the old-soldier routine to dodge out of any really hard graft, but not a bad sort taken altogether. Always prepared to do his bit and be up the sharp end when he was needed. You couldn't ask much more of a bloke than that. Lucas wondered if that was how the others would sum him up if he bought it, or would it be a chorus of 'thank Christ he's gone'?

The Jerries had been quiet for a long time now. It was tempting to think that Kemp might be right. Perhaps they'd already abandoned the hill and monastery. But when he'd last taken a cautious look out of the front it had seemed like the fighting was still a good way short of the foot of the hill. It was hard to believe that the Germans, who had paid for the ground with so many lives, would give it up until they absolutely had to.

Well, he was quite content to stay put and trust in an Allied victory giving them an easy passage out. He'd rather wait for the army to catch up to them, rather than go looking for them, with all its attendant risks.

Another day, two at most, must see them safe. They'd be bloody thirsty by then, and Tatman would have lost his paunch but they'd be alive, and that was more than a lot of blokes would be by the end of the battle.

He pulled back his sleeve to read the time. His eyes were tired and the luminous marks and hands looked blurry. That couldn't be right, getting on for 22.00 and still no attack by, Jerry? They were taking their time. Maybe the hill had been evacuated.

An indistinct shout from the recently constructed post took his attention that way. There was something, about the size of a fist, tumbling on the roof of the shelter.

The blast from the egg-grenade tore his rifle from his grasp but didn't knock Lucas over. As the shock passed he blinked his eyes to free them of the milky haze clouding them, and found he couldn't. The sudden dazzling light of the detonation had destroyed his night vision more effectively than a flash-bulb going off in his face would have done.

He heard the shouts and the brief blurr of nearby sub-machine-gun fire and, knowing what was coming, stumbled sideways a pace to get his back against the wall. As he reached for his pistol a large rough hand grabbed him by the throat and at the same moment the blade of a knife was plunged in through his side with vicious force.

Pain, incredible pain, was Lucas's first sensation as the steel was withdrawn from his body. He could feel the blade scraping along one of his ribs and his skin felt suddenly damp and warm about the knife's entry point. Another instant and a second stab would be made at him. His left hand flailed out, attempting to find the arm that held the weapon, while with his right he sought the butt of the Colt beneath the obstructive stiff flap of its holster. It was in his hand and he yanked it free and without time to think the action through pushed it forward until it met an unyielding bulk; Lucas pulled the trigger twice.

He'd failed to get a grip on his assailant's arm, and the tip of the sharp steel was piercing him again as the pistol in his hand bucked violently, its escaping gases blocked by the object against which the muzzle was pressed.

Lucas thought his wrist was breaking as the second shot repeated the effect and jarred his arm to the shoulder. The hand was still at his throat and a heavy weight was pressing against him. Whoever was holding onto him was slowly sagging to the ground and pulling him down as well. He had just time to club the man's neck twice with the heavy automatic and then they were both down, and he was under-neath.

There was fighting and shouting all about him. Another body fell. Lucas saw a face below a German helmet down close to his own. His one free hand still held the Colt and he put a bullet into the gaping mouth that was so near he could feel the heat of the gasped breaths coming from it.

Another German egg-grenade exploded; its concussion in the tunnel was punishing, tearing at his eardrums, pushing his eyes hard down into their sockets. Anger and frustration at his inability to take any real part in what was going on gave Lucas new strength and he heaved the body that lay partially across him to one side, and struggled out from beneath it.

Dust and stone were showering from the roof of the tunnel as the sergeant made it to his knees. He pressed his hand to his side and the pulsing sensation stopped. From somewhere came a scalp-tingling series of screams that ended in a hysterical, distressed hooting that it didn't seem possible could be the product of any human throat.

Lucas pushed hands aside that came down to help him to his feet. 'I'm all right, leave me alone.' He found he could stand unaided and gradually straightened up. As long as he kept pressure on the wound it didn't bleed.

'Looks like we've got enough new material to build another of Tatman's ghoulish walls, Sergeant.'

'Yes, sir. What are our casualties,' Lucas wondered if his voice sounded normal.

'We are just getting sorted out now. I think even Murray got a shock the way they came at us. I've never seen or heard of anything like it. Are you all right?'

'Just winded, sir. It'll wear off.'

'Good, you had me worried there. Let's get everyone back behind the blast wall. There's no chance of holding the entrance.'

As the British engineers and New Zealand infantry retired behind the chicane of concrete the German machine-gunner opened up once more. A single ball of red tracer flattened itself in a bright splash of colour on the tunnel wall behind them.

'I owe you an apology, Tatty. I thought that was you making all that bloody racket out there.' Harris looked down to where his sleeve had been ripped open to the elbow and the woman was wrapping long turns of bandage about the gash in his forearm.

Tatman didn't hear him, nor could he hear the hideous non-stop screaming to which Harris referred. He would never hear anything again. The grenade that had exploded on the roof of the shelter had destroyed his eardrums. The only sensation of sound that he had was the headache-inducing roar of rushing water, as though he were standing next to Niagara Falls. He had tried one tentative groan when the throbbing in his left hand had started to resolve itself into an acute stab of pain, but had not repeated the attempt. Now he hugged his wounded fingers under his armpit, afraid to look at them, or have them seen to.

When his turn came Murray roughly pulled the hand out and examined the damage. Tatman clenched his eyes and turned his head away.

The sergeant wiped the worst of the blood and dust off the broken fingers. All including the thumb were misshapen; the top joint of the index, and the nails of two others were missing. Murray took the gorget from around the big man's neck and used it as a splint to bind the fingers too, carefully laying them out flat before he started binding them.

'Found a use for your armour, then? Mind some medic don't pinch it when you get to the CCS. Nice souvenir is that.'

Still the sapper paid no attention. Murray reached forward and snapped his fingers beside each of Tatman's ears in turn. He saw that Saville was watching the test, and when it elicited no response, shook his head to the officer.

Lucas watched from the doorway. Having set Reilly on guard, and shut up his crowing about 'the luck of the Irish', he was keeping out of the way as much as possible. He didn't know why he had decided to conceal the fact that he was wounded. Possibly it was because the New Zealand sergeant had come through the fierce hand-to-hand fighting almost without a scratch, although he too had got his man, and he didn't want to be bested by him. During a quiet moment he'd managed to slip away to a corner of the far gun compartment and secure a wad of cloth to his side, lashing it in place with a belt of broad webbing he'd taken from a body. The effect was to make a lump under his battledress top, but with luck no one would notice.

Corporal Mitchell had been laid in one of the bunks to die. The German grenade he had tried to throw back had taken off his hand at the wrist and done terrible damage to his face and chest. There was nothing that could be done for him. When he finished with Tatman Murray went to the dying man's side but all he could do was stand and watch helplessly as Mitchell defied all the odds by dragging out his last seconds of life into minutes.

Saville joined them more as a gesture than in the hope of

169

being able to offer any help. 'Anything I can do?'

Murray laid a handkerchief over the terrible ruin of a face and watched it swiftly stain as it rose and fell slowly. He stepped away from the bedside.

'You've done your bloody job. You've broken in here, you've buggered the guns. Now let me do my job by getting what's left of my men out of this rat trap. I can't stand around and watch them get cut to bloody pieces any longer.'

'What do you propose to do with the wounded?'

'Take them with us, of course. If we can rig up some sort of litter for Nicolson and your bloke, the rest of them can manage.'

'And what about him?' Saville indicated the corporal.

'By the time we're ready to go he'll not need us, you know that.'

'Look, I know how you feel, Sergeant.' My God he did too. 'But we need to have an idea of what's going on in the valley before we make a move. If the advance has made it to the road, or even to the railway line, then fine, we know where we stand. But what if our chaps have been pushed back, or Jerry has managed to establish another firm line? We just can't go blundering off into the night loaded down with a couple of stretcher cases and the woman.'

'What's the bloody alternative? Another day here, or two, or a bloody week?'

Over the Kiwi's shoulder Saville saw that the red-blotched handkerchief had stopped going up and down. He didn't mention it.

'The alternative is that we wait for morning. Use the day to do some careful observing from the embrasures of the fighting in the valley, and then if things look even half favourable, go as soon as it gets dark tomorrow night. We can leave a device in here that will set off the magazine after we're gone. That'll make sure the job's done thoroughly.'

'That's all you're bloody bothered about, isn't it! Breaking your precious bloody lump of concrete.'

'It's my damned job, like yours is to provide our escort, not organise a race down the hill.'

Murray looked like he had more to say, but he didn't, and turned back to Mitchell, to find that the NCO had died all alone, while he'd been arguing.

'Shut up, you noisy bastard!' Reilly was yelling out at the crippled German in the tunnel beyond the blast wall, who was still giving vent to terrible cries and screams. 'Why don't you put a bloody bullet in your gob. Just stop from making that sodding racket, will you!'

Unable to stand the other man's torment any longer Reilly lobbed a grenade around the corner of the wall. At the crash of its detonation lumps of rock fell from the ceiling and the series of piercing yells rose in a single continuous howl that didn't stop until a second bomb was sent after the first.

Lucas had heard the first and been too late to stop the second. 'What the ruddy hell do you think you're doing? If you want to play at fairy bloody godmothers and go about granting dying Krauts' wishes, bugger off out there and finish them with a lump of wood. They haven't done with us yet. We're going to need every grenade and every bullet before the night is out.'

*   *   *   *   *   *

The spectre appeared at the window shortly after the sky lightened. Wolff, woken by its noisy attempts to gain entrance, watched it balance precariously on the pock-marked sill for a moment, then take a stumbling step into the room. He recognised the uniform, what was left of it, a tattered, blood-daubed camouflage smock. The paratrooper wearing it was helmetless and his eyes were glassy. There was a fixed, taut grin on his dirt-streaked face.

Hardly knowing what was happening the Hauptmann struggled to his feet while the figure thumped its chest in a vain attempt to aid articulation. Then, as though poleaxed, and making no effort to cushion his fall onto the stone slab floor, the man collapsed forward. He struck it hard, raising a cloud of dust.

Henschel slithered to him, and felt for a pulse in his neck. 'He's dead. Dead as a bloody dodo.' He scurried back to his place by the wall as a straggling procession of other paratroopers came in one at a time.

Wolff found himself counting them. When he reached five and there was no sign of Kroger his heart lifted, and then sank as the outline of a sixth helmet appeared at the window.

Unteroffizier Kroger reeled from sheer exhaustion, and the cumulative effects of several wounds. His smock was slashed and burned, the camouflage gone from his dented helmet; his face and hands were covered in blood from a network of deep scratches and long cuts. He fixed his eyes on Wolff and headed straight for him.

171

Huge hands fastened on the front of the officer's jacket and he was hoisted into the air.

'You're alive. The worm is alive. Half of the best section in the whole of the Hermann Goering Division is dead and eight other good men with them, and the worm lives. You slept well?'

Terrified that the rough handling might cause his wound to reopen, his mind flooded with that fear to the exclusion of all else, Wolff did not think before answering.

'Only a little. The bodies disturb me.' A groan he heard from Henschel gave Wolff advance warning that his reply was ill-considered.

'Disturb you! Disturb you!' Kroger shook the Hauptmann. 'I'll fucking disturb you. Look at my men.' He indicated the handful of red-eyed paratroops who sat crosslegged on the floor against the walls, going mechanically through the ritual of cleaning and reloading their weapons. 'Those are all I've got left. Nine times we tried to get into your bloody emplacement. It's cost me fifteen casualties so far and we're still no nearer to retaking it than we were twenty-four hours ago. Get out of my sight.'

The Hauptmann felt himself suddenly propelled across the room with such violence that the cupboard he crashed into burst open on the impact. A corpse that had been artfully folded into it flopped out and caught him in its cold embrace. He yelled at the shock and jumped back. The cadaver, released from the confines of its unnatural resting place, lunged after him. Wolff almost felt its clutches a second time as it just missed him and flopped to the floor, its brittle tissue producing a sound like rustling leaves as it settled.

Even Kroger joined in the laugh that brought a temporary look of animation to the faces of his men, faces that an instant earlier had looked as if they were incapable of ever registering a smile again.

Kroger ordered one of his men to get the major on the field telephone. After five minutes of fruitless shouting and cranking, the Unteroffizier himself had a go, also without result. His tactics varied from that of the other man only in that they were louder and more violent. Eventually he smashed the handset down with a force that must have damaged it.

'Come here, worm!' He beckoned Wolff to the middle of the cellar. 'It seems I'm in charge now. That line is still in order. If the major were in any condition to give orders he'd be on the other end. So he must be either dead or have been evacuated. Whichever it is, since we are now isolated, I am taking command. And my first command, worm, is to change your orders. I'm fed up with piling the bodies of my men in the entrance to your bloody emplacement. We're going to blow it up, destroy it. Blast it off the hillside, wipe it off the map. You understand me?'

Wolff nodded frantically. It seemed simplest and safest to take the line of least resistance.

'Oh good, I am glad, because you are the one who is going to do it for me. That's right, you, in person.'

'I . . . I . . .' Wolff sought words, as well as the power of uttering them. 'I . . . I can't, I'm wounded.' A Luger was jabbed at and pushed very hard into his adam's-apple.

'Then I shall have to arrange a miracle cure, shan't I? We are in the right place for one, this is a sort of church. Start marching up and down. If you're still alive in thirty minutes then you're fit to do the job. If on the other hand I'm wrong and your condition is so grave that the exercise finishes you off, then we can regard it as a mercy killing. Now march!'

Stiffly at first, and then faster under Kroger's urging Wolff stamped back and forth across the cellar. He knew fear at every step and at every stamping turn he learned hatred – of the army, of the war, of the paratroop NCO who was humiliating him and putting his life at risk.

'All right, all right. That'll do. You'll have to save some energy for getting down to the emplacement. Now that we know that your miserable body works, let's check your brain. A simple question: how do we blow up the emplacement?'

'It can't be done, not from the outside. We would have to place charges in the magazine . . .'

'Think, Engineer, think.'

'I can't. There is just no way, there is no way . . .' Wolff's throat burned and was harshly painful where it had been jabbed. His eyes were sore from rubbing; and swallowing to try and relieve his terrible thirst was a pointless exercise when he could summon up no saliva. Desperately he looked around the room, but found no inspiration. There couldn't be more than forty kilos of explosive there, even including the remaining bombs for the stovepipe. That was pathetically inadequate for the task of breeching a position he'd designed to be bomb- and shell-proof.

'I see you need help.' Kroger brought up his pistol again and this time he held it against the side of Wolff's head. 'One minute, Herr Engineer. That is how long you have to live.

You will tell me how you propose to destroy the emplacement, or I will decorate the wall with the brains that are failing you so miserably at this moment.'

Out of the corner of his eye Wolff could see the finger on the trigger. Poor Hilda, above all else he hated having to leave her. That was all he could think of. Instead of aiding his thoughts the threat of death had frozen them. Now he couldn't remember even the layout of the Fuehrer's emplacement. To come through so much, and then this. It was so horrible, so stupid. At least he would not die cringing. While every fibre of his body screamed at him to curl himself in a corner to wait for the end, he forced himself to stand erect. He could retain at least that much dignity.

'No, stop, wait! Hauptmann, what about the book, what about the book?'

Wolff didn't dare believe his ears. The voice was familiar, if croaky. It was . . .

Henschel had leapt to his feet. He knew that his execution would follow Wolff's. If he could keep the officer alive he maintained that much distance between himself and death. He grabbed hold of Wolff and shook him.

'The book! You made notes, pages of notes. There must be something, there's fucking got to be something. Think, you shit bag, think.' The Gefreiter's hand cracked across his officer's mouth.

The shake, the blow, the shouting, forced Wolff's brain into activity. Henschel's face was only an inch from his. He could smell the foul breath, see the blackheads and the thick bristles of his stubble. He knew that the man was willing him to think, holding out a lifeline to him. Think, he had to think. Close his eyes, flick through the pages of the notebook in his mind. He sensed that Kroger was about to make good his threat. The words came tumbling from him in a frantic bleat.

'There is a way, there is a way.'

Kroger was suspicious. His long years of acquiring the skill of being able to weed out malingerers made him wary of trusting this last-minute flash of inspiration. 'You had better be right about this.'

'I am, I am. If we can set up a sympathetic vibration in the rock it will . . .'

'Save me the gobbledegook. What do we need?'

Wolff made rapid mental calculations, and topped them off with a guess that tended to the side of caution. 'We will need

174

at least one hundred and twenty kilos of explosive.' To his intense relief Kroger just nodded. He had obtained a temporary reprieve.

'I'll get what you need.' Kroger detailed one of his men to remain behind and guard the pair, and then gathered the others to him as he made ready to leave. 'Understand this, worm. If you are lying, if it turns out you cannot do what you have promised, then by the time I have finished with you, you will have wished a million times that you had never opened your mouth and saved yourself from that bullet.'

After the paratroopers had gone out, and their lone guard had settled himself close by the window, Wolff and Henschel retreated to the furthest corner of the room.

'Will this idea of yours really work, or were you just stringing Kroger along, buying time?'

'No, I really think what I have in mind will work. It has got to, you heard what he said.' Wolff found he was shaking uncontrollably and nothing he did could stop it.

'Hell, whatever happens it can't be much worse than what hung over us a few minutes ago. Mind you, there are ways and ways of dying. We'll just have to hope that this unimaginative load of cruds won't be too inventive. Anyway, if there's any bloody justice in this shitty world, maybe Kroger will get his head blown off, or step on a mine before he gets back.' Henschel made repulsive noises in his throat as he tried to work up a spit, and failed. 'Come on, cheer up, Wolffy. Five minutes ago you were as good as dead. Now you've got another hour or two to live. Enjoy it.'

Enjoy it! Wolff had been through an extreme of terror, what was there to enjoy in that? But perhaps Henschel was right. Another hour to be savoured. Time for memories, if the thoughts of the present didn't make them impossible. He wished he could write to Hilda.

One of the very worst things about all of this nightmare was the realisation that she might never know what had happened to him. He knew his grandmother had gone through a long period of terrible doubt and uncertainty after she had been advised that her husband was 'missing, believed killed' on the Somme. He did not want Hilda to be subjected to that, to the same recurring rounds of despair and false hope. But there was nothing he could do about it. He carried identification, and could only hope that his body would be recovered.

Six minutes of his hour had gone. Every second was beyond value and he was letting them flit by without notice. He must concentrate, make time slow down. But the sweep hand on his watch jogged inexorably onwards, marking off the fractions of his remaining lifespan, despite the effort of will he put into attempting to slow its steady progress around the dial. Seven minutes gone. One more wasted.

It was such a long time since he had prayed, but it could not hurt. He clenched his hands together. There was no cross, no rosary, no wafer or wine and as he didn't want to attract attention to himself he couldn't kneel. So he stayed sitting and bowed his head slowly as if going to sleep. His knuckles were white with the pressure of their grip as he brought his hands to touch his lips and mumbled to himself the words thought long forgotten.

'Holy Mary, Mother of God , , .'

*   *   *   *   *   *

There was some time to go yet before it got dark, but already the few jobs that had to be done before they could leave had been completed. The sappers had worked with a will, setting all of the explosives they had left about the emplacement. It was as though the men wanted to make sure that it would be impossible for them ever to return to that place, by destroying it utterly.

Loops of wire linked all the racks in the magazine, and trailed along the tunnel to the gun room, and both of the eighty-eights. The bodies of Porter and Mitchell had been moved as near to the entrance as was possible, in the hope that they might be recovered for burial later.

They had been very lucky that not more of them were laid there. After the surprise of the first attack they had managed to hold all of the others at a distance and had turned the cleft and entrance into a killing ground. Time after time the Germans had stormed in, trying with every combination of grenades and fire power to reach the defenders, and every time more bodies had been added to the deepening layers on the floor.

Saville was alone with the woman in the magazine. He sought for something to say. 'You will be wishing now that you had not come here.'

'I don't know I come here. Those pigs tell me they taking us to the villa of a big general. They say we go the back way because he not like it known. So we say OK. Then I find we come here. No villa, no general,'

'Oh, I see, I'm sorry.'

'It is all right. This way I go with you. I get to Naples.'

The lieutenant hadn't the heart to tell her that the path for a Nazi whore to the streets of Naples might not be an easy one. There were secrets to be learnt in Naples, and 'I' Corp would not be in any hurry to let a potential spy loose among woman-hungry soldiers. Certainly that was the way the Intelligence boys would look at it, and they might well decide to play safe. She would find little scope for her trade in an internment camp along with other female 'sympathisers'.

'You want me?'

'What?' Saville felt sure he must have misunderstood her.

'You want me? You know.' She winked and hitched up a corner of her skirt. 'No charge. You been nice. I celebrate going to Naples.'

Every sinew, every pumping pint of blood in his body screamed at him to take advantage of the offer. He was hungry, parched and exhausted, but he'd have forgotten all those once he was with her. It wouldn't take him long either, he knew that. But someone might come in, and where would they do it? On the ground? On one of those filthy bloodstained bunks; or maybe standing up behind the screen, straddling the stinking bucket. No, it wasn't practical. No matter how desirable, it just wasn't practical.

'No, no I can't.' Should he thank her for the offer? Damn it, what sort of a twit was he, bolting from a woman? But he kept going, out of the magazine, along the tunnel and into the gun room.

Lucas stood at one of the shutters. It had been partially opened and from behind a sandbag the sergeant was using binoculars to peer down into the valley.

'Can you see anything yet, Sergeant?'

'Not a lot, sir. The fighting is definitely nearer, and Harris reckons he saw a Sherman crossing the railway line a while ago, but at this distance, and with the smoke . . .' He left the sentence hanging.

'Well, keep your eyes peeled. Report any sightings that will give us an idea of how things are down there. I'll be with Sergeant Murray at the barricade.'

Harris was resting against the eighty-eight as Saville went out. He watched the officer go down to the blast wall, and then for a little longer to make sure he was in deep conversation with the Kiwi. A look round to check that everyone was accounted for, and then the sapper quietly slipped down the passageway and into the magazine.

* * * * * *

Wolff had to admit that in a way his prayer had been answered. The one hour had stretched to two, then three, then four. It was five hours after Kroger had left, just as their solitary guard was becoming nervous, that the Unteroffizier returned. Only one of his men was with him and both of them bore the marks of burns from smoke shells, giving a clue as to what had happened to the others.

Four bulky sacks were put at Wolff's feet.

'There it is. That should be more than enough. The price has been paid for it, now you make it work. If you don't then I will use it all on you, one piece at a time.'

The Hauptmann rummaged through the sacks' contents. From the third he drew out a Tellermine, from the fourth an eighty-one-millimetre mortar bomb. 'How can I work with these? I need to obtain a progressive controlled effect. How can I do that with this hotchpotch of ordnance?'

'I do not care how. I just know that you will.' There was not the slightest shred of emotion in Kroger's tone.

A sideways glance that Wolff made to his driver was met with a perceptible shrug, as if to say 'don't bloody look at me, you're the expert'.

During the time the Unteroffizier had been away Wolff had been working on the problem with which he'd been presented, and the more he'd thought about it the more convinced he'd become that he could do it. It was just a case of getting the right amount of explosive into the right place, but now a further complication was added by the unsatisfactory nature of the materials he'd been given to do the job with. It was not what he'd been expecting at all, but it would have to do. He had no choice.

Taking a deep breath, and after wiping his sweating palms on the sides of his jacket, he gingerly emptied the contents of the sacks out onto the floor to see precisely what there was. Yes, it could still be possible. Yes, yes it was.

'Well, first we have to sort out the light- from the heavy-cased charges . . .'

* * * * * *

What a lovely big bum. Harris fought down an urge to rush

178

across the magazine and clutch each well-rounded buttock in his hot hands.

Gina was bent over Russell, wiping his face with a piece of cloth that was kept damp and cool only by his perspiration. She didn't hear Harris come in, and jumped at his voice close behind her.

'You'd look bloody lovely in a nice starched nurse's outfit, with black stockings.'

'What you want?'

'Nothing, I'm fine. I were just sort of thinking, wondering if you'd like to do something for me.'

'You want to fuck?'

The sapper was taken aback at the way she came out with it. He'd known an old scrubber, just before the war, who'd liked talking dirty. She'd kept at it all the time, even while he was doing it, but for some reason he hadn't expected it of this one. 'Yeah, well if you fancy it, like.'

'You pay me. I not do it for nothing.'

His eyes kept roving over her body. 'How much?' The shape of her hips was bloody lovely, and she had quite a tiny waist, for her size. And her tits, they were bloody incredible. This was the sort of bird he wouldn't mind shacking up with for a while. 'Well, how much?' He'd kept a bit of his money back, when the others had pooled all of theirs to get the pistols. Bloody hell, he hoped it would be enough.

She mentioned a sum that he knew to be several times the precise value of the roll of notes in his pocket.

'Come off it. I wouldn't pay that for the best tart in the bloody West End. How much will you really take? And get a move on. I ain't got long.'

'Show me what you got.'

It was tempting at an invitation like that to give her a quick flash, but instead he took the money out and thrust that at her.

Gina flicked through the grubby notes. She hadn't taken as little as that for years, not since she'd started, and not known the rate. Soon though she would be away from here, and that money, added to her own and what she had taken from the girl, would give her enough for a dress, perhaps some shoes as well. Red ones would be nice.

'OK. No, not here.' She protested as Harris's hands grabbed at her skirt and he pushed her towards an empty bunk. Instead she led him behind the screen.

'There's no bloody room. Oh what the hell, come on, get

them down.' Harris was in a hurry. The clumsy attempts he made to speed what she was doing only made delay as his hands got in the way. Oh, he didn't half need this. She was all ready. It was so dark he could hardly see her. He felt his fingers brush her warm belly, it was very soft and yielding. His buttons came undone and he grabbed her to him. His hands fastened on her big bare backside and he pulled her hard against his body.

There was a crash, a horrible stench of stale urine and his boots were suddenly soaked.

'Let go, let go.' She broke from his clawing hands and went back into the main part of the room, sat on the corner of a bunk and with a blanket hurriedly wiped down her legs and feet.

Harris didn't know which of them had kicked over the can, he didn't care. His erection still exposed, he chased after her. 'Come on, you've had your bloody money. I want my screw.'

'You go to hell.'

'Better put that away, before it catches a cold.' Murray stood watching.

With ill grace the sapper tucked himself back inside his clothes and fastened them. 'Bloody bitch.' He felt like killing her, or Murray, or anyone who got in his way.

The New Zealander stepped aside to let him out, then grinned at the woman. 'Nice trick. Better hurry up and fill the can again. You might need it.'

'I not think so. We go soon, yes?'

'Yes. bloody soon. Bloody sooner if I've got anything to do with it.'

*   *   *   *   *   *

The pain in Wolff's back was becoming greater, and the worries it gave rise to were never far from the front of his mind. He was sure that the strain of carrying the two heavy sacks had something to do with it, and he prayed they would stop soon and he'd be able to put them down. Henschel was walking in front of him and was similarly burdened. At every step, and with redoubled intensity whenever he slipped, the Gefreiter was giving vent to his feelings with a string of the grossest obscenities.

Kroger had set a pace down the hillside that had appeared suicidal in view of the large number of mines sown on the slopes. If the Unteroffizier was following a route or path, it was one that only he could see. The continuing deluge of artillery fire had obliterated all features and landmarks except the very largest, and the outlines of those were frequently so altered that they were virtually unrecognisable.

When a halt was called, and Wolff gratefully lowered the sacks to the ground, it was some moments before he realised that they had reached their destination. The mouth of the opening in the back of the ridge had been much modified by the impacts of several rounds since he'd last seen it.

'Where will all this lot have to go?' Kroger unclipped smoke grenades from his belt.

'For the maximum effect you will have to put them about a metre inside the entrance.'

'No, you have it wrong, Herr Engineer. For the maximum effect *you* will put them about a metre inside the entrance. Now get everything ready.'

While Henschel and Wolff fumbled through the process of sorting the sacks and making the charges ready for use, Kroger dispatched his last two paratroopers to round up the machine-gun crews covering the front and back of the emplacement and escort them back to battalion headquarters, where they would be given more valuable work to do.

'You see, Herr Engineer. It is almost over. Now there is just you and me and this ugly specimen you tow around with you.' Kroger brought his submachine-gun to his hip in a threatening manner. 'You both look frightened at the prospect of bombing this place. Perhaps you will be able to summon more enthusiasm for the task if I provide a little cover for you first. No? Well, never mind, you're going anyway. Pick up the sacks.'

One after another, two grenades were lobbed around the corner of the cleft to tumble down its length, over the bodies that carpeted it, and burst in the entrance. Even as they built their dense grey clouds retaliatory fire snapped out from deep within the tunnel. The bullets were sent blindly, but methodically to catch anyone trying to rush the opening.

'You're lucky, they're aiming high. That should suit you two worms. Keep your backsides down and you might make it.' The Unteroffizier's boot lashed out twice and sent both men sprawling. 'Get a move on. That smoke won't last all day. Crawl, you worms!'

A centimetre at a time Wolff edged into the cleft, and towing the two sacks behind him began slowly working his way down its length. Twice he had to pause to push aside stiffening bodies, victims of the night's unsuccessful attacks. The smoke billowed over him and with it came a burst of Tommy-gun fire, mercifully a fraction high.

Halfway there Wolff knew he could go no further, he had reached his limit. Even the threat posed by Kroger on the other side of the impenetrably thick smoke could not compel him to go on. Henschel dragged himself alongside.

'What's up with you? Are you caught on something?'

'No, no, no. I'm finished. I just can't do it.'

'Oh shit, let's dump the stuff here. He'll never know the bloody difference.' He pushed his sacks forward until they nestled against Wolff's. From his jacket he took out the stick grenade that was to be used as a crude detonator, checked that one end of the coil of wire he held was attached to the cord hanging from the wood handle, and wedged the device between two of the sacks. 'Come on, let's piss off before they lower their aim and give us new partings and fresh cracks in our arses.'

Kroger was waiting for them. 'Give me the wire.'

Henschel dutifully handed over what was left of the coil he'd unwound behind him as he came out.

'And where did you place the charges?' The Unteroffizier casualty turned the wire over in his hand.

It was the Gefreiter who jumped in with the answer, though the question had been asked of Wolff. He was afraid that the Hauptmann would once more answer without thinking. 'Just inside the entrance.'

'Then why have only three and a half metres of the wire been used? You just dumped it, didn't you. Just dropped it and ran. I should have done this before now.'

As the sub-machine-gun came up to the firing position, its snout aimed straight at Wolff, Henschel threw himself on the paratrooper with a blood-curdling howl.

Kroger was taken completely by surprise, and sent sprawling by the Gefreiter's shoulder charge. Before he could recover a huge rock was pounded down into his face.

Henschel threw aside the boulder he'd used for the attack and snatched up the wire that had dropped from the Unteroffizier's grasp.

'Now who's the bloody worm!' He tugged at the wire, and turned and ran.

Wolff took off after the Gefreiter, his instinct of self-preservation dredging up a last desperate reserve of energy.

Four and a half seconds, that was the delay on the grenade. The running men used every micro-second of it to put distance between themselves and the massive pile of explosives in the cleft.

Behind them Kroger made his last attempt to carry out the major's orders. Barely alive, he sought round for his MP40. When his questing fingers found it he just had time to get off ten rounds in a rapid burst, before the charges detonated.

The Hauptmann, trailing Henschel by several metres, saw the bullets furrow the dust at his side. There was no cover, only the bare hillside. All he could do was keep going. A sharp pain in his leg made him stumble, and as he fought to stay on his feet and keep moving, there was a colossal explosion behind him. A hail of stones caught him and he was pummelled to the ground. As he went down he glimpsed Henschel, struck by a large rock, throw up his arms and pitch forward onto his face.

Half rolling onto his side Wolff looked back at the scene they had left. Dust obscured everything, but it drifted upwards as he watched to reveal that the back of the ridge had been shattered by the massive blast. Where the cleft, and Kroger, had been there was now a wide expanse of sluggishly settling broken rock.

A gigantic mushroom of grey dust was rising overhead, tainting the white smoke clouds and darkening the sun to a dull, lifeless disc.

Almost afraid to look, Wolff examined his leg. There was a neat round hole in the back of his thigh from which a small trickle of blood was running, but there was no exit wound, only a bulge under the skin on the opposite side. It throbbed, like a low-intensity cramp. After what he had been half expecting to see he was relieved, it could have been so much worse. He tried to stand, but a sensation of pins and needles in his lower leg gave way to a stab of pain when he tried to apply weight to it. There was nothing else for it, he would have to crawl.

The Gefreiter was just pushing himself up as Wolff at last reached him. His face was covered in blood.

'I've knocked me bloody tooth out.' He searched around for it among the scree on which he sat. 'Oh, shit, it was me last one.'

'Can you move?'

'Of course I can fucking move. What do you think I'm doing?'

'I saw you go down, your back . . .'

'Oh it's all right. I'm not such a delicate bloody flower as you are. It feels like an army of shitty paratroops have tramped over it, but it's OK, nothing broken.'

'I can't walk.'

'Yeah, well I didn't think you crawled up here because your knees needed the exercise. All right, let's have a look at it. Bloody hell. You're a bugger for getting nice neat little trip-home tickets, aren't you! Bet I don't get a ticket home for getting me tooth knocked out. God, it's not bloody fair, is it.'

'What do we do now?'

'I know a nice little basement apartment, quite close by. Hot and cold running rats and interesting conversation pieces in every fucking cupboard. Me, I'm going to sit the rest of this battle out.'

'I need help.'

'Don't you fucking always?' Henschel looked about. He picked up a long charred piece of wood. 'Here, use this as a walking stick. I'll race you to the top. Last one there gets smeared by the Allied artillery.'

Henschel began slowly to ascend the hill. Wolff struggled to his feet and, using the cumbersome aid, started after him.

At regular intervals heavy shells were falling on the far side of the monastery, and the ground trembled at each impact. From the far slopes came the continuous rattle of small-arms fire, and the faint echo of it rose from the valley floor. The noise of conflict drifted to them, with the smoke, from three sides of the hill.

The battle for Monte Cassino was still being fought.

*   *   *   *   *   *

Even the high-quality forged steel of an eighty-eight has a limit, and the giant slabs of stone that had fallen from the ceiling had crushed both of them.

'I can't see us getting past that lot, sir.' Lucas crossed his arms casually, but the extra pressure it enabled him to bring to bear did nothing to lessen the strange gushing sensation he felt in his side. It was becoming difficult not to let his growing weakness show in front of the others.

'No. We'll have to try the tunnel. There's plenty of air getting through but we'll only be getting weaker from now on, best if we make a start straight away. Tatman won't be much

184

use shifting rocks with his broken hand but with his good one and his big feet he should be able to break up the bunks for us to use as supports.'

By the flickering light of a single candle Saville could see the large section of the blast wall that had been flattened by the massive shock of the exploding charge. They could only be thankful it had not gone off inside the tunnel. If it had they would all have been pulped by the pressure.

The only sign of Harris was the heel of one boot, protruding at an odd angle from the narrow gap between the jagged broken edge of the fallen concrete and the scarred and scorched wall.

The lieutenant paused at the entrance to the magazine before going on to help in the work of burrowing their way out. The room was a shambles, much of its roof having come down as well. Some of the huge stones had saved Tatman work by breaking a few of the bunk beds. He looked to where Russell's bunk had been.

All of the suffering he'd been through, and the operation, all to end like that, squashed beneath a fifty-ton boulder. Sticking out from beneath the same great slab were a pair of plump bare legs. The hem of a dusty green skirt was visible, just above two well-dimpled knees.

Had she been tending him at the time, or had she thrown herself across him as she realised what was happening? Several times Saville had seen them in quiet conversation as he passed, and when the young sapper had become worse she had done her best to soothe him. They had been alone when it happened, so no one knew. He felt that was best. One of the possible answers would have made him feel even worse about the thoughts he had harboured towards her earlier.

Nicolson had proved once more that he was a natural survivor, coming through everything without further injury. But they still had a second stretcher case. Kemp. He'd been with Harris at the barricade when it happened. Now he sat in a corner of the magazine, swearing like the devil and binding rifle barrels about his broken leg with intricate windings of variously coloured materials. He stubbornly persisted in his efforts, refusing any offers of help.

Lucas had things pretty well organised, and Saville saw no reason to change any of the working arrangements he'd made. He noticed what might have been a degree of sluggishness in his sergeant's movements, but put it down to nothing more than the creeping exhaustion that was taking its toll of them

185

all, as lack of food and dehydration worked on their tired bodies. Still he had expected Lucas to show a bit more staying power. In fact he'd rather expected to cave in himself before the NCO.

The tunnel roof had survived the explosion and subsequent tremors but the passageway itself had been filled from floor to ceiling for almost its entire length by debris that had avalanched in from the cleft, as its walls had broken up and collapsed.

There could be no delusions about the task that faced them. Something like twenty yards had to be cleared, to create a tunnel wide enough for them to be able to manhandle Nicolson and Kemp out. It would have been a daunting task for fit men, and now they were anything but that.

Coupled with their physical weakness was a state of mental exhaustion in which little of what went on around them really registered. The most recent deaths had not touched them. There were periods when their minds went completely blank for minutes at a time. It wasn't a state of sleep or unconsciousness, just a paralysing numbness to everything around them.

The work, hard as it was, gave them something to do, a purpose. Though it was an almost mechanically repetitive task, hauling out the stones and passing them from hand to hand until the last man of the chain tossed them into a far corner, still it kept them busy. It would do so for many hours yet.

Already they had noticed that the few chinks of light visible between the slabs that had come down in the gun room were growing dimmer. The faint sounds of the day's smoke shells was being gradually replaced by the louder reports of high explosive, as the British guns harrassed the German lines of communication and supply, the slim pale paths that looped about the slopes below the monastery.

*   *   *   *   *   *

'I'm cold.' If a tap had been turned on and drained away all his strength, Wolff was certain that he could not have felt worse than he did now. His throat was so dry that opening his mouth was a painful experience, making his cracked lips bleed. Every one of his teeth felt larger and more sensitive; he was conscious of every ridge and texture in his mouth.

'Here, have these.' Henschel threw over a pair of blankets. Wolff didn't pause to consider what they had wrapped

186

before him, he accepted them gratefully. As he hugged the stale material about him and enjoyed the warmth they brought he could scarcely believe he was still alive. There was within him a most enormous feeling of pride, at having come through it all, at having survived, when so many had not.

Outside it was light now. Soon the air would warm and he'd feel better. He disliked being cold; but after the dirt and the pain and the hunger and the thirst he had endured, was enduring, what was that? His Hilda would hardly believe it of him. At home he had been so terribly fussy about his comforts. And here he was, still alive with a fragment in his back and a bullet in his leg. What a sight he must look, with his filthy uniform and his week's stubble.

But he would not tell Hilda everything. The woman and the girl, the bucket, Kroger; all that was distasteful he would leave out. And the Oberleutnant's horrible death. Perhaps he should tell her little, there was not that much to be proud of, except having survived.

They both jumped as the wreckage partially blocking the doorway leading into the heart of the monastery was knocked down. A dusty paratrooper pushed his way into the cellar and, hardly sparing a glance for the two men, headed straight for the window.

'Where the bloody hell are you going?' Henschel was the first to recover from his surprise, and called after the man.

'We've been ordered to withdraw, and I'm getting out this way. The Poles are on the other side of the building. We've been told they're not taking prisoners.'

'Can you get away? Surely if they're that close to the monastery . . .' Wolff didn't understand.

'I'm not bothered about getting away. Fuck that, I've done my stint, I'm the last one left alive in my platoon. I'm getting out through here because the British are on this side and I'd rather give myself up to them.'

'Wait, can you help . . .' But the man was gone, and Wolff was addressing his plea to thin air. He exchanged looks with Henschel.

The Gefreiter climbed slowly and stiffly to his feet. His back was so sore he couldn't straighten up. 'I think that bastard had the right idea. I'm getting out of here.' He suited his actions to his words and shuffled over to the window.

'You can't leave me. I cannot get up on my own.'

'Oh, piss off. You've been a bloody stone round my neck through this whole fucking business. I wish I'd left you in

187

that sodding emplacement, with those ruddy gunners. Oh, give me your bleeding hand.'

None too gently the NCO helped his officer to his feet, and then through the window. They began to cautiously pick their way down the hillside.

The sounds of battle were more muted than they had been, though some were much nearer. There was sporadic heavy machine-gun fire from the far side of the building, and the occasional sharp crack of an anti-tank gun.

'Do you think they'll give us a drink of water?'

'Whatever we get, it'll be better than the Poles would give us.' Henschel pulled Wolff's arm over his shoulder and supported him as they traversed a rough patch. 'Bloody hell. I'm a ruddy nursemaid now.'

*   *   *   *   *   *

It had been a difficult task getting Nicolson out through the narrow tunnel they had made in the debris. The New Zealander had become convinced that they were going to bury him alive, and had struggled against them. Private Kemp had been awkward too, but in his case because he'd insisted on being independent and making it on his own. Consequently he'd taken four times longer to traverse the twenty-yard burrow than if he'd accepted a degree of assistance.

They gathered together outside, before starting down the hill.

'Look up there, on the bloody wall.' Murray pointed to an angle of the monastery.

A small red and white pennant flew above it, looking tiny and insignificant against the extent of the ruination over which it fluttered.

Saville saw it. 'It must be the Poles. They've bloody taken it.'

Tatman watched uncomprehendingly while the lieutenant and Murray indulged in a session of mutual backslapping and handshaking.

Sergeant Lucas didn't join in. He was suddenly very sleepy and just wanted to sit down and rest. Blood had at last seeped through to his jacket and would be noticed soon, but he wasn't bothered any longer. The job was finished and he'd done his bit. God, he was so tired.

The lieutenant walked over to where his sergeant sat, and clapped him on the shoulder. 'Come on, Sergeant Lucas.

Plenty of time for catching up on your sleep later. Can you see the flag? It looks like the Polish lads have done it.'

Lucas didn't move. The lieutenant reached down and gently tugged at the folded arms. As they flopped aside he saw the large dark stain.

Saville felt his eyes becoming very hot. He knelt down beside the NCO and covered the peaceful face with his own jacket. His body didn't have the moisture in it to form the tears the discovery prompted. After going through so much, why hadn't he said . . .

The others gathered round. Murray took off his little woollen cap.

*   *   *   *   *   *

Wolff experienced a feeling of growing relief that it was nearly all over. The small group of British soldiers for which they were heading had not noticed them yet, but he was sure that if their approach was quite open and correct their surrender would be accepted. He could even enjoy a little inward smile at the ridiculous fact that he didn't really know how to go about it. Did one put one's hands up right away, or wait until ordered to do so; or did officers not have to do that?

Well, some sort of gesture was called for. He relinquished Henschel's supporting arm when they neared the group, drew himself erect and stepped forward as smartly as the soreness in his leg would allow.

Almost there now. They didn't seem to have been noticed yet. The British were standing around a man on the ground, doubtless a casualty. He was glad when he noticed an officer among them, that should make things a little easier. Ah, they had been noticed. Yes, now would be the right moment. Wolff's hand went to his holster as he took a pace forward to surrender his pistol.

Henschel's hands jerked high into the air as both the bullets from the British officer's automatic caught the Hauptmann and threw him over backwards.

Wolff's body came to rest on a cradle of barbed wire, and swung gently back and forth as the dust settled on it.

*   *   *   *   *   *

While Murray searched Henschel, Tatman pounced on the

officer's corpse and rifled its possessions. It took a prod in the back from Reilly to draw his attention to the fact that they were leaving.

With Henschel carrying one end of Nicolson's stretcher they started down the hill, turning their backs on the shattered building crowning Monte Cassino.

Saville walked in the lead, still holding the Browning. He found it hard to credit the suicidal stunt the German officer had pulled. The man must have known he couldn't get them all. Coming from the back of the file he could hear Tatman's voice raised in complaint.

'What's he on about, Reilly?'

'Oh, it's nothing much, sir. Nothing much at all. It's just that he's going on about being cheated. He took that Jerry officer's pistol off of him, and he reckons he's been diddled.'

'Why's that?'

'He says there're no bloody bullets in it,'

GREAT BOOKS

E-BOOKS

AUDIOBOOKS

& MORE

Visit us today

www.speakingvolumes.us